Buttermilk Book Publishing

Myrtle Beach, South Carolina

This is the second book in the Foot series written by T. Allen Winn. It is a work of fiction other than some historic references and research. Storyline characters are fictitious and originated from the imagination of the author.

Typecast in Times New Roman

ISBN 978-1-7331576-5-0

Foreword

This is the second book in the Foot series. *Foot, Tree Knockers and Rock Throwers* kicked off the trilogy. It is recommended to read it first as the premise of the storyline continues from the first. While the concept for the story is fictitious, events and accounts of the supposedly hairy beast of lore are utilized in the plot. The premise of the existence of Sasquatch has intrigued many.

Is Bigfoot real? There is no concrete evidence to support their existence, none that the hardcore scientist will accept. Those who have had encounters or have seen them might argue the evidence is plentiful. This series is a work of fiction and make no claims one way or the other. It's a fast-paced fun read and we'll just leave it at that.

The author has never had an encounter but did check one of his boxes in recent years by visiting Willow Creek and the Willow Creek China Flat Museum. The evidence there is quite compelling whether one believes or not. Until indisputable evidence is uncovered, enjoy this fictitious adventure into the world of the *S'cwene'y'ti.*

Another Foot
What Really Happened to D.B. Cooper?

Preface

Dan could have never imagined that his stunt would be a legend maker. His leap would become the ultimate unsolved mystery. Mattie Reynolds after finding her ancestor's hidden journal, and now obsessed with obtaining her own evidence, would unlock a second mystery. Would she expose one at the risk of exposing the other? This decision would weigh heavily on her shoulders alone.

Verifying his flight was indeed on time Dan proceeded to the terminal waiting area marked for Northwest Airlines flight 305. He sipped a cup of coffee while penciling in a black note pad. In his mid-forties and nearly six feet tall he dressed the part of a successful businessman.

His black tie with a mother of pearl tie pin perfectly complimented his neatly pressed white collared shirt and black suit. He carried a black raincoat and had folded it over the arm rest. A black leather briefcase occupied the seat to his left. He retrieved his ticket from his suit's coat pocket to again confirm his seat, 18C, preferring to sit near the back of the plane. He examined the information on the ticket dated November 24, 1971 realizing Thanksgiving would be tomorrow. He would not be spending the holidays with any friends or family this year, but it would be a Wednesday to remember. He sat in the Portland International Airport waiting for the Boeing 727-100 to arrive. The flight would take him to Seattle Washington. He examined the scribbling on the sheet in his note pad. Satisfied he removed it from the binder and meticulously folded it, placing it in his lapel coat pocket.

An announcement blared over the terminal speakers signaling his flight had indeed landed on time and boarding would commence shortly. Slipping on his sunglasses and folding his rain jacket over his arm he grabbed his briefcase and made one last stop at the restroom before proceeding to his gate location. Moments later he seated himself in #18C. Having no fear of flying his adrenalin levels still peaked. His heart pounded as the plane taxied down the runway and then departed for Seattle. He wiped the sweat from his brow and took a deep breath once the plane had leveled off.

He eyed the young and attractive flight attendant sitting in a jump seat at the aft stairway door just behind him. He read the name tag on her uniform and smiled at Florence as he slipped her the hand-written note from his lapel pocket. Florence returned a smile flattered that the handsome young man had apparently given her his phone number. She had grown accustomed to these flirtatious moments. She tucked it away in her pocket and would read it later.

Dan frustrated by her lack of interest leaned over and said, "Miss, you'd better look at that note. I have a bomb."

She quickly retrieved it from her pocket and read *I have a bomb in my briefcase. I will use it if necessary. I want you to sit next to me. You are being hijacked.* Making eye contact with the hijacker the color drained from Florence's face now realizing the severe consequences.

Dan motioned for her to continue reading his demands detailed on the note. He had requested $200,000 in unmarked twenty-dollar bills. He would require two sets of parachutes, two main back chutes and two emergency chest chutes. These would be delivered to him upon landing in Seattle. Failure to comply would result in him using the explosives in his briefcase.

Florence contacted the pilot and informed them of their dilemma. The first officer in turn radioed air traffic control who contacted the authorities. Seattle police and the FBI were soon engaged. The FBI agents informed Florence to return to her seat beside the perpetrator which she did reluctantly. She had been instructed to determine the validity of the alleged bomb if possible. She thought, why her?

Dan sensed that these dumbasses were calling his bluff and decided to show them that he held the winning hand. "Florence, my dear, please look at this and then you tell them what you have seen." He opened the briefcase to expose red cylinders, a large battery and wires. "Does this look real enough to you?"

Florence now in a panicked state nodded he had indeed made a believer out of her. She reported what she had seen to the plane's pilot and first officer who relayed it to the FBI contact on the ground. Speaking to the pilot, Florence stated, "He also said to tell you not to land the plane until you confirmed that his money and parachutes were at the Seattle airport. Failure to do this will prompt him to ignite that bomb. I don't want to die."

Shortly after 5 PM, once they confirmed to Dan that his demands had been met, the plane landed on a remote section of the tarmac. Retrieval of the money and parachutes went off without a hitch. Once Dan confirmed he had what he had requested he released all the passengers and Florence. Dan would not allow the pilot, the first officer, the flight engineer or a second flight attendant to leave the plane.

An FBI agent commented, "Why four chutes?"

A second agent shrugged then replied, "Do you think there's another hijacker on that plane or do you think the chutes are intended for the four crew members?"

"Beats the crap out of me," the first FBI agent stated. "I've never heard of anybody trying to parachute from a hijacked commercial airline before. This bastard must be loony."

"Let's try to buy some time," said the second FBI agent. "Send over the FAA official to the boarding door and have him explain the ramifications of the hijacker's actions to him. We'll fake a vapor lock problem with the fueling. Maybe we can get some snipers in position."

After about fifteen minutes Dan grew tired of this. "Wrap up the fueling or I will blow this," he demanded. They promptly completed the fueling.

There would be no negotiating. The snipers never had an opportunity to zero in on their target. As it stood the FBI could not prevent a departure. Sometime after 7 PM, and once Dan had completed assessing his situation and taking inventory, he barked out his instructions to the crew. "Let's go. Make your new flight plan for Mexico City. Once we are airborne, I want you to keep a minimum cruising speed of 200 miles per hour and hold her at less than 10,000 feet. Keep the landing gear down. Oh yeah, maintain flap at 15 degrees. Do this and you live to see another day."

The first officer engaged in conversation with Dan stating, "We'll only be able to make 1000 miles at that airspeed and altitude. We'll have to refuel before we can make Mexico."

After a few minutes of strategic discussions, they agreed on a plan. Dan gave the command, "Don't pressurize the cabin."

After a successful take off, Dan informed the remaining stewardess, "Please return to the cockpit and stay there." She complied with his request and headed for the cockpit only glancing back once to see him tying something to his waist with a rope before she closed the curtain.

A few minutes later a light flashed in the cockpit indicating the aft door had been compromised. "Is there anything we can do?" Asked the first officer over the intercom.

"No," responded Dan promptly over the intercom.

"He's messing with that door for sure," commented the flight engineer.

Sometime around 8 PM the crew's ears began popping, the change of air pressure a result of a now open aft door and Dan's exit from the plane. Into the pitch-black darkness and a heavy rainstorm Dan plummeted orchestrating the last segment of his plan.

After miscommunications by the news media Dan Cooper, the man, eventually dubbed as D.B. Cooper, had likely disappeared somewhere over northwestern Washington, possibly north of Portland, Oregon. He had parachuted into the unpopulated and dense forest never to be seen again by those searching for his whereabouts.

The saga would not end abruptly here for the man known as D.B. Cooper. While he would make a clean escape there would be no escaping his own personal nightmare on that rainy Thanksgiving Eve night in 1971. He would somehow survive the jump, but the ransom money would not guarantee his safe return. D. B. Cooper would never be found, or would he?

1974
Columbus River
Vancouver, Washington

An overweight and out of shape fifty-two-year-old Anson Parker followed the blood trail from the trophy buck he had wounded just after 4 PM. He had remained in his tree stand as instructed in the hunting magazine for almost an hour to make sure the deer was down before he began his search. Anson, not a seasoned hunter by a long stretch, had forced a shot after being overcome by buck fever, landing a gut shot to his quarry. He now trailed the splatters of dark red on the foliage and sides of saplings. Anson ventured deeper into uncharted forest cursing why he had decided today to hunt alone. Daylight dwindled now. Fatigue was taking its toll on a very pudgy and out of shape Anson Parker.

The trail luckily was not difficult to follow. Trees and shrubs looked as if a paint brush had been applied to them. Anson could not fathom how one deer could lose so much blood and remain on its feet while he labored to stand on his. Determined more than ever he would not be denied his prize. Anson trekked into the darkening and overgrown woods with reckless abandon. He was so focused on the wounded deer he now stalked. Anson failed to notice a bundle of 294 twenties secured with rubber bands. The $5880 rested only inches from his feet on the riverbank he now flanked. Had this been money discarded by the notorious D. B. Cooper? The cash would not be discovered until some six years later by an eight-year-old boy picnicking with his family. The Army Corps of Engineers' dredging of the Columbus River would again expose it for the picking. The D.B. Cooper mystery would continue.

Suddenly Anson's nostrils were slammed with a rotten odor. The stench halted him dead in his tracks. It so overpowered him that he fought back gagging and puking where he stood. "Damn, it's not that warm today. That buck couldn't have ruined this quickly," he spoke out loud. He then spat on the ground trying to expel the nasty taste from his mouth.

He reached in his back pocket to retrieve his flask but even the sweet smell and taste of Jack Daniels couldn't mask that gosh awful smell. He pulled his tee shirt from beneath his camouflaged parker and stretched the collar over his nose and mouth before trudging ahead.

The blood trail ended abruptly in a briar thicket 20 yards ahead where he found a large pool of blood and the imprint of where his trophy had been lying. No blood trail exited the thicket, but he did find long darkish hairs clinging to briars near the spot and indentations, some sort of prints leading from the thicket. Something had taken the buck. His buck. Anson now pissed would not be denied his kill. It had to be a rogue hungry bear. Was he ready to tangle with a bear? Hell yeah. That buck belonged to him.

Stupidly he decided to follow the new trail to apprehend or slay whatever had taken his trophy. He sure hoped it was not a bear, but what else could have so effortlessly scooped up his deer and made such a hasty retreat? He chambered a 30-06 bullet just in case. Even without blood to mark the way the trail was not difficult to follow for a novice like himself. Hell, he could have driven a truck through the pathway. This alone worried him for what he may be about to encounter when he caught up with it. "That buck belongs to me you, sonofabitch. I'll be damned if you'll just whisk it away," he spoke in a very loud and deliberate tone. He hoped to put the fear of God in what traveled the trail ahead of him. He had read somewhere to make plenty of noise when encountering a bear. I read too damn much, he thought.

Anson stopped in his tracks, suddenly stricken with the unnerving feeling that he was being watched, no stalked. Something was out there. He could just feel it. He did a slow 360-degree scan suddenly realizing his visibility had now become less than ten yards in any direction in the thick brush he now found himself standing. Anson had been so possessed in locating his deer that he had failed to notice how the forest had now engulfed him. Becoming panic stricken and claustrophobic the deer didn't seem to be quite as important. He inhaled another pull from his flask, hoping to regain some lost courage. It didn't work. Spinning he now became disorientated and wasn't sure how to back track out even though he had followed the obvious trail to his present location.

His breathing became labored as the panic attack mounted. Anson had read somewhere that he should breathe into a paper bag, but he had no bag. He thought to himself, why he hadn't just stuck to fishing. He liked fishing. Fish were of no threat unless you were in the ocean with sharks. Anson always fished fresh water. He owed plenty of fishing magazines. He realized he had emptied the contents of his flask and was feeling the effects. Lost and now drunk to boot, how stupid was this he thought. Anson flopped down on an old rotted stump to try to gain a little composure. He glanced at his watch; less than two hours of daylight remained.

Lost, drunk and it now getting dark, can it get any worse that this? Yes, it can. That's when he heard something extremely large moving very loudly just out of view to his right. He aimed his rifle trying to detect its origin through the scope. That's when he heard the second similar trampling of forest leaves directly behind him.

This was getting bad, very damn bad. Bears don't hunt in packs, so he ruled out bears. He heard low guttural grunts first from behind. Then something answered from the first location. It had just gotten worse, two of them for sure, whatever the hell they were. He had read to not shoot unless he identified his target. Anson was ready to toss that little lesson out the window. Instead he discharged his first shot into the air and paused to listen for hopefully positive results. He probably didn't breathe for a full minute. Finally, he exhaled after he had heard no new sounds, satisfied that he had scared off whatever had been out there. He chuckled and mumbled, "What are you afraid of Parker, the boogey man?"

As if on cue the boogey man answered, shaking and pounding on the trees directly behind him.
"Now that's not a damn bear," he whispered. "Bears don't drum on trees."

The first series of tree thumping was now answered by a second and then a third. Anson Parker rose to his feet chambering a fresh round, aware he had been surrounded, but by what? He yelled, "I don't know who you damn pranksters are, but be put on notice. I am standing here with a loaded 30-06 Remington rifle and plenty of ammunition. This is no longer funny. I am not afraid to shoot your sorry asses. Safety is off. My shaky finger is on a hair trigger."

The drumming ceased and now the ensuing silence unnerved him even more, because he had no idea where those taunting him were located. The light dwindled under the overgrown forest canopy. Anson figured he best be plotting his escape route. It was time to cut and run and forget that damn deer. Taking a deep breath he relocated and focused on the trail that had gotten him here. He fired two more warning shots into the air and then made a hasty retreat. Foot impacts paralleling him right and left indicated the hunter had become the hunted. The drummers staying out of sight now matched his pace. He huffed and puffed as he tried to maintain a brisk and steady retreat. Brisk was something he did not do well.

He lost his footing stumbling down a slope and into a waiting creek bed. Lying face down and in only a couple of inches of water he elbowed himself up, shaking the water from his face and beard. Anson glanced to the right and then to the left of the creek bed. Anson could see maybe 40 yards to his left before the creek crooked to the right. He could only see less than 10 yards to his right. His view was obstructed by a hard hair pin bend and a downed pine tree stretching from one bank to the other. Still lying on his belly, Anson took one last look in both directions before starting to right himself. Now at the creek bend to his left and 40 yards away stood a hulking hairy something. The approaching darkness and shadows did not offer a clear view, but whatever it was it stood on two legs and was staring back at him.

Frozen, Anson could not stand up nor take his eyes off this animal that continued to stand upright and unmoving. It had to be a bear, but if it was, it was the mother of all bears because this thing was a monster. The riverbank measured a good four feet high on both sides and this animal easily stood another four to five above it.

Studying it he could make out two long arms hanging limply by its sides from extremely broad shoulders and no real sign of a neck. Anson could not see its facial features, but he could tell its body was extremely hairy. The encroaching darkness prevented him from distinguishing its color. The more he thought about it, the shape just didn't match a bear's. But if it wasn't a bear, then what the hell was it? It had to be a bear. What else in these parts matched what stood in the riverbank? He decided he wasn't really that curious after all. Besides, from the drumming he had heard earlier, there had to be at least two more of these things out there somewhere. His assessment had taken less than a minute and minute was all he needed to conclude that it was time for him to make like horse shit and hit the trail.

He looked down to retrieve his rifle, and after ensuring he had a firm grip on it, he turned to face the thing in the creek bed. It was gone. He now leapt to his feet and twirled around to make sure he was not being ambushed from behind. He saw nothing nor heard any strange sounds or footfalls. Being suddenly alone did not calm his nerves. Rubbing his chin, he didn't know quite what to make of his little encounter. He knew one thing for damned sure. He didn't want to get caught in this forest in the dark and got a move on it. No one would ever believe what he had just seen. Hell, his buddies would never believe he had bagged that trophy buck and then just left it in the woods.

He had a lot of soul searching to complete and explaining to do. One thing for sure, his hunting days were probably over, at least in this neck of the woods. Anson had never been happier when his boots finally crunched on the gravel road where his Ford 150 was parked.

Pitch black now, but safely in familiar territory, Anson Parker retrieved the fifth of Jack from behind his seat and took one hell of a draw, but not before switching on the headlights to ensure no demons lurked on the forest fringes. He shook his head, still unsure of what he had just experienced. Something rustled in the leaves just out of view. He snatched up his rifle, clicked off the safety, and aimed in the direction of the approaching sound. Holding his breath, finger on the trigger, he waited. To his surprise out ambled a robust blackjack possum without a care in the world; no clue that it had almost been reduced to hamburger.

Anson chuckled, and then took another swig before relieving his swollen bladder on the gravel. He contemplated just how much of this story he should share with his buddies. He decided to start with telling them he hadn't seen or shot any deer. Admitting he shot the buck would only force him to explain why he had left it. He wasn't ready to share that story and decided to keep his mouth shut on the whole episode. This seemed like the smart thing to do. This decision would forever haunt Anson Parker.

After completing his soul searching he then climbed into the pickup for his one and half hour drive off the mountain and hopefully into the waiting arms of his wife of 21 years. He decided he would not share his story with her either. It just was not worth the consequences. Sometimes things are best left alone and untold. Of course, keeping these things to yourself, especially queer happenings as this, have a way of gnawing at your innards. He had seen what he had seen. He wasn't crazy by a long shot. He was even more certain than ever that it hadn't been a bear. Whatever the hell it had been, this mountain and woods belonged to it now. He had no desire to ever tangle with it again.

1978
Pacific Northwest
Washington

"Okay troop, we'll make camp here," said Scout Master Randy Price. "Grant, Drew gather firewood and pinecones, any small tree branches you can find. We'll need them for our fire. Lester, Manny, Anton, help me with the tents. Let's see if you boys can show me how to set up camp."

Tommy asked, "What about me Mister Price?"

"You can take these pots and fill them with water from that creek down there," Randy replied, pointing down the slope about 50 yards away. "We'll need it come morning to quench the fire."

"Yes sir," answered Tommy, the smallest of the Cub Scouts. Red haired and freckled face, he had the tenacity of a mongoose. The smallest, but he was quite the achiever at nine years of age. He had already earned his Bobcat, Tiger Cub, Wolf, and Bear Badges and was well on his way to earning his Webelos Badge. Randy had sent him to the creek on a nonsense task to allow the other boys a fair chance to shine.

Usually Randy had taken the troop for overnighters in the local park near town, but he now felt they were ready for a true camping experience, a two-night weekender in the great outdoors. Randy Price had been a scout leader for almost 20 years. He loved every minute of it. Nothing made him happier than to see the boys soar like eagles in their accomplishments. This troop had to be his best to date.

He treated everyone as if they were his very own children. Sadly, he and his wife of twelve years had not been able to conceive a child of their own, so doing this helped fill a void for him. Amber knew how badly he wanted children, but due to her many medical problems, she could not give him one. He had just found a note she had wrote and placed in his backpack. Smiling he could not wait to peruse what she had written him.

Reading that note he discovered it had not been what he had expected. Tears ran down his cheeks as each word stole the life from his very soul. He walked off to a stand of spruce trees to conceal his dismay from his troop. She wrote she'd be gone when he returned, no longer able to cope with the guilt. We both need time to think she said. I can't give you what you want most and it's tearing me apart. I can no longer bear that burden. It's time for you find a wife that can give you what I can't.

"Mister Price, what about the tents," interrupted Manny.

He stuffed the note in his shirt pocket, quickly wiped his face with his scarf and joined the boys already trying to erect their tents. He knew their marriage was in trouble but hadn't realized it had reached this point. He didn't need to be here right now. He should be with her. Randy could not bear the thoughts of Amber leaving him. He realized just how foolish he had been and that it could be too late. The boys yelled something. He turned to them and mustered up a smile.

Grant and Drew returned with their first armloads of tree limbs and pinecones. Randy commended them for their effort and sent them to gather more. He glanced toward the creek but didn't see Tommy.

"Lester, how about helping Tommy with that water? Seems he's been down there for a while."

A couple of minutes later Lester yelled from down the hill, "I can't find Tommy, Mister Price."

Randy walked down to where Lester stood holding the two empty pots. The water was no deeper than six or seven inches where it pooled at his feet. He yelled at the top of his lungs, but Tommy didn't answer. The other boys joined him. All began yelling Tommy's name.

Randy hushed them and listened for Tommy to reply. No answer. "Okay boys spread out. Let's walk down stream and see if we can find him."

After about 35 yards the brush became too thick on both sides. The water reached better than two feet deep, prompting Randy to halt the troop in fear of losing another scout.

"Let's try up stream." Same result after about 40 yards, it was too overgrown and even deeper. Randy gathered the boys back at the camp and started a fire.

"Stay here everyone. I'm going to search down the creek bed. Make sure you keep the campfire burning. I promise I will be back before dark. The boys trusted and obeyed their Scout Master, giggling and razzing one another, figuring Tommy was pulling a prank on them.

Randy walked down the creek for almost a quarter of a mile before finding the first tracks in the mud. They did not belong to Tommy. They didn't belong to anything he recognized. He placed his own foot inside the muddy track partially filled with water. His looked like a child's in comparison. The prints resembled a man's, not an animal; barefoot at that, but what man had a foot this large? Something splashed behind him. He turned but saw nothing. A second splash, but Randy didn't catch sight of what had landed in the water, and then came a third splash. He spotted the origin. Someone was throwing rocks at him.

He yelled, "Tommy McAllister. Enough of this foolishness, okay. Jokes over We need to get back to camp."

A cantaloupe sized rock landed just inches from his feet, soaking the front of his trousers, much too large for Tommy to have tossed. The stoning stopped.

"Who are you," yelled Randy. "This isn't funny. I've got a lost scout out here. I'm not in the mood for this crap."

He received no reply and decided he best return to camp because darkness had begun to make seeing difficult. He covered the distance in less than 15 minutes. Exiting the river and making his way up the slope to the camp, he immediately noticed the fire was almost out. He didn't see any of his scouts. Randy should have never left them alone.

Price stopped dead in his tracks 25 yards shy of the fire. He had spotted more of the huge tracks in the dirt; fresh tracks that weren't there before. Panicked he rushed to the first tent and threw back the flap. Empty. He threw back the second. Empty too. His heart was now about to explode. He approached the third and final two-man tent.

Throwing back the flap, he fell backwards to the screams of five terrified scouts crammed and huddled inside.

Manny was crying. "Is it gone?"

"Is what gone?" Randy was playing stupid still sitting on his butt in front of the tent.

"The monster," answered Drew.

Randy then asked, "Did you see something?'

"Not exactly," replied Anton. "But we heard it in the bushes. It growled at us. We think it was a bear."

"We got inside the tent and we heard it walking around outside, real close, snorting, and grunting," added Grant.

"It sounded big, Real big," said Lester, his eyes almost bulging from their sockets.

"A monster," repeated Drew.

"It's all right. Nothing is out here now," consoled Randy.

Lester then asked, "Where's Tommy?"

"I'm afraid I didn't find him, but we will find him I promise."

"Monster got him I bet," said Drew." Ate him right up."

"It was a bear, stupid," said Lester.

"Okay boys. Let's get those fires going again. It's too dark to try hiking out of here tonight. Besides, we need to stay here for Tommy when he returns."

"But what if it comes back for the rest of us. What if it's still hungry?"

Randy didn't answer Anton. He didn't like their predicament any better than the boys, but what else could he do? He feared for what may have happened to little Tommy. He reminded himself that he had seen no blood or signs of a struggle, trying to build on something positive.

Less than three miles away Bubba and Sonny Wilson stood by Sonny's Chevy truck. They were preparing for a night of coon hunting.

"Too early yet," said Sonny. "Might as well have another cold one."

"I don't know why you wanted to come out here so damn early," mumbled Bubba. "We don't usually leave the house until after nine. It's too early by a long shot."

"To be truthful," he explained, "Me and Suzy had us a little fight. I didn't feel like listening to her bull crap."

"You and Suzy are always fighting about something a lot lately," said Bubba, handing him another Miller Light.

"She had that notion about us getting hitched again," he explained. "She acts that way every time they have a girl's night out. You know me. I like it the way it is, no ring on my finger or in my nose. I'm not the marrying kind."

The dogs suddenly began to yelp and howl.

"Looks like they're ready. What you reckon got'um all fired up?"

"Who knows," Sonny replied. "Did you hear that?"

"Hear what?"

"Sounded like a little chap crying," said Sonny.

"Hell, it was probably just the wind."

"Do you feel a wind blowing, dip wad?"

"Maybe it was a bobcat or a coyote," answered Bubba. "Either would have riled the dogs for sure."

"Whatever it was, I don't hear it now, but I swear it did sound like a little chap squalling. Oh well, these woods always have strange sounds. Hold my beer. I'm going to go drain the snake."

"Do I look like a damn cup holder? Take your beer with you," snapped Bubba.

He did. Taking an overdue piss, he spotted something in the bushes as he zipped up. He leaned down, picked it up, but couldn't quite make out the writing on it. Too dark and his glasses were back in the truck.

"Look what I found over yonder," said Sonny. "Fire up your flashlight while I get my glasses."

"It's some kind of 'how to' sign," shouted Bubba, "It's about lowering stairs."

Returning with his glasses, he snatched it from Bubba's hands. "I've seen one of these before. It's off an airplane. That aft stairs mumbo jumbo and 727 are definitely referring to a plane."

"How did it get all that way out here? Did a plane crash in these woods?"

"I don't remember anything about a plane crash. I reckon we best turn it in to the Sheriff just in case."

The placard would later be identified as one from the rear stairway of the plane Dan Copper had jumped from seven years ago, but the mystery remained. Where was D.B. Cooper and all that stolen money?

Numerous searches were conducted for nine-year-old Tommy, but he was never found. The monster tracks had been washed away by a sudden rainstorm before Randy returned with the Sheriff. He drew much skepticism from the townsfolk and the parents with his stories of gigantic tracks and monster sounds. While there was no incriminating evidence, towns folk suspected the scout master may have had something to do with Tommy's disappearance. No charges were ever brought against him.

Randy gave up scouting shortly afterwards; mostly because no one would trust him with their kids. He had lost the passion to do what he had always loved. Parents had given up on Randy, and he had given up on himself after Tommy's disappearance. Randy's wife, Amber never returned, and they were soon divorced. Unable to recover from the anguish of a divorce he never wanted, and a scout lost and never found, and the way people looked at him, one year later, Randy Price committed suicide, one shot under his chin. He died at the location of that last campsite where Tommy McAllister had vanished.

In a note he had written and pinned to his lapel, he expressed his love for his wife, wishing her a long and wonderful life. To his scouts he wrote we know what happened that day Tommy McAllister was taken. We saw the tracks. You heard the kidnapper and we know the monster was real. Never allow anyone to tell you it did not happen. Do not follow in my footsteps. I shame the scouts and for which they stand, and for that I am truly sorry. May God have mercy on my worthless cowardly soul.

February 10, 1980
Columbia River
Vancouver, Washington

Brian, an eight-year-old picnicking with his parents, found that same bundle of twenty dollar bills that Anson Parker had failed to spot six years ago. Disputes surfaced that the 1974 dredging of the river had unearthed the almost six thousand dollars, while others thought it had simply washed ashore much earlier. The FBI matched the serial numbers to the ransom money received by D.B. Cooper nine years prior. This prompted a new interest in the remaining $194,120 still missing.

Reading the article in the newspaper, Maxwell Paxton would be one of those interested persons, planning to conduct his own search of this remote terrain. His close friends, what few he had, called him Mad Max because he too often concocted half-baked get rich schemes. Very seldom did any of them work. The remainder of that missing money had to be out there somewhere. Max planned to stake claim to it.

Max, 41 years old with thinning premature gray hair and a physic that resembled a pear, had never done a tough's days' work in his life. His signature handlebar mustache and pork chop sideburns gave him that dastardly, almost sinister appearance. Most of his gimmicks failed simply because he looked distrustful. Max tried to overcome this with his golden tongue and charming manners. Sometimes it worked. More often it didn't. He could have been a Flim-Flam man in a previous life.
His only loyal sidekick was Bam-Bam Benson, a big slow witted, mildly retarded giant of a black man. Bam-Bam stood 6'8" and well over 300 pounds. He would do anything Max asked, if he understood the request. Poor Bam-Bam had been incarcerated more than once, taking the fall for inflicting injuries on Max's intended pigeons, or those threatening vindication for his detected cons.

Bam-Bam possessed the persona of Lennie Small from Nobel Prize-winner John Steinbeck's' *Of Mice and Men* novel. Max fit the persona of the George Milton character from that same novel. The two were inseparable and a danger to themselves and others they encountered. Because Max had no backwoods experience, he'd have to find a suitable guide to assist them in the search. He was only prepared to offer a 5% cut of anything they found, plus expenses. He had one serious problem, no cash flow to supplement the venture. No one would likely take him seriously, a promise of 5% of undiscovered money. He would require a partner to bankroll the expedition. That was going to take a little work. Most people in these parts knew him too well to offer up the cash. Not to worry, he was up for the challenge.

"Max, what'chu reading," asked Bam-Bam, looking over his shoulder. Bam-Bam could read a little, if the words did not get too long. He was much better with picture books, as he called them.

"It's a story about this man who hijacked a plane and disappeared with an ass load of money," replied Max.

"What does hijack mean?"

"He stole an airplane and then parachuted with bags of money," explained Max. "Then he must have died or gotten lost in the woods because they never found him or the cash. This little boy did find some of the missing money recently, so the rest is out there somewhere."

"Remember when I got lost that time in that mall and you had to find me. That was scary. I didn't have any money though."

Ignoring Bam-Bam's rambling, Max said, "We're going to find that money. It must still be out there, especially if that kid found that wad so easily. D.B. Cooper might just be our ticket."

"Ticket," said Bam-Bam, squinting and scratching his cheek. "Are we going on a trip? I like buses. Remember that time we rode that Greyhound bus to the ocean. You let me put my feet in the water. I don't like it if I can't see my footsies in the water though. I can't swim. You said you were going to teach me to swim, Max."

Max, maintaining his thoughts, said, "Who can we get to finance this little expedition of ours? And I'm going to have to research the files on Cooper to pinpoint where we should broaden the search.

Starting in the area where that kid found the cash might not be a bad idea. Come on, we're going to take a little trip to the library."

"I like the library. Can I get a book while we're there, one of those animal ones with elephants and lions and tigers?"

"I've got to read everything they have ever printed about Cooper. I just vaguely remember his little stunt. It was pure genius what he did, except the landing part. I don't think he got away clean like many people think."

"I don't like airplanes. They fly too high. I like buses, the one with that Greyhound dog on the side. We should get us a dog, Max."

"Greyhound," Max said. "What's all this junk about a dog?"

"Greyhounds are really fast," smiled Bam-Bam, "Except those you bet the money on Max. Why are they so slow?"

Maxwell Paxton just rolled his eyes. "Let's go big boy. If you keep your mouth shut at the library, I'll buy you an ice cream afterwards."

"Chocolate in a cone, Max. I love chocolate."

"If you shut that trap of yours, chocolate it is."

"Zipped up tight," responded Bam-bam, pretending to zip up his lips with his fingers.

February 14th
The Remote Washington Wilderness just south of Mount Saint Helens

"Well, isn't this a wonderful way to spend Valentine's Day, sweetheart?"

"Hey, Mattie, don't look at me. It was your idea to be here, Miss Cupid. I suggested waiting until next weekend, remember? Just be thankful we're not up to our asses in snow."

"And you mind so well," she smiled as she pinched Shawn's butt.

"It's your birth right to do this. Who am I to stand in your way?"

"And you're such an intelligent young man, I could have done so much worse."

"I guess that's why you decided to test drive me first, to ensure you made the right choice." Shawn pulled her close. Her jet-black shoulder length hair brushed his face.

"Daddy always told me to kick the tires first and go for good fuel mileage. He said always pick a comfortable ride." Six years older than his 30-year-old wife, Shawn was in excellent shape. Six feet one and 190 pounds of solid man. He wore his brown hair cropped short like a Marine recruit, even though he had never served in the military.

"I guess you are not ready to trade me in yet."

"Not much trade-in value in an older model like you," she replied, "You're my perfect little fixer upper."

"Whatever you say Professor Reynolds," he said in a mocking tone. "You're running the show as always."

"I'm glad you know the pecking order, Doctor Reynolds. "Now let's get back at it. You're disrupting my workflow."

31

"Always putting work ahead of play," he sighed. "That said, what's the plan?"

"Proof. I've got to find evidence to support my theory."

"Legend and folklore haunt your waking hours, doesn't it? I wish you paid me as much attention as you do your research."

"Like you said, my birth right," she reminded him.

"It's more like a curse. I hate that you found your great, great grandfather's little diary. You haven't been the same since."

Her face reddened from that comment. Shawn could see in her eyes that he had pushed her button. Even when she was pissed, he enjoyed gazing on her smooth dark complexion, her Indian ancestry evident.

"You have to admit you want this as much as I do," she said in a very stern matter of a fact manner.

He shrugged, "It was fun the first hundred or so times but turning up nothing concrete has doused my fire a bit."

"Humor me," she said piercing him with her remarkable almond colored eyes.

"I always do," he smiled. "Are we going to check out that source in town?"

"It's an old lead, but yeah, we'll talk to the guy tomorrow. Let's snoop around here a while for any recent activity. Shame that kid was never found."

"Well it does support your ancestor's tales."

"Sad but true. We still have no evidence we can hang our hats on so until then..."

"We'll keep searching right?"

"Am I obsessed with this?"

"Yep," he answered, giving her a hug, "but if it is that important to you, then it is to me. Did that sound sincere enough?"

"Not really, but you know what to say, don't you? That's why I love you," she whispered in his ear.

"Craziness runs in my family," he whispered back. "I guess that's why I love you back. It's getting colder. Can we wrap this up early?"

"Only because it's V-day and you asked."

Thirty miles north of the Reynolds's location, as the crow flies, Elwood Speed Moore standing beside his girlfriend, Cecelia Velazquez, admired the fruit of their hard labor. The huge greenhouse fended off the cold weather lurking outside. The security alarms had sounded during the night, but all appeared undisturbed. He had blamed it on a deer, possibly a coyote. There was no evidence that anyone had gotten inside.

Nash Hudson surveyed the perimeter for tracks just to make sure. Velvet Tucker, the fourth of their merry little band, should be returning with supplies shortly.

"We've done good here so far, Ceil," commented Speedy, placing his arm over Cecelia's shoulder. Speedy was a 43-year-old biker-thug, just under 6' tall with a stout build, brown hair, and pony tailed. He was an entrepreneur of sorts if growing pot counts.

"Yes, we have. How much longer?" asked Cecelia, a petite Hispanic-American, a natural red head with fiery shoulder length hair, tattoos everywhere. She was quite the looker, 25 years younger, and had been with Speedy since turning fifteen. A runaway, he had found her starving on the streets, and had rescued her from death's door.

"I'd say we start harvesting in another month, or so says our resident expert Velvet."

"Did you hear all that hooting last night?"

"You know me baby, I sleep like a log, especially knowing old Nash is such a light sleeper. It was probably just a screech owl or coyotes."

"It didn't sound like either to me. It was sort of spooky."

"Why didn't you wake me then?"

"It only lasted for a few minutes. I got up to pee and it had stopped before I got back in bed."

"This little lean-to cabin of ours is so damn comfortable. I sleep like a baby. It was a good idea Nash had to construct it under the ridge."

"I just wish we had more privacy than that one room we all share. I saw Nash watching us the other night."

"Let the old fart have some fun. I don't think Velvet is putting out to him."

"I know she's not," she whispered. "She told me the old coot creeps her out, and it would be a cold day in hell before she gave him any."

"Hey kiddies, we had a visitor last night," barked Nash Hudson in a deep gravelly voice from outside.

Nash Hudson had to be in his late sixties, but he acted more like a man 30 years younger. With a full head of thick, coarse, brown hair, he did not look his age. Closer inspection revealed a slightly graying beard and scattered age spots. He had strange eyes, one hazel and the other brown, both seemingly able to look in opposite directions while you talked to him. He was an old mountain man throw back. Nash had grown up in the backwoods of Alaska, somewhat of a hermit, a recluse.

Speedy had only known him for less than a year, but trusted him with his life for right now. Speedy never trusted anyone long term.

He was too paranoid. Of average height and weight, Nash didn't take crap off anyone, including Speedy. Speedy knew better than to challenge him or piss him off. Pound for pound, he'd be no match for the old coot and he damn well knew it.

Speedy stretched and scratched his groin. "Okay, so what did you find?"

"Tracks around the back," he replied. "The ground is too hard to really make them out, but whatever it was, it carried some weight."

"Was it a bear?"

"Didn't look much like bear tracks. I've already ruled them out."

"Coyote, deer?"

"Too light weight. I scratched them off the suspect list too."

"A buck can top 220 in these parts."

"Still too light. Tracks don't belong to a deer or anything hoofed. I'd say closer to man shaped tracks but a hell of a lot bigger."

"Hold on, Nash. Iif it's not a man or a bear, then what?"

"I'd rather not say right now," spoke Nash with a somewhat puzzled facial expression.

"What the hell does that mean, rather not say?" snapped Speedy in an aggravated tone." Cough it up old man."

"Have it your way. You ever heard of a Sasquatch," asked Nash, as serious as a heart attack.

"Whoa, you trying to tell me that you think we've had one of those big old ape men checking us out. That's total bullshit. That's made up stuff, fairy tales, Indian folklore. Bigfoot…cut me a break, Nash. They ain't real."

"I know. I've never seen one myself, but even in the back country of Alaska they mention the Giant Hairy Men. Tales have been circulating up there long before you and I existed in this world."

"Bullshit, I'm telling you. You're crazy, man."

"Do you reckon that's what was making that noise I heard?"

"What noise, Cecelia?"

"Nash, I heard this weird hooting last night. The more I think about it, it sounded like the noise those monkeys make at the zoo when they're exited."

"All right. Enough of this horse crap you two," ordered Speedy. "What are we going to do about our intruder?"

"I'll bait and set a couple of those steel traps I have," replied Nash. "If there is something out there, one snap of those giant jaws will stop it dead in its big old tracks."

"Cecilia clapped her hands. "Hey, we'd be famous if we caught one, wouldn't we?"

"Cecilia, I don't think we need any publicity up here with what we've got in this greenhouse," said Speedy pointing to where the 6' tall marijuana plants were located.

"I'll set the traps," repeated Nash. "We'll see what we get."

"I think we take turns staying in the greenhouse tonight just in case," added Speedy.

"Like hell," spoke up Cecilia. "I'll be damned if I'm staying out here by myself, waiting on this damn Squash-thing to show up."

"Nash, you and me will take turns, okay?"

"Fine by me, I'll take the midnight watch.

"Don't take any chances. Shoot first. Ask questions later."

"Bad idea, Speedy. We don't want to wing one of these things and piss it off."

Speedy eyed to old fool. "You're setting bear traps and worrying about pissing off Bigfoot. Give me a break, Nash. Where's that damn Velvet? She should have been back hours ago."

"Hon, you told her to make sure nobody trailed her, remember," said Ceil.

"I suspect she stopped in at that bar where that asshole Booger Rhodes works. She can't keep her hands off that bastard."

"Well, sweetie, she's not getting any up here, so you can't blame her for catching up a little?"

"That bitch better keep her damn mouth shut. Booger has been known to have diarrhea of the mouth too. He would blab our business to anybody that would listen and buy him a whisky. He would probably want us to include him in on the action if truth be known."

"Come on. Cut her some slack, baby."

Speedy grabbed Cecelia by the wrist. "I still can't believe I let you talk me into cutting her in on this at all. Hell, we don't even know if we can trust her."

"Look, she had the experience raising the weed and we didn't, so end of story," said Ceil, pulling free and standing with her hands on her hips.

"Forget it. Sorry I brought it up. I'm going to help Nash with those traps. How about throwing steaks on the grill?"

"We're out of charcoal but have no fear I wrote it on Velvet's list."

"She better get her ass back here then, and she best have kept that mouth of hers shut if she knows what's good for her."

"I'm sure she's on the way. Just calm down."

"How about a cold one, then?"

"On the list," she answered. "We're out."

"Damn," grumbled Speedy. "What did we do, run out of everything before we sent her for supplies?"

"Just the good stuff," Ceil smiled. "We still have plenty of dried beans and toilet paper."

"This was a bad idea coming out here in the godforsaken wilderness. We don't belong out here."

Saturday
Amboy, Washington

"Nice to be back in civilization," commented Shawn Reynolds. "The fireplace feels wonderful."

"Enjoy," advised Mattie. "Tomorrow I plan to talk to that local gent about his little experience while he's still willing to meet with us."

"One more day, then I must return to work before my patients think I've deserted them."

"I promise we will head back afterwards. Thanks for being so patient"

"Just keep it short. We have a long ten-hour haul back to Sacramento before Monday morning."

Shawn had met Mattie while attending college at UCLA. She had not warmed up to him at first, but he had worn her down. Both, career professionals now, these little weekend excursions took a significant amount of planning. It was tough scheduling and coordinating to pull them off, but he saw how important they were to her, so he did his part to make them happen.

Shawn, a gynecologist, had a medical practice with two partners. Mattie, an expert in anthropology, cryptozoology, primatology and paleozoology, was more of a gunslinger for hire. She conducted seminars and lectures on the various subjects She didn't come cheap, earning a six-figure annual salary.

They wanted for nothing, except the time to reap the benefits of their labor. They had been married for only three years. Neither had a craving for children right now. Both enjoyed life and what freedom they had. They took it to the limit as often as possible. Mattie had become obsessed after finding the memoirs of her great, great grandfather, Matt McGregor, stashed away in a forgotten trunk in her parent's attic while helping them move last year. Her ancestor had spun some interesting tales of the backwoods and wild northwestern frontier.

Matt's stories of a hidden valley and cave inhabited by a race of giant hairy creatures did suck you in, Shawn had to admit. Stories of Bigfoot and Sasquatch had always been part of the Indian culture and the northwestern folklore. Until reading Matt's writings, he had never heard the name, *S'cwene'y'ti*. Apparently, this had been the name used by Matt's Indian wife, Morning Flower. From best they could tell Matt had not told his wife of his writings. He did not seem to share her deep-rooted belief that these creatures should be protected at all cost, and that no man should ever know the location of this cave and hidden valley. Members of a wagon train had sworn to a pack to keep it their little secret.

Matt wrote that his friend BN the wagon master had settled down with an ex-madam Lillian Staggs when they had arrived in California. He had taken on work as a lawman and they had planned to marry, but he had been slain, shot in the back on the eve of their wedding day. Lillian Staggs had moved on to parts unknown. Matt mentioned that he never saw Jim Creswell and his children again but was sure Jim would keep their secret. Neither he nor Morning Flower ever returned to the tribe of her brother, and he often regretted that, knowing how much she loved Panther Claw.

Matt true to his word, had never revealed the whereabouts of the *S'cwene'y'ti* or had ever admitted their existence, but it had haunted him to the grave. That's why he had written about it in his personal diary, a simple man's way of maintaining his sanity. While he did not map out the location, he did indicate an area in the northern woods, near a mountain that fit the description of Mount Saint Helens.

The infamous Ape Canyon was near the dormant volcano. He and Mattie would focus on that area when they returned in the spring, unless they received a new lead from the gentleman they planned to interview. Mattie's research had uncovered many interesting events in the terrain near St. Helens.

One such encounter happened in 1924 in Ape Canyon, when a bunch of miners were attacked by hairy ape-man. The documentation on that incident indicated the miners had shot at and possibly wounded one or more of these things. They eventually retaliated, attacking the miners trapped inside their cabin, pelting their cabin with rocks while trying to gain access. The miners escaped without injury the next day.

Ironically, Matt McGregor had recalled a similar attack in his writings of a group of mountain men. The creatures in that attack had eventually sought out and abducted the five men responsible for shooting one of them. These things murdered the original shooter and had taken the remaining four to the hidden valley. None of them survived their ordeal. There was mention of some of them becoming breeders, but Shawn wasn't sure he understood McGregor's meaning behind this brief statement.

His scribbling stated that there had been a wagon train involved, more kidnappings and several rescue parties, all ending under very tragic circumstances. He indicated he too had been taken and rescued, but not before being subjected to some more embarrassing situations.

He didn't elaborate on these situations either. In all, it appeared that maybe a couple of dozen people had lost their lives surrounding these events and other skirmishes pertinent to his accounts. Among the dead, besides the five mountain men, were various members of that wagon train and a small band of Indians.

Other incidents uncovered by Mattie too eerily resembled the accounts in Matt's journal. Reports of prospectors being abducted while still in their sleeping bags concurred with McGregor's own tales. Ungodly smells, the rock chunking, and pounding on trees and the cabin walls, drew similarities to what had happened to him and others during that 1800's account. It was no wonder that Mattie had allowed this quest to devour her. History pointed to some truth in their existence.

Tomorrow she would interview an eyewitness, the first actual eyewitness since she had begun her little investigation. Shawn hoped for her sake it would pay off. He had to admit that the thought of these creatures existing and living in the deep woods of Oregon and Washington did intrigue him too. He would not admit that to Mattie though.

Unlike her, he needed concrete proof, not smoke and mirrors and fairy tales. Seeing one with his own eyes would be the only way he would buy into it. He hoped this character tomorrow wouldn't be a local crackpot or the perpetrator of a hoax. Time would tell.

That very afternoon, the eve of their scheduled meeting and on the fringes of the deep woods, Bert Thomson and his stepson, Bob, loaded the last of the hard wood in his old pickup. The load rounded off some three feet above the truck bed's side walls. Once seasoned, this would burn just fine in his Buck Stove insert. What Bert or his young son had failed to notice was that the weight of the firewood had caused the truck's four tires to sink several inches deep into the soft ground. Not until he attempted to drive his truck from the remote trail did reality slap him between his eyes. The truck didn't budge.

Bob, nearly thirteen, had just reached puberty and was still amazed by the changes to his body lately. He had started sprouting blonde hair where none had been, and he had been experiencing feelings that would not go away without a little persistent persuasion. His stepdad had smiled and told him he had arrived and assured him contrary to tales taking care of it would not make him go suddenly blind. That had been way too much information from his stepdad.

Wearing faded camouflaged overalls and a matching hat, Bob enjoyed spending afternoons like this in the woods. He enjoyed most of the man talk. His stepdad called it male bonding. He even allowed him to chew tobacco. Times like this he really like being around his stepdad, but there were those other times that frightened and troubled him. Bob had tried to tell his mom about those times, but she has shushed him, not wanting to upset the good thing they had with Bert. Bert had a darker side. It worsened when he drank Scotch.

"Damn it," he cursed, climbing out to assess the dilemma.

"What's wrong, Papa?"

"Ground has thawed I reckon," he answered, squatting down by the driver's side back tire. "Let's see what we can do to get her going, boy."

Bert grabbed his ax and began cutting down several small saplings to wedge underneath all four tires. These would be used for runners. Bob helped him drag them to the truck. Bert on all fours started positioning the trees under the tires.

"Whew boy," he yelled, taking off his Seattle Mariners ball cap and fanning the air. "Did you cut one?"

"No sir," grinned Bob. "You always told me to claim the nasty ones and that one doesn't belong to me."

Grinning, Bert patted Bob on the head, that's my boy. He then stood up and scanned the small clearing near the trail. The smell felt like it was settling in his clothes, like when you're cooped up in a room full of smokers. He thought maybe it might be a polecat, but he had smelled them often and this was ten times worse.

"What is it Papa?" Bob was now gagging and spitting.

Before he could answer something grunted loudly in the thick overgrown forest on the opposite side of the truck. It repeated the sound with an extremely deep and commanding tone. Bert strained his eyes, trying to zero in on the source in the thick stand of firs. He saw nothing.

"Hand me my shotgun," ordered Bert. Bob quickly retrieved it from the gun rack on the truck's back window.

Bert broke open the double barrel to ensure buckshot occupied both chambers. He surveyed the tree line, waiting for the next sound. After a couple of minutes of silence, he shrugged, leaned the gun against the truck, and returned to his task of freeing up their ride.

"Was it a bear, Papa?"

"Could have been I suppose, but I've never seen one around here before. They usually keep to themselves. It might have been an old buck I reckon. Sometimes they grunt and stomp at you." That was no grunt he had ever heard from bear or deer, but there was no need to spook Bob. Whatever it was, it must be gone now.

Bert finished placing the limbs in front of the driver's side tires and walked around to do the same on the passenger side. When he did, something shook the bushes like it meant business. He had made a very bad decision leaving his shotgun on the opposite side of the truck.

Sunday Morning
Amboy Waffle House

Mattie and Shawn Reynolds entered the doors and every head turned their way as if choreographed. They were obviously the only strangers in the establishment and the Waffle King was for locals only. The waitress motioned them to seat themselves, so they grabbed the only open booth.

"Coffee," the waitress asked.

"Yes, please," spoke up Shawn, noticing the tag on her shirt indicated her name was Norma. "Thank you, Norma."

"Do you know a Mister Anson Parker?"

"That would be him coming out of the Men's restroom," said Norma nodding in that direction.

Anson spotted them and pegged the strangers as the ones he was supposed to meet. He looked much older than fifty-eight. These last six years had taken their toll on him. Losing his wife to cancer last year hadn't helped.

"You must be the Reynolds' couple," he said, extending his hand.

Shawn chuckled and then asked. "How could you tell?"

"Please, have a seat," motioned Mattie.

Anson slipped into the booth and flagged Norma for a coffee refill. He eyed the couple sitting across from him intently. After a few seconds he said, "Small town. I heard why you were snooping around up in the backwoods. Did you find anything worthwhile up there?"

"Not so far," answered Mattie. "What do you know about these so-called forest legends, Mister Parker?"

"Getting right to the point aren't you little lady, I like that. Legend would imply there's no fact. I assure you what I saw was very alive and real."

Shawn cut to the chase. "Well, time is short. We have a long drive. Just what did you think you saw, Mister Parker?"

"What's in this for you? I mean do you work for like a newspaper or something. I don't want my name plastered all over the news. This is between just me and you. And for the record I did not think I saw something. I did see something. I don't need these folks looking at me like they think I'm crazy. I have to live here you know."

"He didn't intend to insult you sir. We have no affiliation with a paper, magazine, television station, or any other news media. This is personal."

"It is to me too. Other than my wife, may she rest her dear soul, I've kept this bottled up for the past six years, because I don't want people thinking old Anson Parker is a fool or raving lunatic. Hell, lot of time passed before I even shared it with her. Sometimes you just need to get it out in the open and let somebody else weigh in on it. I'm not sure she totally believed me, but she didn't call me crazy. I'm still struggling a bit in telling strangers."

"Understood," she assured him.

"Mister Parker," said Shawn.

"Anson," he replied.

"Anson why are you willing to share your story with strangers now, after all these years?"

"I don't really know. I guess after hearing what you two were looking for I figured I might finally have somebody to talk to that wouldn't think I'm touched in the head. That means a lot to me."

Norma returned to refill the cups and Anson fell silent until she completed her task and moved on to the next table. "Don't say anything that you don't want repeated in front of that busy body. She's the town gossip and this here Waffle King is like a canker sore for rumors."

"Okay, Anson," said Mattie. "Tell us what has haunted you all these years. Maybe we can help?"

Anson took them back to 1974 and his encounter with the giant hairy creatures. It flowed so effortlessly and vividly that Mattie felt she was there with him. It even captivated Shawn, but he would never admit it. Without a doubt this man believed what he had seen was real.

"So now that you've heard my story do you think I am a damned old fool?"

"What you experienced has been documented many times by people who smelled, saw, or heard what you did," explained Mattie. "So, no, you're as sane as the next person."

Anson nodded, relieved to hear her response.

She continued, "My great, great grandfather reported similar incidences in his chronicles from the mid 1800's. That's why I want to get to the bottom of this phenomenon."

"That makes me feel a hell of lot better," said Anson. "You don't know how good it feels just to get this off my chest. So, all the stories that have been around for ages are real?"

"My ancestor apparently believed they were real enough to put it in his writing. Would you be willing to take us to this place?"

"Now?"

"Not now. We must get back to Sacramento today," again interrupted Shawn.

"We'll plan a return trip," she replied giving Shawn *The Look*.

"Let me think on it," he answered, scribbling his phone number down on a napkin for them. "You call me when you settle on a date for coming back. I'll let you know for sure then."

"Fair enough," she said, folding up the napkin and putting it in her purse.

Anson slid out of the booth. Both Shawn and Mattie stood, shaking his hand and bidding him farewell. The man did look like an enormous weight had been lifted off his shoulders. Confession is good for the soul, whether it is real or not, speculated Shawn.

"What do you think?"

"Well, like you told him," answered Shawn, "It supports your old great grandpa's stories and reports from many other countless witnesses."

"But," she finished.

"But we have no real evidence, do we? We're still at square one. I'm the relentless skeptic without it. Don't you think if a tribe of these things exists like in his little diary that mankind would have stumbled up on them by now? Where's the concrete evidence, the smoking gun?"

"Honey, you're missing the point. People report seeing them all the time, so there has to be more than just one of them out there."

"Yeah, just like ghost, UFOs, and the Loch Ness Monster. They're everywhere."

"You left out the Tooth Fairy and Easter Bunny," Mattie snapped, not appreciating his sarcasm.

"And Santa, the Stork and the Boogey Man..." he continued, just to fuel the fire.

"You know you're really acting like such a smart ass," she said, now fuming. "I thought you were with me on this!"

"I'm just saying we need to move forward cautiously and keep this close to the vest. We certainly don't need any unnecessary publicity. The fewer people that know what we're doing, the better."

"I don't think you have to worry about Parker if that's what you're concerned about."

"No, I'm sure old Anson won't say anything. He was thrilled to just have someone to talk to, but others would go into a feeding frenzy and make us look like flying saucer hunters. Neither of us can afford to lose our credibility. We do have to work for a living."

"Noted," she said.

"Let's hit the road. We have a long drive."

"I'm going to get to the truth and that's a promise."

"Never doubted it for a second," smiled Shawn.

In the deep woods...

"Hey man, it has been a damn week and you haven't caught that sneaky bastard that keeps tripping our alarm system," complained Speedy.

"Bastard is right and it's a pretty damn smart one. It keeps breaking into our storage shed and stealing food, mostly sweets or prepackaged goods, no canned items," answered Nash. "It intentionally trips the traps every time. I've never seen anything do crap like this."

"Well, aren't we lucky? I guess it doesn't have a damn opener then or your phantom would take the canned goods," said Speedy, in a smart-ass tone. "And it's smarter than you, old man. What does that make you?"

"Good news," said Nash, ignoring the sarcasm, "It hasn't breached the green house."

"So, I guess it doesn't have a bong, rolling paper or matches," snapped Speedy. "We're so frigging lucky, aren't we? We can still get stoned but won't have food for the munchies."

"And it doesn't appear to have an arrest warrant," replied Nash, with a face showing no emotion.

"Screw you Nash. You still think it's Bigfoot, don't you?"

"Well, we're still seeing some mighty large footprints. You've seen them. What do you think? It's not our imagination, that's for damn sure."

"Big sonofabitch, whatever it is. I don't buy into this giant gorilla crap though. I think it's probably a bear or somebody just messing with us. Maybe it's that sonofabitch, Booger Rhodes trying to spook us off our little operation so he can steal it from us?"

"You heard Velvet. She said she didn't tell him anything."

"Yeah, right. You believe that bitch, don't you? If she's humping him, she's doing more with that mouth of hers than just giving hummers. You can count on it."

Speedy didn't care much for Velvet. She seemed to think she was running the show just because of her knowledge and expertise of weed growing. If not for Ceil, he would have gotten rid of Velvet long ago. Getting rid of her now would mean killing her. That didn't sound like such a bad idea to him. He had killed before for lesser reasons, but he would abide by Ceil's wishes, for now.

Speedy continued his ranting, "Booger would just love to cut in on this action. I've had past dealings with him, and none have been good. He has gang connections too and loves strutting for the big dogs. I'm not willing to share this with anybody else, especially not that sonofabitch, Booger Rhodes."

"Got it, but I don't think our intruder is Booger. I don't think he has the smarts to pull this off. What you say I do a little tracking and see if I can trail it back to its hiding place?"

"Fine by me. You should have done that weeks ago. I bet you find it leads back to tire tracks that belong to Booger."

"If it does, let me deal with him. I have some old backwoods' ways of persuasion that might just work on our wise guy."

"He's all yours. Just don't tell me where you buried the body. I know where far too many are located already."

Nash cracked an uncharacteristic smile on that one. "What if it's not Booger?"

"And that alternative would be one of your imaginary gorilla men. Same applies Use whatever persuasion you see fit to get rid of that marauder too."

He nodded. "I'll follow the next fresh trail."

"Just see to it that you put a stop to this crap, even if you have to bring down old King Kong.

April 30th

Mattie eyed her Franklin Planner. She couldn't believe it had been almost two and half months since their little jaunt to Washington State. Tomorrow would be May 1st. Her lecture calendar had filled, offering no breaks for a return trip. Her research of Sasquatch sightings and historical information had taken a setback too. She had not intended to shelve it, but the travel and personal appearances had taken a toll. She regretted having to back off now.

Shawn had been extremely busy too. One of his partners had opted out of the practice because of family issues. He and his remaining partner had absorbed the patient workload. They had little free time for each other lately, much less sleuth time. She glanced at her watch, 2:45 P. Her plane would be arriving in Sacramento within the hour. She had nothing on her calendar until Saturday, when she would depart for LA for a weeklong conference. It was Wednesday, April 30th. She hoped for a little downtime with Shawn if his calendar was open Thursday too. She needed it.

Shortly after 7 PM Mattie heard Shawn entering the backdoor. She greeted him with his favorite drink, a Manhattan. Showered and perfumed, she stood there naked as a Jaybird. He set his second favorite thing on the table and opted to partake of his most favorite thing instead, her. He drank his fill.

Basking on the den floor, his clothes strewn everywhere, she asked him, "Can you take tomorrow off for more of the same?"

He sighed, "I can think of anything that I would rather do but..."

"But?"

"Neil and I are buried in patients tomorrow. I don't even have an open slot for lunch. I suspect by the time I make my hospital rounds I won't make it back here until after ten tomorrow night, at the earliest."

"Bomber," she whined.

She didn't hear Shawn leave the next morning and only woke when the morning sun slammed directly in her eyes through an opening in the blinds. She had slept to almost 9 AM, something she normally never did. She needed coffee and a shower. She still smelled strongly of sex, not a bad smell she thought to start off one's morning. After the shower, her third cup of coffee, and a slice of cheese toast she flopped down at her desk and began paging through various books she had purchased on Sasquatch, Big Foot, Yeti, and other hairy ape men literature. She had read most of these accounts way too many times. All the stories consisted of people smelling awful odors, hearing weird inhuman like cries, and growls or the discovery of gigantic footprints. All good stuff, but it didn't prove a thing.

The rock throwing and tree knocking seemed to be a common theme. Rarely did these alleged creatures ever inflict any physical harm to their victims. Matt McGregor had indicated in his journal that the *S'cwene'y'ti* were for the most part peaceful creatures. He did go on to state that you did not want to cross them though. They had the memory of an elephant and would seek justice if harmed.

Some of the more intriguing stories included testimonials of sightings. Creatures were often seen crossing old logging roads or highways in remote areas. People reported hearing or seeing them rummaging through their trash cans or stealing food items like fish. By nature, they didn't appear to be overly carnivorous other than fish, and they were not cannibalistic by nature, despite the belief by many. Matt reinforced this fact in his memoir. Of course, Anson had been convinced that these creatures had stolen his deer.

Her ancestor's writings and other accounts, a splattering of the 1800 and even early 1900 tales, described actual abductions. These were rare now, the Tommy McAllister case being the exception. Males seemed to be their primary targets, but females were taken as well. The Indians seemed to accept these kidnappings as part of their culture more so than the white man.

Morning Flower, her great, great grandmother and wife of Matt McGregor, a full-blooded Indian, apparently believed these creatures were godlike and should be protected. Matt gave into her wishes and kept the secret until just before he died. His own abduction had continued to haunt his dreams. He had struggled to distance himself from the apparent anguish and humiliation he had suffered while being held captive. His breeder reference while not detailed, spurred her curiosity. She felt that somehow these comments offered a key to solving the mystery. He described the humiliation of this but was apparently embarrassed by the ordeal. What did it really mean? What had happened to Matt McGregor and those others?

Another strange phenomenon he had described had to do with the glowing bright fires he vaguely remembered seeing in the far reaches of that canyon. There were no such artificial lights during that time, at least none that would produce the brilliance he said he had encountered. He felt these were somehow associated with his memory loss and possible brain washing. He couldn't really describe or recall the actual source of these bright fires, even though they were etched in his memory.

From his writings Matt McGregor never got over the fact that they had left others behind when he had escaped. He mentioned a couple of fellow mountain men, a Calvary Lieutenant, and a young Indian brave. He often wondered if they had survived and remained prisoners to do the Foot clan's biddings. He did not elaborate on what those biddings included, again uncomfortable in filling in the gaps in the story.

She glanced at her watch, almost 11 AM. She decided to head over to the library and peruse the newspaper microfilm for the past couple of months, specifically focusing on those from the northwestern region. Sightings had been a rarity lately, but maybe she'd get lucky.

Mattie arrived just before noon at the library. The librarian greeted her saying she had not seen her in a while. They exchanged the usual pleasantries. Rather than backtrack, starting with today's May 1st date, she decided to go back and work her way forward. She started with the week before Valentines, primarily because she hadn't been to the library since their last trip and the meeting with Anson Parker. The first several days of perusing proved uneventful. She skipped ahead and then on February 15th the headlines knocked her breathless.

She read the article; reread it two more times, and then located several follow-ups in the regional paper for the next couple weeks, and then the story simply died. She fumbled in her purse until she found the phone number, and then proceeded to the payphone to make the call. Her breathing by now had become labored from a mixture of shock and excitement. The phone rang six times before the party on the other end picked up.

"Mister Parker, I mean Anson, this is Mattie Reynolds. My husband and I met with you at the Waffle King a couple of months ago," she said, trying to calm down her tone.

"How are you doing, Mrs. Reynolds? I thought you had forgotten about us crazy folks."

"I never said you were crazy."

"I know, and I appreciated you hearing me out. Does this mean you and your husband is planning a return trip?"

"You can be assured of that. Why didn't you call to tell me about that other abduction, the one that happened the day we left?"

"You didn't give me your phone number. I figured you did that because you didn't want me to call you anymore with my foolish talk."

"Crap, trust me, it was just an oversight, I assure you, Anson. I just read several articles on that episode. What can you tell me about it?"

"Probably not much more than what you done already read. It happened north of here. I don't know the feller, but it was a shame what happened to his boy."

"And they never found him."

"Not that I've heard. Sounds like one of them things like what I saw might have snatched him up. Of course, nobody believes his poor old stepdaddy. They still think he had something to do with it.

That's why I kept my mouth shut when it happened to me. People around here don't take kindly to such foolish talk."

"It sure does resemble what happened to that Cub Scout a few years ago, doesn't it? They never found him either did they?"

"Nope, and they drove that poor scout leader to suicide. He just blew his head off. Some people say he killed himself because he was so torn up about it. Others think he did it because he was guilty of doing in that boy like some kind of crazed pervert or something. Guess we'll never know what really happened. Dead men are not much for talking."

"I'm looking at my calendar. I have an opening starting on the 10th and don't have anything else scheduled until the 23rd. What you say we plan to meet you for breakfast same time at the Waffle King on the 11th?"

"I'm usually there on Sunday mornings anyway, so I will see you then. Do you think one of the hairy monsters really got that boy?"

"Well, it resembles what I've read from my long lost relative. Somehow I just don't buy into both a scout master and a father being guilty of the crime."

"Me either, but I've seen one of them things firsthand. Like I said, you tell anybody, I will deny it, you hear."

"See you on the 11th, Anson."

She hung up the phone and then asked the librarian for printed copies of the specific articles she had just read. Shawn needed to read these. Shawn arrived home just past midnight. Even though Mattie had a five AM flight to LA, she waited up for him. She watched him patiently while he read the clippings.

"What do you think?"

"So, this Bert Thomson and his stepson, Bob, crossed paths with one of your *S'cwene'y'ti* and it snatched up the kid and disappeared while his stepfather stood there holding a loaded shotgun?"

"He couldn't shoot without jeopardizing hitting the boy."

"Why didn't he just rush it and pound it with the gun instead? It had the boy. He should have done something. I would have."

"He said in the article that it was huge, over eight feet tall and it completely caught him off guard."

"For Christ sake Mattie, it had his stepson, if we can believe a single word he said. You wouldn't have stood there with your thumbs up your ass, would you? Something is hokey about this story."

"Well he didn't expect it to sprint off with the boy like it did," she again tried to defend the man's position. "You just don't see something like this every day."

"Okay. I will give him that. Then why didn't he chase after it?"

"It did say in one of those follow up articles that he tried to follow it, but it was much too fast and quickly disappeared in the dense growth, but you're missing the point, honey. We have a fresh sighting."

"The local authorities didn't sound like they bought the man's story. It sounds like they still suspect him. They didn't find any tracks or sign of his alleged creature."

"It doesn't matter what the police think. It's just all adding up. Can't you see?"

Shawn just rolled his eyes and shrugged, no creature, no hard evidence, end of story.

"My calendar is open after the 10th. Once I wrap up in LA, I say we go check this out. It's too fresh to pass up."

"Can't do. I'm booked solid all month. You know how my business is going right now. We're swamped. Can it wait until next month?"

"June is a bad month for me. I really want to dig into this while I have an opportunity and it's still sort of fresh."

"I know you. There's no talking you out of this, right?"

"Not a chance."

"Are you coming home first?"

"As it stands, I am thinking of flying from LA to Portland and meeting up with Anson Parker. I've already phoned him. He's agreed to meet us...me I suppose."

"Anson seems to be a trustworthy guy. I suppose you'll be safe in his hands."

"I'll be fine, but it would be much better if you were by my side. My flight is in a couple of hours."

"I'll drive you to the airport. I love you, Mattie."

"And I love you too, but I have to know the truth."

"I know you do. What do they say? Oh yeah, the truth will set you free."

"And it will knock science on its ass if I can photograph one of these things or bring back hard evidence that they really do exist."

"Is that what this is all about?"

"You know me better than that. I just want to experience what old great grandpa McGregor experienced."

"Watch what you ask for my darling. It screwed up the old man and he never got over it. I like my women better if they're not in straitjackets."

"I love you, Shawn."

"Ditto."

May 3rd 9:00 AM
Castle Rock, Washington
Mountain Joe's Diner

"Tell me Mister Paxton. What makes you think you can do something no one else has been able to do in the nine years since he jumped from that plane?" The lily-white complexioned man, sitting on the opposite side of the booth, chewing on a rather large stogie, seemed a bit intimidating.

"Call me Max. I believe the others have been concentrating their efforts too far south of where I believe D.B. Cooper landed and most likely met his untimely demise, Mister Spencer Underhill. Can I call you Spence?"

"Underhill will suffice. Do you know this country?"

"No sir, but I know somebody that does. His name is Elijah Franklin Payne and he has lived in those woods and mountains all his life. We can secure his services with a thousand bucks plus expenses."

"Are you acquainted with this Payne gentleman?"

"Not personally, but I know him by reputation. The guy that runs that outrigger store down the street referred him; claimed he was the best and worth every single penny."

"Do you know that large black man waving at the window? He seems to want something."

Max turned to see Bam-Bam with his hands cupped around his huge round cheeks and nose pressed against the glass. Bam-Bam grinned and started waving again.

"Don't worry about Bam-Bam. He's just a little slow witted. I'm sort of his guardian."

"It appears he would like to come in and join us."

"He's fine. I told him to wait there until we finished our business."

60

"Indeed, so you assume we can do business?"

"Well, you're the one that called me after you saw that add I ran in the state paper."

"Let's say I'm interested and will finance this little expedition of yours. What's your cut? I would think carefully before you respond, Mister Paxton. Something tells me I could do this without you."

Max could read people and he sensed that this man Underhill sitting across from him could not be conned and should not be crossed. "How about a 60-40 split when we find the cash?"

"And if we don't, I'm out of everything and you aren't out of one red cent," replied Underhill. "I tell you what Mister Paxton. I'll give you 25% of what we find and will allow you to slither back in that hole you crawled out of, if we find nothing."

"But it's my idea and," Max attempted to say.

"And my money staking it," interrupted Underhill. "I would take my offer if I was you, and I handle all cash transactions. You supply the manpower."

The man's eyes were cold, inhuman, and unemotional. Shark eyes. They were eyes that you shouldn't cross or bare awful consequences. Max had crossed men like this before and had no fond memories of those encounters. Max calculated that his cut would be less than fifty thousand dollars, if they found the remainder of the missing money intact.

"35%," countered Max, pushing his luck.

"You'll take 30% and consider yourself fortunate that I'm feeling generous today."

Max conceded, but he did not like how this had gone. He sensed this Underhill would have just as quickly walked away. He wasn't willing to let this fish off his hook. He had no other nibbles.

"What's your story, Underhill?"

"Closed book to you. Arrange a meeting with Payne this afternoon. We purchase what we need and leave in the morning."

"Level with me Nash. You've been at this for weeks, trailing apparitions into those woods, and what have you got to show for it, absolutely nothing and our goods keep being raided. By any chance did you trail our intruder back to a hiding place this time? We have gotten out the first crop of weed and the second is almost ready. Tell me something good for a damn change."

"Sorry. Trail went cold like always. This time on that hard ass rock surface in Ape Canyon. I think it knew I was following it again."

Speedy stood there, arms crossed. "Ape Canyon. Now doesn't that just sound appropriate. You still think it's one of those hairy gorillas, don't you?"

Nash just shrugged. "How much longer before we can harvest the balance of the crop and leave this mountain?"

"Velvet said the second one should be ready within the next week or so. We add that to what we already have, and we get the hell out of here. I can see it on your face. There is something else. Spit it out."

"I saw Booger's truck about a mile and half back. It looks like you were right. He has been snooping around here. I figure he's chomping at the bits since we've already harvested some of our crop."

"So, Velvet did blab her mouth to that worthless piece of crap. Do you think he's out there watching us?"

"Yep. He's a couple hundred yards back, over your left shoulder, and up on the ridge. I saw the reflection from his binoculars."

"Do you have any of those traps left?"

Nash grinned. "Where do you want them?"

"Around that bastard's ankles," remarked Speedy. "And he won't be needing that truck either. Let's keep this our little secret. There's no need to stress out the girls."

"Give him something to watch and I'll take care of the rest. I'll leave him a little surprise back at his truck."

"Nash, you get rid of the evidence afterwards. Are you okay with this?"

"This isn't my first rodeo, if that's what you're asking? I don't like to make a habit of it, but I'd say this garbage needs to be buried. It stinks to high heavens and will only get worse if we don't get rid of it. I don't like claim jumpers."

"I'll sweeten the pot for you, no pun intended. It is the least I can do."

"Just for the record, I still don't think Booger is our culprit. This is the first time I've seen him around and I would know." Nash then nodded and ambled off to retrieve and set the traps. Booger Rhodes would not be returning from his espionage trip.

Speedy began staging the distraction. He allowed Booger to see him hauling some of the weed to a table in the yard where he pretended to strip and harvest the bounty. He figured old Booger's eyes were popping out of their sockets about now at the mere sight of it.

Velvet walked up behind him. "What are you doing with that? You shouldn't have pulled that plant. It wasn't mature?"

"I guess you forget Princess. This shit belongs to me. If I want to pluck a plant or two it's my damn call," snapped Speedy very loudly, already looking forward to silencing the stoolie.

"I thought that's why you brought me on board, to make sure this was done right." She questioned him as if she thought she carried the big stick

"I did think that's why I cut you in on this, but..."

"But what? Finish it. It sounds like you've having second thoughts about our little arrangement."

"But nothing," he smiled. "You're doing such a fine job that I'm going to hate to see it end."

Velvet, now rattled by this conversation and Speed's tone, felt things might be going sour. "I need to do another supply run. I'll probably stay the night and come back in the morning."

"Since I'm damn clueless about taking care of these plants, why don't you stay here and retrain me. I'll have Ceil do the run this time."

Now she knew something was fishy. He was on to her. He had to be, but how? "I'll just plan to return tonight then."

"Ceil will do it. You and me, we need a little one on one time. Take me in under your wing and teach me a few things."

Velvet didn't appreciate his ridiculous smile. Yep, something was up. She needed to alert Booger and the Calvary. It was time to move in on this operation and eliminate the competition.

Speedy had also read her perfectly. She was squirming. Nash wanted a distraction, so why not give him one. He reached over and grabbed Velvet by the arm, twirled her in one swift motion. He held his Bowie hunting knife to her throat. Booger watched helplessly from his hiding place on the ridge.

Velvet wore no bra and Speedy fondled her huge fleshy breast, 100% real to the touch. Black as an ace of spades she lived up to her African heritage with a womanly sized body and corn rolled hair. Shame he would not be sampling her. She would have been quite a ride, he thought. He then slit her throat and let her fall to the ground like a bleeding hog.

Booger almost yelled out aloud not believing what he had just witnessed. He slid back from his hiding place, leapt up, and hauled ass for his truck. Vengeance would be his once he rounded up the boys and returned up here to kill that bastard and confiscate that crop.

Booger was a big ole mountain boy with a barrel chest and anvil sized arms. He was almost as wide as he was tall, and he was less than five feet eight inches. He looked more white than black, having had a black father and white mother. His broad nose and full lips were about the only signs linking him to his father. He had been deserted by both parents when he was seven. His aunt had done the best she could raising him, but he fell in too easily to a life of crime and running with the wrong crowd. Drugs had been his major means of revenue, but he never touched them himself. He was a boozer, having a weakness for dark Rum. He wished he had a bottle right now.

He and Velvet had been together for the past seven months. He enjoyed the sex with her, but there was no love between them. He had never loved anyone and probably never would. He was a loner. He suspected they would have parted company after they split the profits of their planned little acquisition. Things work out for a reason, he supposed. It now all belonged to him. He traveled the one and half miles in record time, returning to what he thought was a concealed vehicle. Booger and Velvet had kept their little opportunist venture between them until now, but he intended to call in a few favors and return with a small army to take the prize. Then he would make these bastards pay for what they had done to his accomplice. He had originally planned to kill them anyway. He would make them suffer instead, a slow death.

Booger saw the truck ahead and stopped for a second to catch his breath. That's when he sucked in the foul odor that caused him to gag. He thought *had something just died here*. He heard the grunt from his left and turned to see the inhuman face towering above him from the fir trees less than six feet away. Too terrified to run and knowing he could not fire his pistol without alerting the others of his presence, he did the only thing he could do. He quickly retrieved the blade from its holster on his belt. He held the machete for what seemed like minutes, maintaining direct eye contact with this face from hell. Locked in a stare down, neither of them moved.

Finally, the creature stepped into full sight, and what a sight it became. Massive, muscular and huge, eyeing his adversary, Booger realized he was badly overmatched. He did the only thing he knew to do and charged this nightmare before it had a chance to make a move on him. Booger had always been a master at the element of surprise. There was no such thing as a fair fight or allowing your opponent to get the advantage. That's why he never lost a fight. He didn't play by the rules. He lunged and slashed simultaneously, drew first blood. An inhuman scream came from the thing that stood before him. As planned, he had caught it off guard.

The creature moved with lighting speed, much quicker than Booger could have ever imagined possible for such a large animal, if it was an animal at all. Falling lifeless to the forest floor, neck broken, Booger Rhodes would never get the upper hand again. He was at least spared a more painful and agonizing fate awaiting him at his truck. The steel traps set by Nash would not claim their intended quarry. Booger's body would never be found. Such is the way of the *S'cwene'y'ti.*

The wind carried the ancient spoken warning of the long dead Indian Chief; *Heed these words from Lone Bear. Stay east of the big water. Do not travel into the mountains of the north woods for the S'cwene'y'ti lives there. The sacred ones welcome no intruder to their land. Be wise. Set your traps in the streams south of the mountain forest. Take not from the S'cwene'y'ti for they do not forgive easily. Anger them and they take your spirit. You disappear as does the melting snow.*

Wednesday May 7th

Mattie Reynolds sat in her hotel room reviewing her literature for tomorrow's lecture. Her allotted time slot would begin after lunch and would close the day's events at four. She had only to make it another three days and her flight was scheduled to depart at 8:17 Saturday morning. She knew her topic backwards and frontward, so she required no rehearsals. Glancing over at the digital alarm clock, 7 PM, it was too early to phone Shawn He had told her he had been roped into an advisory meeting at the hospital and it would probably be after 10 before he arrived home.

With no new articles to read she searched in her briefcase until she located Matt McGregor's journal. She had read it cover to cover so many times she could almost recite the entries. Morning Flower McGregor had been true to her convictions of protecting the *S'cwene'y'ti*. Matt had remained silent, but he didn't share his wife's stubbornness to protect the legend.

True to her and the others, he had honored the pact the survivors had made. Something unimaginable had happened to Matt while being held captive by the Foot clan. He struggled with this occurrence his entire life but continued to support his wife's wishes. Even after her death, just two years before his own, he remained silent. Code of the mountain man, she surmised.

He had once contacted his old trapper buddy BN to see if he felt the same. BN told Matt he had long ago put the ordeal behind him. His nightmares were still haunted by those murdered while under his leadership of the wagon train. He didn't blame the giant hairy ones for this treachery. Men had been responsible, and they had received due punishment. Sadly, this man Bad Nose Carlson had been gunned down after surviving the ordeal in the wild. She read again how Matt had never seen the young farmer and his two children, the remaining survivors from the wagon train after they arrived in San Francisco. He had hoped the man had remarried and had lived a long and prosperous life.

He and Morning Flower had raised three children of their own, two boys and one girl, in addition to Peter and Pamela, who each lost both their parents during the unfortunate event of that ill-fated wagon train. Matt received word about Morning Flower's brother after her death, that Panther Claw had become chief and lead the tribe for almost twenty years. He was found dead one winter morning by his son, slumped over a smoldering fire. He had not been sick. Matt suspected he had died of heart failure or possibly a stroke. His son succeeded him as chief. Matt nor Morning Flower had ever returned to the land occupied by her tribe, nor ever saw Soaring Eagle again. She had never met her nephew.

Mattie ran her fingers over the penciled words trying to connect with her ancestor. She wondered what she would do if she found concrete evidence that the legend lived. Being a professor, her intellect dictated that she owed it to the world to acknowledge an undiscovered species, possibly the mythical missing link, but her heart tried to convince her to uphold her great, great grandmother's wishes and tradition. She couldn't say which would win out. She would cross that bridge if she ever had the proof.

Mattie regretted that Shawn would not be able to join her, but that didn't deter her decision to go without him. She certainly didn't relish journeying into the deep woods alone. Injured and isolated in the great forest, one would most likely face certain death. She wasn't ready to face that outcome yet. Her mind raced, and she spun a plan. She hoped it would work. She would know for sure in less than four days.

Mattie wondered what Matt McGregor would do in her situation. What had been his real reason for writing this journal? Had he intended for one of his ancestors to reveal the secret or had this just been a way for him to cleanse his mortal soul, to die knowing someone else knew of these awful and eventful happenings? Could this be a test to determine if his heirs would remain loyal to the family promise?

Mattie wished she had lived in those times. She could just picture herself living among these creatures and learning everything about them. She could have been both student and teacher. Ah, but had these creatures really existed or had they been the ramblings of man who might have suffered from some sort of mental disorder?

No, Matt McGregor had not been crazy. His writings didn't come out as one written by some raving lunatic. Matt had written with conviction. She could see this in his penmanship. He believed in what he wrote. He experienced this phenomenon. He had been changed by his encounter and had suffered emotionally from other horrors in the secluded canyon. To solve the riddle, she must first find that canyon and evidence of the *S'cwene'y'ti's* existence. She must do this for Matt and more so for Mattie.

Destiny waited. She could sense it. She had never felt it any stronger than she did right now. One way or another, she would bring closure as had Matt McGregor. After all, it was indeed her birth right. Finding his journal had been the sign. She would not squander it. The mystery of the great northern woods was hers to solve.

One thing for sure, when she set a goal, she always reached it. This would be no different. Mattie Reynolds didn't know how to spell failure. She smiled. Her destiny awaited her in just a few short days from now. It felt like an eternity.

The D.B. Cooper Fortune Seekers

Elijah Franklin Payne eyed the motley crew standing before him. He rubbed his chin then subconsciously scratched his ass, contemplating whether he had made the right decision to take them into the high country. The old blue tick hound stood obediently by his side and yawned, not nearly as impressed by the strangers' presence.

Max broke the silence. "What would you like us to call you?"

"I don't give a rat's ass what you call me so long as you give me the money you promised me for dragging your butts around them northern woods," answered the old backwoodsman, spitting an impressive splatter of tobacco juice in the dirt less than an inch from Underhill's pristine polished black laced shoes.

Arms folded, Underhill clinched and then unclenched his hidden fist. He disliked this worm almost as much as he despised the con artist, Max Paxton. Jury was still out on the retarded black giant he had only formally met less than an hour ago, but he seemed harmless enough.

Obsessed to solve the mystery of D.B. Cooper he would make the most of it until either they achieved their goal, or it proved to be another wild goose chase. He had done worse over the past nine years in his search, so what was one more? At least they would be searching an area never considered or searched.

Underhill finally spoke up, "Mister Payne, if you would be so kind to acquire the supplies and gear we will need and bring me the receipts, I will reimburse you immediately."

"Tell you what. I have a better idea. You come with me and pay as we go. No need to let that money exchange hands so many times."

"As you wish," replied Underhill, almost regretting his decision to go through with this.

"How many days you fellers want to stay out yonder?"

"However long it takes to find what we're looking for," advised Max. "P to camp out for a while."

"We're going camping, Max," said Bam-Bam. "Are we going to roast marshmallows? I like marshmallows. I like those little weenies in the cans too, the ones with the beans. They make me fart though, but I still like them."

Both Elijah Franklin Payne and Underhill stared at the humongous Negro, wondering why in the hell Max Paxton would even consider bringing him along. Underhill sized him up, figuring he would at least make a good pack mule. He might be good for a few laughs too. Elijah Franklin Payne already had a pack mule named Old Bertha, so that thought never entered his mind.

"Have any of you got experience in the Washington north woods?" Elijah Franklin Payne was sizing them up and betting none had.

"That's why we're hiring you," said a very impatient Underhill. "We're relying on your expertise."

"I can tell you something right now," spoke the old mountain man as he spat another good one. "I'm not expecting to be your babysitter. You boys best be prepared to pull your own weight because we'll be crossing some mighty rough terrain. You better learn right now to shit or get off the pot. This ain't no place for whiners or drag asses. You keep up or get left behind. You boys hear me."

"I think we can keep up with you, Old Man," responded Underhill.

He smiled and spat again. "Best you remember that, because I'll remind you what you said when your tongue is hanging below your chin and you're blowing like an old has been moose."

Max wisely stayed out of this conversation. He figured the less he said the less likely Elijah Franklin Payne would be apt to rub his nose in it if he floundered out there.

"Let's go get those supplies. You best have cash because where we are going the proprietor doesn't like that plastic stuff. After we get what we need, we can drive up there at first light. We'll need a trailer to haul Old Bertha."

Underhill asked, "What's an Old Bertha?"

"My mule," he spat, and then answered, "Old Bertha and Blue Boy, my hound, go where I go."

"Very well," said Underhill. "We'll rent one for your animals."

"Can I pet the animals, Max? You remember that time you took me that petting zoo and the goats and reindeer almost knocked me down. They sure were hungry. You remember, don't you Max?"

No one responded to the slow-witted giant's question. Underhill just shook his head in disgust, dreading the extra baggage the big darkie would add. He didn't have much use for the Negro race, especially a retarded one. He believed slave traders had ruined this country. Funny he thought, everyone had always wanted to blame slavery on the confederacy, but those ships bringing them over flew United States colors and not those of the confederate flag. Northerners had been just as guilty as southerners. Americans were responsible for them being here.

Either way, in Underhill's mind, they contributed nothing to society. They were all just worthless criminals and they multiplied like rabbits. Steal and procreate, what other purpose did they have? He wasn't prodigious. He hated everyone, regardless to race, color or gender. He just disliked the darkies more than the rest. This world required another good purging. Where were one of those biblical floods when you needed one?

"It'll take us about six hours to get to that area you boys have in mind; two hours by automobile and the rest on foot."

Max grumbled to himself. *I cannot believe I agreed to just 30%. If we find all of it, my cut is less than sixty grand. But if I find it first, maybe he won't get any. Accidents can happen out there in the wilderness. Bam-Bam can see to that. Might be that the old mule skinner buys the farm too. Things have a way of working out. Sometimes all it requires is a little nudge.*

72

May 10th

Mattie Reynolds sat in the airport waiting for her flight to arrive. Still on schedule, she'd be in Portland shortly. She would meet with Anson Parker Sunday morning as planned. Hopefully by Monday. She'd be at the scene of the last alleged encounter. She had time for a quick phone call to Shawn. Using the payphone, she dialed home. No answer. She tried his office and the receptionist said he was in surgery.

Returning to her seat she began thinking just what she would have really done if her child had been snatched by an *S'cwene'y'ti*. She couldn't answer that question. She wasn't even sure how she would react to just seeing one up close and personal. It both excited and scared her with the prospects of encountering one of Matt McGregor's beasts.
Mattie really wished Shawn could have joined her this time. She felt like this might be the one. She retrieved her camera from her carry-on checking the battery and making sure the film had been properly advanced.

Mattie played with the focus on the zoom lens. If offered the opportunity, she didn't want her photograph to be one of those fuzzy out of focus shots that seemed to make the tabloids. She wouldn't allow pour quality to have the skeptics saying hers was just a man in a monkey suit. Mattie smiled, thinking how confident she was to already think she might have a photo in the can. Instinct my dear, she reminded herself, the advantage of having a women's intuition.

The announcer over the PA system bellowed that her flight had just arrived at the gate and boarding would commence in 15 minutes. She had time for a quick bathroom visit, and then she would be trekking toward her destiny, she hoped. How would she really respond to an actual encounter, side with Matt or Morning Flower? She just hoped she had that choice.

"Nash, it's been three days and there's still no sign of Booger Rhodes."

"Not a hair and that truck of his is still parked in the same place. The traps haven't been tripped either." Nash was rubbing the side of his neck, not liking this. "This is damned peculiar. It's like he just went and disappeared."

"You did bury Velvet deep, didn't you?"

"Speedy, for the one hundred and tenth time, the answer is still hell yeah. When I bury them, they stay buried," snapped Nash. "Is Cecelia still asking about her?"

"All the time, and I keep telling her the same damn lie, that she must have run off with Rhodes."

"She's not too bright, is she? She should be asking you how she got off this mountain with our truck still here."

"She has. I told her Rhodes must have snuck up here and whisked her away."

"And just walked away from her cut?"

"Enough, I've already been drilled a new butt hole without having to put up with your crap."

Nash gave him that possum grin and strolled off toward the green house. It still worried him about Booger. He had found more of those big tracks in the general area of the truck. Something stunk to high heaven. Nash had found a set of Booger's boot prints within a rock's throw of the truck then they just vanished, like he just grew wings. He had seen a set of the Bigfoot prints right next to Booger's. Nash had kept this information to himself for now, because he didn't want any more of Speedy's crap. Another week and they should be harvesting what were left and could kiss this place goodbye. A three-way split, and then back to Alaska for him. Sweet!

Mount Saint Helens

Damien Dark stood in the shadows of Mount Saint Helen. He scanned the mountain with his binoculars, but the surrounding forest appeared tranquil and undisturbed. The mountain had not rumbled since yesterday. He took that as a good sign that maybe the experts were wrong about a pending eruption. Damien flipped out his binder and reviewed his most recent entries.

He had certainly met some interesting characters over the past few days. Harry Truman said he had lived here for over fifty years and there wasn't a person man enough to make him leave. He wasn't afraid of this mountain; Truman had told him. That old guy had character appeal for sure, he thought.

Then there was that Johnson fellow he had stumbled up on over near Coldwater Ridge. He said he was some sort of expert on volcanoes and was living his dream, waiting and watching for what he had called an eminent eruption. Damien understood dreams. He was here because of his lifelong dream. Neither of these two gentlemen seemed concerned about the potential for the mountain to blow its wad, so he didn't heed the warnings either. Things like this didn't happen in the United States, if you discounted Hawaii and Alaska.

Damien had also crossed paths with a splattering of campers and loggers. None of these people had said they had seen what he was looking for, so he wasn't sure if this sighting would pan out or not. Most looked at him like they thought he was crazy. He would find proof this time or he wouldn't, such was the life of an amateur UFO Investigator.

Washington State was a little-known unidentified flying objects hotbed and ripe for his picking. His real name had not always been Damien Dark. He had been born Donnie Grubb, but that just didn't sound like a very impressive name for someone who hunted flying saucers and space men. Two years ago he legally became Damien Dark, UFO Investigator extraordinaire. His family had all but disowned him for doing it. His mother had cried for a week. His dad had kicked him out of the house because of the hat he called, nonsense.

Damien, barely twenty years old, fair haired and just as fair skinned, extremely nerdy and skinny as a toothpick, had yet to strike notoriety among the UFO investigating society. He had been hooked on UFOs since reading about the Roswell incident. He opted to take this year away from college to prove that they really existed. With that proof he would achieve recognition from his peers. While not a pledged member of the UFO Investigators League, he still admired the original UFOIL founder, Timothy Green Beckley. Damien's dream, to start a chapter of UFOIL in Washington State had thus far been unsuccessful.

Taking a break for lunch, Damien retrieved his book with documented encounters and sightings. These always got his juices flowing. In 1973 in Goshen, Ohio, a man walking his coon dogs had spotted a saucer and three aliens in a ravine. He watched them board the space craft and fly off. Amazing! He wished he could see a saucer. Maybe he would have better luck if he had a coon dog, a UFO tracking hound.

One year earlier in another part of Ohio, a short lizard or frog faced human had been spotted. No saucer had been seen with this little green man. Why didn't any of these people own a camera? His favorite had to be the Mothman back in the mid-sixties. A huge winged man like creature with red eyes had been spotted numerous times in West Virginia. Again, no UFO was ever seen, and no one ever figured out what this thing had been, but it had received plenty of publicity.

Ohio had a lot of UFO reports. He wished there were more in Washington. It would only take one encounter to get him noticed. Maybe he would get lucky. Even though the area was more famous for Bigfoot encounters, there had been reports recently of strange lights in the sky and power outages. Could the two be related? He doubted it. Little green men were always associated with UFOs, not Bigfoot.

He shoved his literature back into his backpack. Sitting on an old pine stump he ate his bologna and extra sharp cheese sandwich, and then he washed it down with a warm Pepsi. He rummaged through his backpack until he found his M&Ms. He loved these covered peanut delights and the slogan, melts in your mouth and not your hands.

Grabbing the bag with his teeth, he tugged on it to breach an opening. A much too large tear ripped down the bag spilling his gold onto the pine needles, just his luck. Scrambling to retrieve everyone, he crawled around on all fours. That's when he made first eye contact with two of the largest hairiest feet he had ever seen in his life. It would be the last thing he remembered. He hadn't told anyone where he had planned to hike today, a very big mistake.

Underhill had rented the trailer to haul the old coot's jackass. He cursed himself for being so stupid. The four of them rode in a 1978 Jeep Wagoner loaded to the hilt with gear and supplies. Blue Boy sat up front with his master and Underhill. Underhill didn't like the slobbering hound, but at least it didn't possess the gift of gab like its owner.

"Guess you boys heard that the mountain is cutting up a tad," stated Elijah Franklin Payne. "Some say she's just aching to blow her top and drop the mother lode."

Bam-Bam grinned as only he could. "Max, you always drop a load at the dog racetrack, don't you? Are you going to bet on Blue Boy, Max?"

"I did hear on the news that the volcano has been acting up since sometime back in March," commented Max, leaning over from the backseat, ignoring Bam-Bam.

"Yep, she's become quite restless the past month," he continued. "You boys are not scared of a little eruption, are you?"

"Are you," rebutted Underhill.

Cackling like a hen laying the big one, Elijah Franklin Payne answered, "Hell no, she'll probably grunt a little, spew a little more, and then slip back into her sleepy ways. That old mountain does this sometimes just to let us know she's there."

"Then I guess we proceed," answered Underhill. "Why are you stopping this vehicle?"

"I got to see a man about a dog," replied Elijah Franklin Payne.

"But you got a dog sitting on the seat beside you," said a puzzled Bam-Bam. "What kind of dog are you getting this time?"

"He means he's got to take a dump, Bam-Bam," explained Max.

"Number two," said Bam-Bam, holding up two fingers.

"Number two," confirmed Max.

Underhill rolled his eyes, thinking I've got these two talking in baby talk and the old fart is crapping while the meter is running. This venture stinks, literally, thought Underhill. We better find Cooper, or I'll have all their asses, including that stupid donkey and mangy hound.

The old man soon returned from his visit with nature and they were once again underway. Elijah Franklin Payne had been a backwoodsman for his entire sixty-seven years on this good earth. He was a man of average height and size, clean shaven except when he let his beard grow out in the winter. He still had a full head of gray bushy hair. Elijah lived a satisfying existence. The rustic log cabin where he resided had been constructed by his own hands. He lived off the land as much as possible, but still enjoyed the perks of civilization.

Payne had to have his chewing tobacco and coffee, store bought boots, long johns and overalls. He had a sweet tooth for crunchy peanut butter and semi-dark chocolate. He had no problem purchasing the other staples to survive in the wilderness.

While he paid no water or electrical bills, he did maintain an emergency generator and used it sparingly. He drew his water from a local stream, had a two-seater outhouse, and chopped his own wood for burning in the stone fireplace. The old mountain man used a wood stove for cooking and kerosene lamps and candles for light. He read the Good Book almost every night but kept an old ragged and torn copy of Playboy for special occasions. He would have to buy him a new issue one of these days.

His only electronic equipment, an old battery-operated AM-FM radio, kept him company on those long winter nights. He could receive only two stations, both country music. One did provide local weather updates weekdays, something you needed to stay one step ahead of in the backwoods.

He took work where he could, made a meager living as a guide for hunting and fishing trips to supplement his cash flow for the finer things. Payne had never paid any taxes or collected welfare or any other government handouts. He didn't believe in either. He had never been married and saw no need to ruin his life that way. Payne had not been with a woman in over forty years, didn't miss their comfort or troublesome nature. Sex meant no more to him than the need to piss. He took care of both by hand when he had to, and he did a lot more pissing now days then worrying about the other.

Payne thought about how he had certainly taken on a strange job with this trio. He had easily pegged Max as one of those snake oil peddlers. Knowing that, he could deal with him and wouldn't get snookered with his scheming. The big old black boy seemed like a likable and humble sort, but he'd keep an eye on him too, because something told him that he would do anything that Max asked him to do.

That left that Underhill feller. He didn't really like or trust that one either. Underhill talked too uppity for one thing. He didn't like people talking down to him. He didn't believe fancy-britches were in this just for finding old D.B. Cooper's hijack money. Old Elijah would figure him out, if given enough time. That man somehow smelled of government. He didn't like government folks in any form or fashion.

The prospect of them finding that missing loot worried Elijah Franklin Payne even more. That much money could influence the way a person thinks. Sometimes people could get downright vicious and ruthless if a pile of money was waved in their faces. Greedy men were the worst of the worst. Yep, he would have his hands full keeping an eye on all of them while protecting his backside. If it came to it, he could handle himself and put these folks in their proper place. He figured this was a damn witch hunt at best.

"Are we there yet? I'm hungry."

Underhill thought, for Christ's sake, that black boy sounds like a snotty nose kid on a vacation road trip. What a dingus? How in the hell did Max Paxton allow himself to get hooked up with such a moron?

Max chimed in, "Yeah, how much longer before we arrive at this trail of yours?"

"Another 40 minutes we should be there," replied the old man. "You better enjoy the ride because once we hit the woods, we got to hoof it to make it to a good camping site before dark-thirty."

"We have ample daylight remaining," stated Underhill. "I believe you said we had only four hours of hiking ahead of us."

"That's four hours at my pace," he said, spitting a wad of tobacco out the window. "You boys are too out of shape to make it in less than six."

"You establish whatever pace you desire old man," challenged Underhill. "I'll be your damn shadow."

Elijah Franklin Payne glanced over at Underhill. He rubbed Blue Boy lying on the seat between them. He predicted these boy's butts would be bouncing off the forest floor within the first hour. He looked forward to that sight. Breaking them would be a sheer delight.

Sunday Morning, May 11th
Waffle King Rendezvous

"About time you showed your face Missy," said Anson Parker. "I had just about given up on you."

"Sorry, I had problems securing a rental car and I also had to purchase some hiking gear. My bag was full of business clothes from my week in LA," Mattie Reynolds explained.

"You had any breakfast?"

"I snacked on the drive, but I will take a cup of coffee."

Anson flagged down Norma and motioned for a refill for him and cup for his guess. She signaled she would be there after she took the order from the booth full of ladies.

"I guess you're going to want me to take you to the spot where those things chased me out of the woods. I'm not real anxious to go back up there. I haven't been back since it happened. They might not even be there now after all these years."

"Actually, I had something else in mind." She paused while the waitress delivered their coffee. "I'd like to go to the sight where that kid was recently abducted."

"What's that got to do with me?"

"I thought you might be so kind as to take me. I'll pay you for your time."

"Look little lady, I'm not a wilderness guide," he explained, making a screwy face and throwing his hands up in the air. "I've never been that far north and I'm not familiar with that neck of the woods."

"I thought you were a seasoned hunter. Besides, it might help you bring closure to your ordeal."

"I gave up hunting after that day in the woods and I don't need any damn closure," he said in a much higher pitched tone. "I know what I saw out there. I don't need to see it again to make a believer out of me. You go if you want to. That's your business, but don't blame me for nothing that happens out there."

"Please calm down, Anson. I'm sorry. I just thought you would be willing to accompany me since my husband couldn't make it. It's not safe out there for a woman alone. I promised him I would not venture out there by myself." She began turning on the charm and playing the sympathy card.

Anson expelled a lung full of air that blew the napkins off the table. He rubbed his hands together like he was trying to wring out a dirty dish rag. Attempting to compose himself, he picked up his cup of coffee the spoon resting in the cup rattled like chattering teeth in the winter. He did not like being put in this position. He wasn't an explorer and sure didn't need to be a hero. Lost or dead didn't wear well either.

"Seriously Anson, I'm sorry that I presumed too much. I just thought this had haunted you all these years and this would be a way for you to conquer your demons."

"Demons," he grunted. "That's what's in them woods, all right. Mark my word. Conjuring up one of them ain't going to happen on my watch. You don't know what you're signing up for, little lady; hunting them out there in their own backyard."

"I'm sure you're right, but it's just something I must do. I'm very hardheaded and persistent. My husband reminds me of this all the time." Mattie smiled, pouring on the charm.

Anson now subconsciously patted both feet like he was tap dancing. The table shook as if it was in the middle of a moderate earthquake. Perspiration dripped down the back of his neck soaking his collar. This conversation had taken an ugly twist, something he had not signed up for.

"Haven't you read or heard about that mountain acting up for the past month? This is no time to be going up there, period."

"Mount Saint Helens?" she confirmed. "Yes, I've been following it on the news."

"They say it could blow any minute. If we go up to that Ape Canyon area, we'll be at hell's back door if it does," warned Anson.

"You just said we, so should I take it that you are at least considering accompanying me?"

"I didn't mean anything," he now stumbled on his words. "I didn't say I meant I would. This could be very dangerous is all I was trying to infer."

"The volcano doesn't scare me," she replied. "They usually give plenty of warning just like hurricanes."

"What the hell do you think it has been doing for the past month? I've been thinking about this since we last talked. Have you given it any thought what might happen if you come face to face with what I saw?"

"All the time," Mattie smiled. "I live for that possibility."

"It doesn't worry you that these things might have been responsible for kidnapping children."

"Well I guess it means we're safe," she grinned. "They don't seem to have a fondness for tasty little woman and crusty old men, or you wouldn't be here, now would you?"

Anson almost broke a smile on that last comment but fought it back. "Just what do you plan to do if you see one of these things, or maybe more than one?"

"Well, I would certainly like to photograph them for sure."

"Don't think I'm going to pose in a picture just to provide you with a scale or a reference point."

"If we're lucky enough to locate their habitat, I would love to observe their activity, study them for a while."

"Most likely they would be observing you. That's would they did to me."

"The homerun would be to actually communicate with them, if that is a possible assumption."

"I heard how they sound. Trust me. It didn't sound like a language I ever heard anyone speak. What makes you so sure they wouldn't consider us part of the menu instead? What I saw didn't get that big eating pine nuts and wild berries."

"You're still here, aren't you? And the way you tell it, they had you surrounded and if they would have wanted you, they would have taken you, right?"

"There really isn't any winning with you is there? Your mind is just plum made up, isn't it?"

"On the contrary, just ask Shawn, I let him win sometimes, when it's convenient."

"Let him win when it's on your terms," he repeated.

"Yep, when it's to my advantage to do so," she replied, taking a sip of her coffee.

"And this is not going to be one of those times is it?"

"Nope, I'm going up there with or without you, but I certainly could use your help and would appreciate your company."

"You do realize that I'm no spring chicken. And I bet I am some sixty pounds heavier than I was the last time I tried to outrun Bigfoot."

"You won't have to outrun him this time," she smiled. "You just need to be able to outrun me."

84

"Hell, I probably couldn't outrun a one-legged tortoise right now, but I am damn good a tripping people," Anson grinned.

"So, I guess we'll be taking a little trip in the morning, then. I promise you I will compensate you well for it."

"How about you writing that check out for me now, just in case I make it back and you don't."

"Deal," she said, offering her hand and they shook on it. She wrote the cheek, filling in a generous offering. "And feel free to go ahead and deposit it in your banking account if it will make you feel better."

"I hate Mondays," he sighed.

"I thought you were retired. Why would tomorrow be any different to you than any other day?"

"Why, you ask. Not much of a mystery to it. It's simple because I'm going with you to look for Bigfoot in the backyard of a riled-up volcano, against my better judgment, and it so happens to fall on Monday."

"We could leave today."

"Monday will do just fine. We need today to plan and get our crap together."

"Consider yourself on the clock starting right now then."

"I never did like working weekends."

"You're not going to make this easy, are you, Anson Parker?"

"I don't believe you have either, have you missy?"

"Bigfoot might be a welcomed sight after wrestling here with you, Anson."

"Watch what you wish for, little lady. I've seen them and believe me, I'm a sweetheart in comparison."

"You really have a problem with me having the final say, don't you?"

"Might," he replied, as they both busted a gut laughing.

Cecelia Velazquez asked, "Was that another damn earthquake?"

"St. Helens again," answered Nash. "I heard on the radio that they're still predicting an eruption."

"Well, don't we need to get the hell out of here then?"

"Remaining crop should be ready to harvest by the weekend," stated Speedy. "We're not leaving until then."

"By the way, I moved Booger's truck, so it didn't block our way out. I had to push it down the ravine though. There was no sign of any keys or Booger." Nash blurted it out before thinking.

This raised an eyebrow with Cecelia. "Whoa, I thought you said Booger and Velvet ran off together, Speedy?"

Fast thinking, Speedy replied, "That's' what the hell we thought happened to him and her. I reckon we were wrong."

"So, what happened, Nash? He couldn't have just dropped off the face of the earth and he certainly couldn't have gotten out of here on foot. He wouldn't have left that truck behind. And what the hell happened to Velvet? Did she just up and disappear too?"

"We don't know, Kido, and that's the truth."

"Hey Cecelia, could you get us a coffee refill," asked Nash uncharacteristically.

"What am I now, your frigging waitress?"

"Ceil, don't be a bitch. Just get us some damn coffee, okay?"
Speedy patted her on the ass and smiled.

"Somebody best be telling me what the hell is going on here," she
mumbled a few more obscenities, and then walked back up to the
cabin as requested. She glanced back over her shoulder and gave
both the finger.

"I thought I told you not to bring up Booger and that truck in front
of Ceil," warned Speedy. "You know how that gets her started
with all those damn questions."

"Sorry, I let it slip," answered Nash, ready for what Speedy could
dish out.

"Forget it for now. I'll handle Ceil" said Speedy, lowering his tone
to almost a whisper. "Are there any more signs of our night
visitors?"

"Fresh tracks around the perimeter from last night, and it brought
company this time."

"Are you telling me that there's more than one?"

"At least three to be exact and ones a big son of a bitch, bigger
than the original one," stated Nash as he illustrated by widening his
hands to about eighteen inches to indicate the size of the footprint.

"Holy crap," blurted Speedy. "And you're still thinking that it's..."

"A group of Sasquatches," he finished the statement. "Yes, what
the hell else could it be? Do you have a better answer?"

He shrugged. "What do you think they want?"

"Food probably," answered Nash. "If they wanted anything else,
they would have probably already taken it by now."

"You don't think they eat people, do you?"

"Well we're still here, aren't we?"

"Booger is missing. Maybe they have enough to last them for a while. He was quite the porker."

Nash gazed toward the ground and began rubbing the back of his neck with his left hand, while he fiddled with the knife strapped to his belt with his right. He kicked at the dirt.

"What? Cough it up, Nash."

"Velvet's body has been dug up," he replied, making eye contact with Speedy, while waiting for his reaction.

Speed lurched and grabbed Nash by his shirt. "What the hell do you mean, it's been dug up," questioned Speedy, much too loudly. "I thought you said what you buried, stayed buried. This is getting crazy."

"First time for everything," answered Nash, pulling Speedy's hand free and shaking his head from side to side.

"They're eating people, aren't they," shouted an obviously panic-stricken Elwood Speed Moore. "This isn't good. This so isn't frigging good. What the hell are we going to do about it?"

"Calm down. We don't know that for sure."

"What else could they be doing with the bodies?"

"Don't know, but I say if they wanted us, they would have already attacked. And if they attacked in force, I'm not sure we could stop them."

"We have frigging guns and plenty of ammo. What the hell do they have that makes you so damn sure we're easy marks?"

"Size and numbers. These aren't a bunch of dumb ass monkeys. They appear to be social, organized and intelligent. They have tripped every trap I've set and continue to raid our supplies. We're dealing with intelligence here. And they're coming closer every night."

"Oh great, coming closer and in bunches," said Speedy, throwing up his hands and now walking in circles. "Anything else you haven't told me?" He hadn't even noticed Cecelia standing behind him holding the two mugs of coffee.

"What's going on here? You boys look and sound like you need something stronger than coffee. I heard that last part about the monkeys. It's time you two fess up and quit whispering behind my back. What the hell's going on damn it?"

Speedy sat down in one of the aluminum folding chairs. He rubbed both eyes, and then looked to the sky for answers. "Get us a bottle and three glasses, Ceil. We need to have us a little discussion."

"It's about them, isn't it? This is about those damn squash people, isn't it?"

"There's more and best you know the whole frigging story, since you're up to your neck in it with us," said Speedy. "We're going to need every shooter we got."

"Hold your horses, Wyatt Earp," warned Nash. "This isn't the OK Corral. They've given us no reason to shoot at them."

"Who said shoot at them? I'm talking killing the muthers before they kill us."

"That is crazy talk. I really don't think you want to provoke them."

"Who's provoking? Like I said, I'm talking about killing the bastards before they kill and eat us."

Nash realized now that he should have stuck to his gut instinct and kept his mouth shut. Pandora's Box had been opened and there would be no closing it. He only hoped that these scavengers didn't show their faces before they harvested the rest of the weed. These things were monstrous, and they were smart, and he didn't want to make them angry.

A week was a long time and unfortunately the Sasquatches were becoming bolder. Anything could happen. With Speedy, he expected the worst. He thought seriously about folding up the tent and getting the hell out of here. Money was of no use to a dead man, but to the living it meant everything. The key was to remain alive long enough to cash in and spend it. He suddenly didn't like their odds.

"You boys okay back there," asked Elijah Franklin Payne, seeing the con man and the big ole black boy dropping further behind.

Underhill, rethinking the situation, should have never gotten hooked up with them. He had given Max Paxton the benefit of the doubt, hoping there were a few more stones to uncover in the D.B. Cooper mystery. He wasn't sure if that was true now. This may be another snipe hunt, but it certainly wasn't his first.

"Oh hell, old man, let's take a little breather and let them rest for a few minutes," directed Underhill.

"What's the matter, you winded too, city boy?"

"I'm fine but the slow wit can't keep up this pace."

"I told you before. I'm not here to baby sit. We should have never brought him along."

"And I'm paying for your services, so I say we stop," stated Underhill as he sat down on a boulder and waited for the other two to catch up.

"Tell me Underhill. Are you a cop?"

Underhill didn't answer.

"Bingo," Payne said, as he spat tobacco juice on the base of the boulder Underhill was sitting. "I knew I was right. I'm figuring you're a fed. You look and smell like a G-man to me."

"You don't know anything old man. I'm not in any mood for your little guessing games. How much further?"

"Our first campsite is just over that ridge yonder, and then down in the draw below," he said pointing up the incline.

"I didn't ask where," he repeated. "I asked how long?"

"Another couple of hours if you boys can pick it up a tad. If not, dark is going to get us and trust me, you don't want to be stumbling around on these ridges at night."

"What difference does it make where we camp tonight? Here, over the ridge, under the ridge, around the damn corner or under the damn rainbow?"

"We don't have water on this side, and down the bottom of that ridge will shelter us from tonight's dropping temperatures. That's why you hired me, to know this sort of stuff, right mister secret agent man."

"Forget I asked," grumbled Underhill. "And refrain from calling me that."

"Forgotten," he grinned, winked then spat, landing an impressive wad of thick tobacco juice inches from Underhill's boots.

Old Bertha suddenly seemed spooked and stomped her feet nervously. Big Blue stood up and began sniffing the air, emitting a low grinding whine.

"What's up with your damn animals?" Underhill didn't like the mule's antics.

"They've got wind of something," answered Payne, as he surveyed their surroundings.

"I've never seen them both act like this, not at the same time." He inhaled a deep breath though his nostrils. "You smell that?"

Underhill drew in a whiff. "I don't smell anything but those stinking animals."

"Never smelled that smell before," Payne continued. "Almost like burnt animal fur, mighty peculiar, mighty damn peculiar and that's a fact."

A slight rockslide started at the top of the ridge. Payne caught a glimpse of something large flitting about. He strained his eyes to pick up more movement, but whatever he had seen, had disappeared on the back side of the ridge. He rubbed his arms. The hairs were standing up on both as well as the back if his neck, and he didn't like it one damned bit.

"Stay alert," he warned. "That might have been a bear up there." Payne really thought *that wasn't a bear*. What he had seen was bigger than any of the local bears and it moved too quickly on hind legs. He tried to shrug it off as an overactive imagination, but he knew this was untruthful. He recalled the stories, but they were just stories, right?

"You boys rested and watered," he asked, looking back at the still winded duo. "And you best make sure you take a piss or dump if you've got to go."

With that Max walked over to a tree and relieved himself. He cadvised Bam-Bam to do the same. In the middle of pissing, Bam-Bam placed his hand on Max's shoulder and let out a little chuckle.

"You better not be laughing at me," warned Max. "It's damn cold out here." He glanced over at Bam-Bam's uncircumcised and useless member as it hung like a garden hose.

"Magilla Gorilla," laughed Bam-Bam, patting Max on the back with his free hand.

"Why are you babbling about that cartoon gorilla in the Hanna-Barbera Saturday morning show," asked Max, removing the giant hand from his shoulder.

"I saw him over there in the bushes," he said in an excited tone. "He wasn't wearing any clothes though. He usually has on them funny little short pants with suspenders and a bowtie and hat. He sure looked different naked."

Max glanced over to where Bam-Bam pointed but saw nothing but dense foliage. It wasn't uncommon for the overgrown kid to possess a vivid imagination, especially when it came to cartoon characters. He thought all of them were real.

"Shake it off before you put that Anaconda back in your pants," Max told him.

"I don't have an Anaconda in my pants," replied Bam-Bam. "But I saw Marlin Perkins and Jim wrestle one on Mutual of Omaha's Wild Kingdom. It wouldn't even fit in my pants, Max. It was too big and way too long."

"Exactly," said Max, as he zipped up.

"What's holding you boys up back there," asked Underhill.

"I saw Magilla Gorilla."

"Whatever," sighed Underhill, rolling his eyes skyward.

Elijah Franklin Payne rubbed his chin, and then looked back in the direction of the ridge, spat and again surveyed the perimeter. He eased the rifle from his shoulder and checked to make sure he had a bullet chambered. He always did, so it unnerved him that he was going through the motion of checking.

"All right girls get a move on it," he ordered. "Daylight is burning. I want to make camp on the other side of that ridge before dark."

Bam-Bam mumbled, "We're not girls. Why did he call us girls, Max? He's a funny old man."

No one answered.

Monday May 11th

"You look like you could use a break," commented Mattie Reynolds to Anson Parker.

The grossly overweight Anson just nodded to confirm he did and then flopped down on an old spruce log. He wasn't much good at this hiking stuff several years back, and he certainly hadn't improved like wine with age. Mattie checked her map then the compass. They appeared to be still on track for Ape Canyon, but the terrain had been much rougher than she had anticipated. While she thoroughly enjoyed Anson Parker's company, she had regretted dragging him along. He was in no shape for this. Their progress had been hampered by his much slower pace. She feared he would have a stroke or worse.

She passed her canteen to him. "Here. Have a drink, then wet your handkerchief and place it behind your neck."

"Sorry," he said, still very winded. "I'm just holding you up. My old body just isn't cut out for this. I told you that before we left. I guess you believe me now, don't you?"

"You're doing fine," she lied, worried about his deteriorating condition.

"I hope we don't run up on a Sasquatch because I sure wouldn't be able to outrun you right now," Anson said, managing a smile.

"I thought you had that tripping technique down pat," she said, breaking a smile of her own.

"How about you just do one of those Chevy Chase falls if we see one and we'll call it even?" Anson managed a little laugh and sounded less winded. "You're the one that wants to encounter one. I've already been down that road."

"Deal," she answered.

"You really want this bad don't you, missy?"

"Not for the reasons you think, but yes, I do."

"Who said I was thinking? I'm just trying to survive this nightmare hike and make a little conversation."

"I'm not looking for any fame or fortune. This is just for me to validate what my ancestors experienced and tried to preserve and protect. Well, that's a half truth. My great, great grandmother who was an Indian stuck firm to her convictions. Her husband, Matt McGregor reluctantly went along with her and carried it to his grave."

"So, he didn't buy protecting them, then?"

"Not totally," she explained. "In his words, he was abducted by a large clan of them, twenty or so. He was then taken to a hidden valley with a cavern as the only way in and out. He didn't elaborate in his writings, but something inexplicable happened to him while being held captive. He was also haunted by leaving others behind when he escaped with his rescuers and a handful of kidnapped children."

"Did he ever seek vengeance?"

"I don't think so. He sounded levelheaded to me, but maybe he wanted someone to put a stop to the abductions."

"Is that someone going to be you, gal?"

She shrugged. "Jury is still out I suppose."

"I get it," he nodded. "You've got to see this firsthand. You believe the entrance to that hidden valley is somewhere in Ape Canyon, don't you?"

"Could be," she said. "It makes sense."

"Tell me this. What makes you think the one I saw even belongs to the same group your old grandpa encountered? You read where these things have been seen in almost every corner of the world."

"Are you the expert now, Anson?"

"Well, I have to admit, after it happened to me, I started paying more attention to the news clippings and magazine articles. My ears always perked up when I heard tell of someone seeing one. Out here in the northern woods it seems to occur a lot more than people have the inclination to admit. A lot goes unreported, just like mine."

"I think it is a hot bed for sure, and to answer your question, I believe that whatever populates this general area are possible ancestors of the ones they encountered in the 1800's."

"How long do you reckon they live?"

"Hard to say," she said scratching her ear. "No one has ever found any bones or fossilized remains."

"Why do you think that's so?"

"I think they dispose of their remains."

"How come no hunter has ever bagged one?"

"I'll ask you that question. You had your weapon when you encountered yours."

"I reckon being scared shitless had a lot to do with it. These things were smart. They were messing with me...stalking me. I suppose they sort of looked human too."

"If they're so smart, why didn't they capture you then?"

"I've thought on that subject now for over six years. They obviously had me out numbered and on the run. You are the expert. You tell me why they didn't do something to me, other than about make me soil my drawers."

"They didn't want to harm you," she explained. "They just intended to scare you out of their territory."

"It worked. I got the hell out of there and never returned. Well, I hadn't returned until now, anyway, so I guess I didn't completely learn my lesson."

"Think about it. They utilized perfect tactics. They kept their distance throwing rocks and beating on trees, making nightmarish sounds. They even made sure you knew you were surrounded. Then finally, they gave you a quick glimpse just to add the icing to the cake."

"You make them sound way too human, organized, soldier like."

"It explains why and how they stay one step ahead of us, doesn't it? I think they are seen only when they really want to be. Sure, they stumble like anyone else, crossing a road or clearing at the wrong time, but for the most part they've learned to survive by being ghosts or UFOs or any other of mankind's many myths."

"You believe in ghosts and UFOs too, gal?"

"Well, my ancestors never wrote about ghosts, but since you brought up the subject," she took a deep breath and continued, "Strange bright fires or some sort of illumination was seen in that hidden canyon. Matt McGregor and his fellow trappers experienced memory loss afterwards. They succumbed to the control of their captors. Does that sound familiar?"

"Hold on missy," exclaimed Anson, now standing up and nervously clarifying, "You're talking, now what do they call it? Oh yeah, the Enquirer calls it alien abduction."

"I'm just reporting what I read. I've never witnessed a UFO before nor am I drawing any conclusions or parallelisms." She smiled seeing how antsy he had become.

"Bigfoot is one thing but Little Green Men; this is getting way too weird, even for me."

"Are you rested?"

He nodded yes, to confirm, then shook his head back and forth in disbelief of what he had gotten himself into and then he said, "I'm way too old for this crap. Martians and Bigfoot. How do I outrun a dang UFO?"

"Calm down before you work yourself into a stroke. Frontiersmen probably saw a lot of things they couldn't explain."

"What worries me most is I've seen one of those hairy ones. I know they are real, so if they think they saw flying saucers, who am I to argue with what they think they saw?"

"Matt didn't see anything flying. He just saw bright lights or fires as he called them. It could have been anything."

"Name one of these any things then."

"Enough, we need to get moving," she said, not knowing how to answer.

Mattie certainly concurred with his suspicions but left it at that. She felt sorry for him and would have suggested that he turn back, but she feared he could not make the return trip safely alone. She hoped her obsession would cause poor Anson no harm. Mattie Reynolds found herself between a rock and hard place. She pondered turning back but couldn't muster the will to do so. If only Shawn could have made this trip, she thought.

"Speedy old buddy, I've walked the perimeter again," Nash acknowledged, returning to a now blazing bonfire in the center of their camp.

"And," asked an anxious Speedy.

"And, why in the hell do you have such a huge fire burning in the middle of the afternoon?"

"Couldn't hurt," he answered, throwing another log on top. "Most animals stay clear of fire and smoke."

"Like I keep telling you," replied a frustrated Nash, "These aren't most animals. I'm not even sure we can honestly classify them as animals."

Speedy scoffed at this then asked, "So what the hell did you find out there this time, mister super sleuth?"

"I didn't find any fresh tracks if that's what you're asking."

"See, the fire is working."

Nash just shrugged. He doubted the fire to be a major deterrent. Most likely the creatures had enough of their supplies for a while, but he felt sure they had not discontinued their raids long term. The blood curdling scream caused both men to jump. Weapons drawn they rushed to Cecelia's defense in the green house.

Speedy flung open the pothouse doors to eye Ceil cowering behind a cluster of mature plants, clutching a small hand-held spade like a dagger. She was focused on a tear in the plastic wall. Seeing the torn opening, Nash backed out and circled the greenhouse in pursuit of the bold intruder. Up until now the creatures had conducted their raids under the cloak of darkness and had never disturbed the greenhouse. Something had obviously changed its routine. Nash didn't like it.

"What happened, Ceil," asked Speedy, pulling her in his arms. "Did you see it?"

Trembling almost convulsively Cecelia stuttered a reply, "I heard it ripping through...and I turned...I saw the shadow...a monstrous shadow. I mean...that thing ...was huge. Then the hand...holly crap... that hand. It was something out of a nightmare. It reached in. We've got to leave...leave now. I mean it. We need to go."

Nash poked his head through the hole. "It's gone, but these footprints are the biggest ones I've seen to date." Then he spotted the open honey bun less than a foot away. "It has a sweet tooth," he said, pointing to Cecelia's half eaten pastry. "I agree with

Cecelia. We should cut our losses and take what we can and count ourselves lucky."

"Like hell," shouted Speedy. "In just a few more days the crop will be worth a lot more. No snack loving ape men are going to make us alter out plans."

"We don't get a vote."

"Nash, I don't run a democracy when it comes to this. You leave. You leave with nothing and get nothing later."

"I'm not so sure that's such a bad deal. I've never been a very materialistic man."

The sudden crash and sounds of crunching metal sent the trio scurrying to identify the source. The discovery sent chills up their spines. A massive tree had careened off the cab of their only vehicle, a four-wheel drive pick-up. It now lay across the crushed hood. Damages appeared to be significant.

"What the hell," Speedy managed to spit out.

"Was the tree rotted," asked Cecelia.

Nash inspected the tree's base, took a deep breath, and said, "Uprooted and it was deliberate." He knelt and placed his hand inside one of the prints. "Our friends were responsible."

"Those things did this," whined Cecelia.

"Afraid so," answered Nash, inspecting their transportation. "We don't need a mechanic to tell us the Ford is shot. The tree has crushed the engine block for sure."

"Bastards," scoffed Speedy. "We needed that truck to haul that eighteen-foot box trailer. How are we going to get this reefer out of here now?"

"Screw that," replied Nash. "How are we going to get our sorry asses out of here?"

"These monsters don't want us to leave, do they," asked Cecelia.

"What about Booger's ride?"

"Remember, no keys and at the bottom of the ravine," Nash reminded him. "It's flipped over on its top anyway."

"Damn it," exclaimed Speedy.

"Good news is we can hike out of here." explained Nash. "Bad news, it will take several days."

"I'm not leaving here without that reefer," growled Speedy.

"Please, let's go now," whimpered Cecelia.

"Hold on everyone," cautioned Speedy. "Take a deep breath and let's figure this mess out."

"Nash, I'm with you, if you're ready to leave now," said Cecelia, standing by the old woodsman to show her support.

"Too late today but we can leave at first light." replied Nash.

Speedy sported his rifle for full affect and spoke up, "We're sticking together. Nobody is leaving just yet."

"Don't threaten me, Speedy boy," warned Nash, meaning every word he said.

"Not a threat. We are leaving, but we'll be leaving together. We are carrying as much of the reefer as we can."

"Oh, you need us for pack mules?"

"Something like that, partner," smiled Speedy. "Three can carry more than one. We can come back with a new set of wheels and get the rest."

"Like hell,. I'm not coming back up here," exclaimed Ceil. "Not with those squash-things just waiting to eat us."

"Yeah, I think I can live without a return trip too," added Nash. "The rest is all yours."

Speedy said nothing. He just caressed his rifle and tallied his new profit margin. No damn big old monkeys were going to screw this up for him and that was a fact.

Underhill glanced at the illuminated hands on his wristwatch. It would be daylight soon. He had only slept for a couple of hours, about an average night's sleep for him. His thoughts turned to Cooper His thoughts always ended up on that notorious scoundrel. He needed answers. He required closure to that damn stunt he pulled. He despised loose ends. This cold case had left a permanent blemish on what could have been an exceptional career otherwise.

Revisiting November 24, 1971 as he did routinely, he recalled he and his partner's futile attempt to thwart Cooper's hijacking. Cooper had screwed up everything with his little get rich scheme and worst of all, had outsmarted them. Now retired from the bureau, he had devoted entirely too much of his time and his own money to solving the mystery.
Underhill had followed every lead no matter how weak. He had certainly proved that by being here.

He didn't really care whether Cooper had died or survived, and he wasn't that interested in finding the money. He just needed to put an end to his torment and solve the case. His partner had died in the line of duty a couple of years after the hijacking and had been spared the same anguish. Then again, his partner had never been as obsessed as him.

Reaching into his pocket, he retrieved the pearl tie pin and gazed upon it like some miniature crystal ball. Underhill had taken it from the evidence room just before his retirement. He forever kept it in his possession. He had earned it. No one else could appreciate its significance. It served as his constant reminder, his motivation, and his curse.

As ridiculous as Max Paxton's theory had sounded, Underhill had this uncanny feeling he was close to solving the mystery that had drove him to the brink of insanity. While he had no hard evidence to support this, his instincts rarely let him down. His skin tingled, and goose pumps rose on his arms as he fingered the pin. It had belonged to Cooper, his nemesis. Unable to induce sleep, he climbed from his sleeping bag and decided to take a piss. The almost full moon offered plenty of light to maneuver, even in the bottom of this godforsaken ravine where they camped.

The old scout had been determined that they made it to this spot below the ridge before dark and they had done so, just barely. Zipping up, he suddenly had a sense of being watched. He turned to the encampment, but the remaining three bedrolls were occupied. He still couldn't shake the feeling and decided to patrol the camp's perimeter. His pistol was holstered underneath his jacket and easily retrievable.

Completing the sweep, he had detected no intruders, man nor animal. It still didn't change the fact that he had felt being watched. Underhill stoked the fire and added several pieces of dried wood. Soon the flames danced and illuminated the encampment, casting an assortment of shift changing shadows on the surrounding trees and brush. Still he saw no watchers, but he struggled with his own demons.

Elijah Franklin Payne, aware of the sudden change, cracked an eye to see who had been responsible. He saw Underhill, his back to the fire and to him, standing there like some eerie apparition.

"Couldn't sleep, lawman," asked Payne, still confined to his bedroll.

Underhill didn't flinch and slowly turned to face the questioner. "Disturb your beauty sleep old man?"

"Apparently you don't think you're pretty enough either, G-man," spoke Payne, scooting from his bedroll.

"How much further?"

"By way the crow flies it's probably less than a day. Since we don't have wings, more like two, that is if you boys can keep up a decent pace. We'll be doing a lot of up and downing today. Down one hollow and back up another, and then we do it all over again."

"Isn't there anyway to go around them?"

"Sure, there is," he smiled, stuffing his mouth with his morning chew. "Take about a week to do it though. It would be a lovely stroll for you greenhorns."

"Guess we'll do it the mountain goat way then, old man" replied Underhill, spitting on the ground at Elijah's feet.

"Fess up with me boy. What are you, FBI or CIA? You're too cool and hard nose to be county or state."

"Neither," answered Underhill. "Since this is eating at you like a cancer, I'm retired, FBI and on vacation. I did work with the bureau once upon a time."

"I knew it," Payne slapped his knee. "You looked like one of them agents all along. What you say I make us some coffee?"

Underhill nodded his approval. He eyed old Grizzly Adams, admiring the old man for what he was. He pegged him for a straight shooter. Underhill trusted his ability to read people. The old fart was growing on him. He would never admit that to the old man though, but he did respect him. Liking him would be going too far though. He didn't allow himself to like anybody; always a loner and he intended to keep it that way.

Payne passed him a cup of coffee, hot and black. He eyed him while taking his first sip. "Ready to tell me why you're really here mister secret agent man?"

"D.B. Cooper's money like the rest of you," answered Underhill.

"Bullshit," spoke Payne, spitting tobacco juice into the fire. "It's more to it than just that. You are not the sort of feller that cares any more about money than I do. You and I are a lot alike in a damn crazy sort of way."

Underhill broke a smile before taking his next sip. He remained silent for almost a minute before replying, "Pretty simple. I was there when Cooper hijacked that plane. It really pissed me off that he got away clean and we never found him."

"Your kind don't like leaving nothing dangling, do you?"

"I expect I'm worse than most. This one really left a bad taste in my mouth," explained Underhill. "And on my watch; unfinished business."

"Are you looking for a skeleton out here or something? You're wasting your time. Critters would have gotten rid of it long time ago."

"I'll settle for fragments of his clothing, pieces of a parachute or the missing money. I just need evidence to justify that it's over." Underhill spilled his guts for the first time in years.

"What if you don't find anything out here?"

"Then I look elsewhere," he replied. "I have nothing but time."

"You're really screwed up, you know it?"

"Yeah, it's a curse for damn sure."

"If he's out here, we'll find him, and if he's not?"

"Like I said, I'll keep searching. I'm retired, and this is my new hobby."

"What if old D.B. Cooper is somewhere living the high life? Maybe he spent some of that money and got a face change. Maybe I'm him."

"Well then I suppose I've found my man if you can prove it, but you could have certainly bought a better-looking puss. Hope you didn't use all the money."

"You make me laugh secret agent man. You're a real hoot. You want a chew?"

Underhill waved him off.

"Then can I pour you another cup?"

Underhill nodded, allowing the old man to refill his cup. The old man poured himself a second. They never spoke another word. The chirping birds indicated morning approached. Max stirred, followed by Bam-Bam.

Tuesday May 13th

"Smells good," commented Mattie, as she climbed from her tiny domed tint.

"I figured we could both use a hot breakfast before we got started," answered Anson. "You sleep okay?"

"Soundly. I hope I didn't snore."

"I thought woman didn't snore," he grinned. "Just like they never fart. At least that's what my wife always said "

"Smart lady and don't you ever forget it," she warned. "What are you cooking?"

"Canned sausage and some quick bread," he replied. as he handed her coffee. "Nothing fancy, but it'll stick to your ribs."

"How are you feeling?"

"Old, aching, too fat, and pretty damned useless," answered Anson.

Forty minutes later, they had broken camp and were on their way. After the first half mile of rigorous hiking over unfriendly terrain, Anson had begun to breathe deeply and sweat like a mule in heat. Mattie monitored his condition and she didn't like what she was witnessing. Anson never complained nor asked her to stop or slow her pace. Somehow, he pushed on and kept up with her.

Her map indicated they were half day away from Ape Canyon, if they could maintain their present pace. She wasn't so sure they could or should, given poor Anson's laboring. They faced their steepest upward climb just ahead. She pretended she needed a break. Anson obliged. He looked pale. His breathing was very irregular. He didn't complain, drank some water, and on her cue, rose and started the long climb. The man had true grit and balls to match.

Anson shocked her. He completed the hour and half climb without stopping. They both sat exhausted at the top, now looking at an equally scary descent. Anson motioned that he needed to relieve himself and walked to an outcrop of overhanging rocks, just out of her sight, for a little privacy. Finding the perfect overhang, he dropped his pants to his ankles and released his bowels. He felt clammy and woozy from the ascent. His stinking release even surprised him, and he hoped it hadn't drifted towards Mattie. His face reddened worrying about it. After one last long strain, he opened his eyes to see standing on a boulder about 20 feet above his location, his worst nightmare. He knew at that moment that the stench did not exclusively belong to him.

Panic stricken, he tried to rise and became entangled in his trousers and fell face first, mouth open and eating pine needles. How come every time he encountered one of these things, he found himself on his belly? He tried to right himself and that's when the pain hit him. He clutched his chest and managed a faint call, "Mattie," then he fell backwards plummeting over 400 feet down the slope, bouncing off trees like a ball in a pinball arcade machine.

Mattie had heard her name, then the series of crashes. Approaching where she had last seen him disappear, she first noticed Anson's steaming crap, but no Anson. Scanning the area, she still saw no trace of her hiking buddy. Then she looked over the edge of the overhang and could just make out his body below. She detected no movement, nor did she see the creature watching her from above.

"Anson," she called out, but received no response.

She yelled his name several more times, but he remained quiet and motionless. There was nothing left for her to do but climb down. Weighing her options, she could not make it from her present position. She spotted some sort of winding animal trail twenty yards to her right. Travel even on the narrow trail was difficult because of the slope and loose rocks and dirt. She almost fell several times, but understandably so, because she had thrown caution to the wind with the pace she tried to maintain. It still took her almost an hour to reach the bottom. All the while, others watched her curiously.

Ten yards from Anson's body, she knew he had to be dead. Misshapen like a contortionist, the old man's limbs were bent in the wrong directions. Only one foot remained in his pants legs. She figured that he must have lost his balance and had fallen while taking a dump. What she didn't know, Anson had died of heart failure before he tumbled over the edge, because of coming face to face with his worse fears. His worse fears now eyed Mattie from its hiding place.

She sat down by the lifeless Anson Parker, placed her face in her hands and began to weep. This had gone so badly wrong. Shawn should have been with her, not Anson. Wiping her runny nose and tears with her sleeve, she tried to think through her options.

Obviously, she would not be able take his body out by herself, but how would she protect it from marauding critters? She was so close to Ape Canyon, should she finish what she had started first? Anson was dead, and he would still be dead if she went for help or not.

Something suddenly clicked. She remembered Anson had a walkie-talkie in his backpack. She glanced back up to where she had just climbed from, realizing that both hers and his backpacks were still in their camp at the top. She whispered, "No need dreading it, I've got to climb back up there regardless. If I can radio for help, I can finish this with a clear conscious."

She first pulled up Anson's pants the best she could, and then dragged his body to an overhang. Just dragging the portly man's body ten yards had been a major ordeal, especially with the configuration of his distorted and broken limbs. Jutting bones from one leg and an arm plowed through the ground making a furrow. Resting briefly, she decided to cover his body with rocks. She figured this would at least keep the larger predators from dragging off his corpse. She labored at this task for what seemed like forever.

Exhausted, she collapsed alongside the stone grave and finished with a little prayer. She took another quick look up the side of ravine, dreading her next mission. It had taken her over an hour to climb down. She figured it would take twice that long to climb back up. She was in no condition to climb right now. Woozy headed and dead on her feet, attempting to rationalize her next move even exhausted her.

She glanced at her watch and was shocked to see it was half past 1 PM. She had lost all track of time and the morning had left her in its wake. Still, she needed some rest before she could make that climb. She decided to close her eyes for a few precious moments. She had always been the master of the power nap. Giving in to it, her eyelids fluttered, and then closed. Her mouth fell open and she began to snore very unladylike. Her power nap had commenced immediately. Out now she watched in slow motion as her dream unfolded.

Anson Parker screaming and falling forever. She followed floating like a balloon downward from her perch high above and landed beside the man's distorted body. Two children, both young boys, stood over his body and giggled. Standing behind them in the shadows lurked a huge ominous figure. She strained her eyes to focus on the dark apparition but could not bring clarity to whatever watched from a safe distance. The two children constantly glanced over their shoulders as if asking for permission to be there. They seemed to have no fear of their overseer. The younger kid wore a Cub Scout uniform. The other boy wore a red plaid cotton shirt and looked like a junior lumberjack. Each poked at Anson's stomach with sticks and laughed when the man's belly jiggled. She yelled at them to stop.

Suddenly Anson sat up and asked the boys if they had seen his trophy buck. The scout formed antlers with his hands on his head and the other pretended to shoot him with the stick he held. Both danced and giggled and again looked to the stranger behind them. It hooted and drummed a response in Morse code on a tree trunk.

The boys appeared to understand and stepped backwards, and then vanished as if never there. In her dream, she too tried to back away from the scene, but her feet felt like lead. She looked down finding her legs spread wide, held in place with stones piled up to her knees. The two boys laughed and clapped somewhere in a distant fog.

Anson sitting now, held a walkie-talkie in his one good hand and she could hear Shawn's voice calling her name. She tried to answer but could not form the words. Anson Parker just smiled and tossed the radio toward the shadowy figure. A huge hairy hand emerged from the darkness and caught the radio, and then crushed it like paper. She now heard Indians chanting and erythematic drumming. Shawn appeared from the tree line wearing a huge coon skin cap and trapper attire. She heard the Davy Crocket theme song and began mouthing the words. "Davy, Davy Crocket, king of the wild frontier." Shawn smiled, began clapping, pleased by her performance.

The craziness continued. He walked over and began removing the stones to free her. The raccoon hat, now alive, reached for her hair, entangling its little probing fingers. Shawn's lips were moving, but she could not hear his words. Free, she now reached for him, but Anson and the creature from the shadows grabbed her dragging her away. Shawn tipped his restored raccoon cap and waved goodbye. The young boys reappeared, grabbed him by both hands, and led him into the forest. She struggled, but Anson and the unseen one held her firm in their grasp.

The hairy one tossed her like a ten-pound bag of potatoes over its shoulder and carried her away. She attempted to scream but felt too groggy. Mattie could feel the creature's every stride, long and deliberate. It was so powerful. Its muscles rippled underneath her torso. Its fur cushioned the bouncing motion and comforted her. She was no longer afraid. She had found what she had been looking for, evidence and then some. She smiled, thinking she would have a new entry for Matt McGregor's journal. Unable to keep her eyes open, Mattie Reynolds returned to a deep sleep.

Tied up in the greenhouse and sleeping very little last night, Nash tried to clear his head and decide how to handle Elwood Speed Moore's fragile emotional state. He had come dangerously close yesterday to losing what sanity he had left and Nash had to be careful with how he approached their fearless leader. Cecelia ironically had become his ally. That did make it two against one, but still there was no easy solution to their precarious situation.

111

Speedy, too damn determined to leave here with the pot would complicate matters tremendously.

The larger piece of the puzzle, what did the Sasquatch have in mind? Once myth, now reality, would they allow them to leave peacefully? Why wouldn't they? They had done nothing to threaten them, except set those traps. Up until now, none had been harmed. Nash firmly believed it should remain that way. He didn't want to piss them off. Nash thought maybe if given free rein to the supplies the creatures would forget about them. He would make that pitch to Speedy. He wasn't very happy with not having any weapons. Speedy had confiscated his gun and knife then tied him up for safe keeping. How stupid had that been?

There was no possible way for the three of them to haul out all this marijuana. Speedy unfortunately had delusions that they could make it happen. Nash had to gain control of the situation. Killing Speedy would be the last resort, but he would not hesitate if given that as the only option. He wasn't so sure Cecilia Velazquez would support that decision. He really didn't care. Speedy, accompanied by Cecelia, entered the greenhouse. He noticed immediately her black eye and split lip. Speedy had not taken her comments lightly. Staring through glazed eyes, she stood obediently by his side, obviously a broken woman.

"Well, Nash, old buddy, have you had a chance to change your mind and work with me," asked Speedy as he cut Nash's hands free.

Nash wiggled his fingers trying to stimulate the circulation back in his hands, and then reached down and untied his feet. He eased up, bracing himself as he did, because of leg cramps. Rotating his head, his neck snapped loudly as he appeared to realign his spine from being locked in the same position all night. Finally, he spoke.

"How do you propose we leave here on foot and take some of this with us?"

"Some, we take it all," responded Speedy in a very relaxed and deliberate tone.

"Do you realize how much weight you're talking about? Sorry, the three of us can't possibly haul it out of here on foot. Explain to me how you plan to make this happen?"

"So, you're in," said Speedy.

"I'm listening."

Speedy walked Nash outside and pointed to his solution. He had constructed a pull sleigh like those the Indians or frontiersman used to haul the sick behind a horse or by hand. Basically, he had tied a tarp between two tent poles and all they now had to do was fill the tarp with weed and drag it behind them.

"You do realize how far we'll have to drag one of those things, don't you? We'll never be able to drag what we have in that greenhouse."

"Once we reach the dirt road it'll be mostly downhill and a piece of cake," boasted Speedy.

"And another 28 miles before we reach the paved road, and then we'll look just a little too conspicuous dragging bails of reefer behind us, don't you think?"

"We'll catch a ride."

"Who in their right mind would stop for a trio like us?"

"Ceil will be our bait then we'll hijack us a ride."

"You're frigging loony," snapped Nash, almost instantly regretting he had let that comment slip out.

Speedy placed the pistol against his forehead and said, "You've really run out of options. You're in this to the end or dead. You choose."

"Guess I'm in," smiled Nash. "But when this is over, you and I need to clear the air of our differences."

"When this is over you can count on it, old buddy."

Nash took that as Speedy intended it. The sorry bastard would certainly kill him and Cecelia once they hauled his bounty off this mountain. "We still have one little problem, the Sasquatch."

"You let me worry about the monkey men."

"Might I make one suggestion?"

Speedy answered sarcastically, "More traps."

"Allow them access to the food."

"I thought they pretty much had that already."

"I mean place it somewhere to preoccupy them while we make our hasty retreat," clarified Nash.

"Fine by me, but if they show their ugly faces, I use the Uzi and make hamburger meat out of them."

"I really don't think you want to pick a fight with them," cautioned Nash.

"They'll be picking the fight," he smiled. "I'll just finish it."

Cecelia had not uttered a word, but she had watched the two men intensely. She occasionally rubbed her swollen face and took deep breaths. She still cared for Speedy, but right now feared for her life and not just from more of his abuse. She was terrified that these things would not let them leave. She did agree with Nash their safety outweighed hauling the reefer off this mountain. Ceil kept those thoughts to herself.

Elijah Franklin Payne moved down the trail, tugging Big Bertha. Blue Boy sniffed out the trail ahead. Underhill walked out of kicking distance of the old mule, followed by Max Paxton and Bam-Bam. They must have looked like a circus parade, thought

114

Underhill, a dysfunctional one at that. Payne held up his hand, signaling everyone to stop. He placed his finger to his lips, giving the quiet sign. He tilted his head and listened, and then knelt and patted Old Blue. He bobbed his head up and down.

Underhill finally asked "What?"

"I heard voices ahead."

"Voices, I don't hear anything?"

"Two. Men's voices. Blue heard them too."

Max asked loudly, "Who in the hell would be out here?"

"Keep your voices down until we know who we're dealing with," warned Payne.

He listened for a couple of more minutes but heard no more chatter. "All right let's check it out."

They traveled for another twenty minutes before the dense forest broke into a man-made clearing. Standing at the edge, Payne could see the dwelling tucked into the side of the ridge, but from their vantage point he could not see the greenhouse. Two men and a woman stood chatting about 60 yards away.

Nash facing their direction spotted them first and nodded to Speedy. He turned and saw two men with the mule and an old hound dog, but Max and Bam-Bam were still in the edge of the woods and not presently in sight. Speedy eased the pistol to his side and then waved a greeting.

Payne waved back, and then he and Underhill began walking in their direction. Seconds later the other two of their merry band stepped into the clearing. Nash counted four and watched to see if there were any others. No one else appeared. Speedy slipped the pistol into his belt in the small of his back and covered it with his shirt tail. Each group walked meeting halfway, sizing up one another.

Speed took the lead. "What brings you fellows out here in the great outdoors?"

"We're just on a little camping trip," lied Payne. "I'm Elijah Payne and these boys hired me for a wilderness adventure trip."

"Pleased to meet you," said Speedy, extending his hand. "My name is Speedy. This is Nash and the young lady is Cecelia."

Payne immediately noticed the woman's battered face and smelled something fishy. The setting was all wrong. These people didn't belong out here, but he suspected they could say the same about his band of unlikely hikers.

Underhill spoke up, "I'm Spencer Underhill."

"You can call me Max. This is Bam-Bam."

Payne played along. "What are you folks doing out here in the middle of nowhere?"

"We have been lodging here, doing a little hunting and fishing," answered Speedy. "Nash is our guide and buddy."

Realizing what Speedy had blabbed, Nash spoke up, "Fishing now since hunting season is over. We really enjoy the backwoods lifestyle, real laid back. We're taking a little extended vacation."

Underhill spotted the greenhouse. He immediately recognized the set-up and knew this was no regular greenhouse. They certainly were not vacationers. He rubbed his shoulder fingering his gun in the shoulder holster underneath his jacket. Speedy picked up on Underhill's reaction and reached back as if to scratch his back. He too sensed something wrong with this picture.

Max, oblivious to it all asked, "What's in the greenhouse? You grow your own vegetables out here?"

"I love carrots," commented Bam-Bam. "Do you have any carrots? Bugs Bunny eats carrots. I like him and Daffy Duck."

Payne saw this coming unraveled and pretended to rub Old Bertha, placing his hand on the shotgun he kept in her saddle pack. The rest unfolded in slow motion. Speedy grasped the pistol from his belt, while at the same time Underhill reached for the revolver underneath his jacket. Payne readied the shotgun. Shots rang out as bodies dove for cover. It was a scene out of the Wild West. The first shot from Speedy's pistol struck Payne in the chest killing him instantly. Underhill grazed Speedy on his left cheek as he spun behind a tree. Speedy's second shot struck Underhill in the forearm of his shooting hand. He dropped his revolver to the dirt and tumbled backwards.

Blue Boy leapt toward Speedy, defending his now very dead master, but fell short on his lunge to the pot growers third shot. Max threw his hands in the air, screaming, don't shoot, mimicked by Bam-Bam doing the same. The mule veered to the left kicking and hee-hawing. Nash grabbed its reins. For what seemed like an eternity no one spoke a word.

"You boys have any more guns," asked Speedy, waving the pistol around.

"We're unarmed," answered Max, nodding toward Bam-Bam.

"Ceil, get those guns," ordered Speedy, pointing to the pistol and shotgun. She did exactly what he asked.

Underhill held his free hand over the bleeding wound. The bullet had hit no bone and passed through cleanly. He stared at Payne who had not been so fortunate. The old man's lifeless eyes were wide open, the dirt soaked with his blood.

"Ceil, check their pockets for any concealed weapons and get their IDs." Again, Cecelia complied almost robotically.

No other weapons were detected. She handed Speedy two wallets. Neither the giant black feller nor the dead man had identification. Bam-Bam had simply smiled at her while she searched his trouser pockets.

"Sonofabitch," exclaimed Speedy, examining the wallets. "You're with the FBI."

"Retired," explained Underhill.

"Fed just the same," snapped Speedy. "You faked this little camping trip just to sniff us out, didn't you, asshole?"

"Retired and on vacation; I have no interest in your little enterprise, nor do these other two."

Liar," yelled Speedy. "Once a Fed, always a Fed and I do hate you bastards. I never had me a chance to kill one though." Speedy smiled and winked at Underhill.

"What are you going to do with them," asked Nash, still holding onto the mule.

Grinning, Speedy replied, "Between them and that mule, we have a replacement for our truck and trailer."

Nash hated to admit it, but he certainly had a point. The bad news for them, they too were dead men once their task had been completed.

"Nash tie them two up," he motioned to Max and Bam-Bam. "I'll take care of the Fed."

Nash didn't like the look on Speedy's face. He still looked just a tad too deranged for his taste. He feared the agent would not be accompanying them when they departed. Killing a federal agent whether retired or active would be a grave mistake. What a cluster this had become he thought.

Wednesday, May 14th

Mattie opened her eyes to pitch black darkness. She was lying on her back. Strange, she looked skyward and saw no stars. Must be overcast she thought. A dank musty smell clogged her nostrils. She squinted, trying to see Anson's grave, but she could not penetrate the darkness.

She sat up, and then vaguely remembered her nightmare, and instinctively ran her hands down her torso, relieved to find herself fully clothed. Dreams can sometimes feel so real. Mattie reached around to try to find something that she could use to pull herself up but located nothing close by.

Finally, she pushed up with her hands and made it to a crouch, and then fully erect. Her eyes were starting to become adjusted to her dark surroundings. She could hear dripping water not far away. Mattie fingered her parched lips. Hands out in front, feeling the way, she took a couple of baby steps. She could barely make out a sliver of light somewhere ahead. To her shock, she surmised she was in some sort of cave. How in the hell had she gotten inside a cave? She had never been one to sleepwalk.

Becoming more and more adjusted to the darkness, Mattie Reynolds slowly moved in the direction of the only light. She jumped when she encountered the cold dripping water. Coupling her hands she caught a few drops, sniffed then tongued it. It tasted fresh with a glint of limestone, so she licked her hands, and then captured a few more drops. The little dab of moisture rejuvenated her. She rubbed the next few drop over her eye lids, then her face. Taking a deep breath she continued her trek toward the light source.

As she drew closer it didn't appear to be a natural. It danced and flickered, casting irregular shadows on the cave wall ahead. The cave narrowed considerably. The height shortened to less than four feet. Crouching, she entered the passageway and it almost immediately hair pinned to the right, then again back to the left before opening into a second cavern. The source of the light came from a rather large fire pit in the center of the huge cavern.

This cavern reminded her of one she had visited as a child in Sweetwater, Tennessee. The Lost Sea caverns had been a series of cathedral like rooms, many previously occupied by Indians, moonshiners and ancient cave dwellers. She remembered it had been advertised as the largest underground lake in the United States and even had glass bottom boat tours. Divers had mapped over a dozen acres of underground lake and had never found the end of it.

This cavern reminded her of the one they had dubbed "The Counsel Room", once used by the Cherokee Indians. All the Indian artifacts found there proved how they must have used it. The Lost Sea remained her most favorite caverns. Mattie marveled at the size of this one and wondered who had built the fire that blazed so brightly. Inching her way toward the flames, she continued to assess the cavern for any signs of its occupants. Her footfalls echoed. She still had no memory of arriving in the caverns, and last remembered deciding to take a break after finishing Anson's grave.

Standing only a few feet from the roaring fire, Mattie saw firewood a plenty piled on the other side. She still saw no signs of life, but she knew someone had to be nearby. The fire had not started nor maintained itself. The cavern must have been the size of a football stadium. Its deepest reaches disappeared into the dark shadows. Mattie saw no other light sources indicating a passageway out. She edged herself along the shadowed furthest points and began to spot spurs or possibly exit tunnels. She couldn't be sure how deep they were without venturing down them. That might come later.

Mattie started to call out, but something deep inside tugged at her, telling her that might not be such a wise choice. She continued to circle the far edges of the gigantic room staying inside the fingers of light. Looking ahead, she failed to see the obstacle at her feet and tripped, catching herself on the palms of her hands and knees. Brushing off her clothes, she turned to verify what she had tripped over, and to her shock she spotted a complete human skeleton. The tattered and almost deteriorated clothing indicated it had been here for a while.

Mattie knelt to examine it closer and immediately recognized both legs had been broken at some time and had not mended completely, indicating this person had probably been incapable of walking. The clothing resembled that of a man's business suit. Why would a man be dressed like that inside a cave? In a crevice, just a few feet away she spotted a jumbled mass of some sort of fabric compressed into the hole. She inched her way over and touched it. Tugging on it, she pulled it from the crevice. It was a parachute. Something shifted inside the fabric.

Mattie began to unfold the chute. It had been meticulously folded to hide the object inside. She unfolded it until she discovered a worn black journal. Rubbing the back of her neck with her left hand, she held it in her right. Just as she began to open the cover, she heard movement behind her. The distorted shadows on the wall told her someone approached her position. A chill ran down her spine. Swallowing deeply, she slowly turned to face the owner of the shadow.

Underhill's arm had bled freely until finally it had stopped on its own. His captors had not offered to bandage the wound. The one called Speedy had tied him securely to some sort of storage or supply cabinet. The sweet smell of honey buns infiltrated his nose. Speedy had strewn them all around and had even smeared several over his clothing.

He had heard of the Indians burying their captives up to their necks in the sand and leaving them for the ants and buzzards, but Underhill didn't follow this honey bun approach. Maybe the pot grower wanted wild animals like possibly a bear or wolf or something to do his dirty work. The gutless bastard.

From his vantage point, he had been able to see them harvesting and packaging the marijuana. It appeared that they planned to use Old Bertha, Max and Bam-Bam to transport their pot. Darkness approached, which meant they would not be leaving until daybreak. He had to figure a way to free himself. Underhill regretted that the old man had fallen prey to their ruthless ways. He certainly hadn't deserved that fate. This Speedy character obviously hated cops, especially the Feds. He probably had quite an impressive criminal resume. Experienced murderer had to top his accomplishments.

The nylon rope that bound his arms and legs would not enhance his chances of escape. His arms were tied behind him to some sort of heavy metal chair and against the cabinet. At least he found himself in a sitting position. He could watch the camp activities.

He detected all was not well between the three pot growers. Speedy had been the only one with a gun. The woman had been kicked around recently. The older gentleman just didn't fit in and reminded him a little of Elijah Payne, a sort of frontier throwback. He interpreted that the female had either been disobedient, not loyal, or not submissive to his qualms. Jury was still out on the one called Nash. He had detected no weapons in his possession, but he had rallied to the support of the leader against them.

The one called Speedy approached. "Well mister Narc, your covert operation didn't go as planned, did it?"

Underhill said nothing. He stared Speedy down and then eased into a smug smile. Speedy landed a boot to his right temple blurring his vision.

"It is not in your best interest to be a smart ass," cautioned Speedy. "What tipped you off to our little enterprise?"

Underhill figured he better play along, if for no other reason than to stall for time and stay alive for as long as possible. "You really have to watch who you associate with now days," he bluffed. "Informants are cheap or at least willing to cut their own deals to protect their asses."

"Who was it? Don't tell me. It was that damn worthless Velvet, wasn't it?"

Underhill gave him the, *you got me* look, but said nothing. He figured he'd give this Velvet the credit.

"If she was in it, then that means so was Booger," grinned Speedy. "It all makes sense now, Velvet making all those trips to town and Booger parked up there and spying on us."

Speedy gave Underhill a solid backhand across the face, blooding his lip. "Guess what, Velvet is dead, and Booger just plain disappeared. Two of your paid informants are history. You'll be joining them soon."

"Just curious, what happened to your transportation?"

"What makes you think something happened to it?"

"Well, you would have killed the others if you didn't need them and seems you have a fondness for Old Bertha. You're not a mule poker, are you?"

That drew another backhand, this time leaving a cut above his left eye. Well, at least he wasn't taking it out on the woman for a while.

Speedy squatted and grabbed Underhill by the chin. "You just sit here and watch those woods, smart ass. You'll find out soon enough what happened to our truck and probably what happened to old Booger. You're not going to like it. I can assure you that."

"Letting the little wild animals do you dirty work, you, little shitless coward?"

"Keeps your blood off my hands. You're dead either way."

"Seems to me you have plenty of blood on your hands, he thought, but didn't say it. Underhill gritted his teeth and managed one last statement. "The bureau knows your location and agents are just waiting to swarm this place. If I don't report in as scheduled..."

Not allowing the agent to complete his threat Speedy pulled his knife and cut off Underhill's right ear. Then he placed it in his shirt pocket. Underhill grimaced but did not scream.

"Just a little souvenir from you to me to remember you by Agent Underhill," he said, as he patted him on his cheek. "Listen for those footsteps with your left one."

Speedy stood and walked off. Once he was out of sight, Underhill let out a little muffled cry. Tears rolled down his checks. For the first time he took stock that he just might not get out of this one after all. Something in those woods put the fear of God in the one called Speedy that smelled to high heavens for him, the now one eared ex-FBI agent.

"Nash how are our other two guests doing?"

"How do you think? They're tied up like good prisoners."

"You sound like you don't approve."

"This little venture has gone very badly. Velvet and that Booger dude are dead and now the old guide as well. For Christ's sake. You're holding an FBI agent hostage. As far as we know the woods could be swarming with them."

"We'll be leaving in the morning, so stop your whining, Nash."

"You forget we may still have them to contend with somewhere out there."

"Underhill and the supplies should keep them occupied. Must I remind you? That was your idea."

"I don't remember saying use an FBI agent for bait."

"Are you with me or not, Nash? You best decide."

"I'll finish what I started."

"What you bury stays buried too, right?"

"Do I get my weapons back?"

"I'll have to think on that a bit longer. Where's Ceil?"

"Feeding that jackass," he answered.

"Underhill isn't hungry right now," Speedy laughed. "I just crack me up."

Just after midnight the hooting began. It echoed from various locations around the camp.

"That's them," whispered Cecelia. "That's what I told you I heard. What do they want with us?"

Pissed off or scared, only he knew for sure, Speedy stepped outside their little modest dwelling and sprayed his Uzi along the tree line. The hooting ceased.

"See Nash. They're no match for our fire power."

Nash said nothing. He watched for a reaction from the two captives bound in the corner. The big black one looked highly agitated but said nothing. The other one finally spoke.

"What the hell is going on out here other than your weed farming?"

"Have you not ever heard of Sasquatch?"

Max shrugged.

"Bigfoot," clarified Nash.

"We've got a Bigfoot out there," Max exclaimed. "We're sitting on a goldmine."

Nash was taken off guard by that reaction. The response got Speedy's attention. "What do you mean ... goldmine?"

"Forget this stupid weed you have here," Max continued. "Catch that Bigfoot and you lay claim to fame and fortune."

"I'm listening," said Speedy.

"No one has ever caught one. It would be the scientific discovery of a lifetime. You could name your own price for it dead or alive. This could be worth millions."

Nash interrupted, "Maybe you don't get it. We've got several of these things out there circling our camp. They've been stealing our supplies. They trashed our truck. They dug up and stole Velvet's body and probably killed Booger Parks. And I don't think they want us to leave or hell maybe that's exactly what they want, who knows."

"You have more than one," shouted Max, "Correction, this could be worth billions!"

"Did you hear nothing I just said?"

"You have more than one," answered an excited Max.

"We don't have anything you damn fool. They have us surrounded and possibly outnumbered, and we have no clue what they really want."

"Enough, Nash," barked Speedy, walking over to Max, knife in hand.

Max's eyes enlarged like saucers, and then he closed them, waiting to be dead. Speedy cut his hands free. "And do you have a plan in mind for capturing one of our hairy visitors?"

"Not now, but just give me a little time and I'm sure I can come up with one," smiled Max. "Can you cut Bam-Bam free? I'll probably require his assistance."

"You two are crazy," shouted Nash. "I've said it once and I'm going to say it again, don't piss these things off. You're not dealing with dumb animals."

The night became filled with the blood curdling screams, and then just as quickly became deathly quiet. They listened but heard not another sound.

"It's those creatures," said Ceil.

"Not this time. That was Agent Underhill," answered Nash.

"I knew they had a sweet tooth," smiled Speedy.

"Max always fusses at me for having a sweet tooth. I like sweets, especially Hershey bars," said Bam-Bam.

"Or they're carnivores," spoke up Max, "Poor Underhill."

Ceil lost her cookies and began to scream. "Get me the hell out of here, Speed. I want to leave now. Do you hear me? We've got to go now before they eat all of us." She clutched Underhill's revolver and waved it around wildly.

"Ceil, stop your damn foolish talk and hand me that pistol," asserted Speedy.

She pulled the trigger, firing a single shot into the wooden entrance above Speedy's head. He didn't take that very well and unleashed the Uzi, nearly cutting her in half. "Stupid bitch, you know better than to shoot at me."

Nash sighed, and then exhaled, "Unbelievable, you certainly know how to treat all your partners. I guess I'm next?"

"Two ungrateful dead bitches, that's all they were."

"That was just like in the movies," said an excited Bam-Bam.

"I say we stick to the plan and leave at daybreak with our crop," advised Nash, attempting to refocus Speedy.

"Chicken feed if our new buddy Maxwell is right."

"My friends call me Mad Max."

"Then Mad Max it is. How about you and the nigger bury the bitch?"

"He doesn't like being called that name," warned Max.

Bam-Bam opened and clinched his fists in response to the unnecessary name calling. He suddenly didn't like the shooter man.

"Bury the bitch, now," he ordered.

They picked up her body, trying to keep it in one piece. Once outside Max whispered to Bam-Bam, "When I give you the signal, you break his neck, you understand?"

"I don't like him. He called me that name. I don't like it when people call me that name, Max. I will break his neck when you say so."

"Only on my signal," explained Max. "You must not harm him until then."

Bam-Bam nodded he understood.

Max grabbed the shovel. It was too dark to wonder off very far. He found a soft spot just a few yards away and handed Bam-Bam the shovel. "Dig her a hole."

Inside Speedy discussed the possibilities with Nash. "All right, we leave in the morning with our reefer, but if these things try to stop us and we nail one, it's a win-win situation for us."

"You're hoping they do, aren't you?"

"I can think of a billion reasons for it." Speedy tossed Nash Underhill's revolver. "You may need this if they attack."

"And if they don't," answered Nash.

"You'll still need it," winked Speedy.

"Who the hell are you," asked Mattie, after she stopped screaming.

"Damien Dark at your service. Is this cool or what?"

128

"What are you doing here?"

"Same as you," he explained. "They bought me here too."

"They?"

"I came here in search of UFO's and found the Holy Grail."

"We've been abducted by aliens?"

"Better than aliens and I never thought I'd say that," he giggled like a little schoolgirl.

"Damien Dark cut the crap," she yelled. "Who brought us here?"

"Bigfoots of course," he smiled. "And me without my camera. My backpack is back at Saint Helen. You know they keep saying it might blow any day. No problem. You will be able to support my story when we return. We'll both be famous. Who are you by the way?"

"Reynolds, Professor Mattie Reynolds."

"I knew I recognized you. I've attended one of your seminars before, Professor."

"You've seen the *S'cwene'y'ti*?"

"The what?"

"A Sasquatch, a Bigfoot, a damn American Yeti, you've seen one."

"Several, Professor" he answered. "They are indeed real."

"You built the fire."

He shook his head. "No, they did. They're more human than we could have ever imagined in our wildest dreams. I'm sure glad no hunter ever shot one of them."

"How long have you been here?"

"Only a couple of days as best I can remember."

"They haven't attempted to harm you?"

"Not so far, Professor. They showed some interest at first then sort of just left me alone. It's kind of embarrassing what they did to me."

She inquired what with her eyes.

"This enormous leader forced me to ejaculate in its hand, and it smelled and tasted my semen, then just walked away. I expected something like this from aliens, but not from Bigfoot, unless they are one in the same. How cool would that be, Bigfoot being an alien."

"I bet that's what troubled Matt. That's what he was too embarrassed to mention in his journal."

"Who's Matt? What journal?"

"Never mind. Are there any other humans here?"

"I haven't seen anyone else."

"No kids, no boys?"

"Afraid not. Were you expecting to see some boys?"

"I don't know what I expected to find," she said in a frustrated tone.

"Where are they now?"

"Don't know. I haven't seen any since they brought you in and built up the fire. Here, they left us some potato chips and honey buns. There's a spring at the far wall over there if you're thirsty."

"Where did they get these supplies?"

He shrugged he didn't know.

"Do you know who this dead guy is?"

"I guess I've been so enamored by this find I never noticed the remains."

She decided not to share the journal for now. This Damien seemed just a bit too publicly hungry for her taste. He was one of those freaked out UFO hunters.

"Have you found a way out of here?"

"I haven't really looked. Isn't it great to be part of the discovery of a lifetime?"

Dark was going to cramp her style for sure. This was supposed to be her day under the sun. And only she would decide if or when it reached the public eye. He offered her food again, but she declined. His lips were plastered with the gunk from one of the honey buns. She motioned to his mouth and he wiped if off with his sleeve. Damien Dark smiled. She could see chips caked between his teeth. This boy was quite the slob.

"Tell you what," she whispered. "You check that far end over there and I'll do the same in that direction." She pointed. "We can make a couple of torches from our dead friend's clothes and search for an escape route."

"What's your hurry? You just got here. You haven't even seen them yet."

"Snap out of your star struck state," she raised her voice and shook him to reinforce her meaning. "Look at this dead man. They could be responsible for his demise. We better have our ducks in a row if they shift gears and attempt to do the same to us."

"They could have killed both of us already if they had wanted to. Tell me. What is your real problem?"

"Do what you want to do, and I'll do what I think is best for me. Just stay the hell out of my way."

"Boy, there goes the neighborhood," he said rolling his eyes. "Are you on the rag or something?"

Wham, he never saw that one coming. She abruptly slapped him across the face, jarring his teeth and blurring his vision. "Manners, and respect for your elders," she said in a very pissed off tone. "Learn it, live it and we'll get along just fine. Now just stay out of my way before I aim lower next time."

He cupped his groin with both hands and stepped aside. "You better not try that with one of them."

She ripped strips from the dead stranger's shirt and layered them around a tree limb she had recovered from the wood pile near the fire. She moistened them slightly in the spring then returned to the fire and lit the torch. She followed the contour of the opposite side of the cavern for three or four hundred feet but discovered no exit tunnels. She returned to the fire pit when her makeshift torch flickered out. Mattie scanned the perimeter but saw no signs of Damien. Sitting, she pulled the journal from her jacket and flipped it open to the first page and began to read.

I awoke in this strange cave. My memory is a little fuzzy but coming back to me gradually. Due to my injuries I felt compelled to write what had happened. This could serve as my last will and testament I suppose. I didn't figure on that thunderstorm when I made my jump. I also underestimated the difficultly in making a jump like this. I do remember crashing through the trees and my chute becoming entangled. I hung there for what seemed like forever in the darkness and blinding downpour. I heard the branch break and down I plummeted. Hell of a fall it was. I landed feet first and heard both my legs snap like twigs. I must have blacked out from the excruciating pain. Now here I am. I have no clue where that is. There must be people around because there is a fire burning. I have not seen them yet. I feel too weak to yell out. I only write this now because I feel my injuries are life threatening. I'm repeating myself I know. I did this for the money and now I have no idea where it is either. I guess the ones that brought me here have it. The airlines will have me listed as Dan Cooper. I'll just leave it at that My real name is not that important. I don't have any close relatives. Cooper will serve me just fine. I bet the news is a buzz with what I did. No one would have ever guessed what I had in mind. They do now but it's too late. You'd think I'd be hurting more than I am with both legs busted up like this but funny I don't really feel much pain. My watch tells me it's Thanksgiving Day now, November 1971. I'm just not sure if it is AM or PM. I guess I should be thankful I'm still alive. I'd feel more thankful if I had that 200-grand by my side. I'm mighty thirsty. I'm not real hungry right now but a turkey leg doesn't sound half bad if I had one. I can't believe I still have this notebook and pen. I guess the ones what found me either didn't search me or were too excited about the money to care. So much for a bargaining chip. Some mess I've gotten myself into. I'm feeling a little lightheaded so I

"Damn, this poor bastard is D.B. Cooper," Mattie whispered. Matt McGregor's journal brought me here to find answers and now Cooper's journal is unraveling another one of man's biggest mysteries. What ever happened to D.B. Copper? Now I know. I'm in his shoes, she thought, except I have no broken legs. I wonder how long he survived in here.

She saw Damien Dark returning from the shadows and tucked the journal back inside her jacket. The little freak would just love to get his hands on it.

"Well, you aren't gone yet."

"You can continue acting like a little smart ass or we can work together, your choice."

"I guess I'm a better smartass than a team player, huh?"

"Live out your little fantasy, wonder boy, but I'm going to find a way out before your alleged *S'cwene'y'ti* return."

"You still don't believe me, do you?"

"I deal in evidence and so far, all I've heard is your wild tales," she scoffed. "And from a boy who soils his breaches at the thought of flying saucers and little green men, it's just not that convincing."

"Make fun of me if you must, but you won't think it's so funny when that ten-foot Sasquatch returns. Maybe he'll make you do what he made me do," he smiled. "If he's anatomically correct, you're in for quite a thrill ride. He'll bust you wide open."

"You're a regular little trash mouth, aren't you?"

Damien said nothing, turned and walked toward the far reaches of the cavern, in the same direction that he had just appeared. Mattie pulled out the journal once she had seen him sit down with his back to her.

My watch tells me I was out for almost three hours. Someone was here while I lay unconscious. The fire is blazing again. Someone placed a handful of wild berries on top of my notebook. I tasted a couple of them and almost puked. My stomach just isn't ready for food yet. My right leg has started hurting badly. I pulled up my pants leg. I wish I hadn't. The bone is jutting through just below my knee. I decided not to look at my left leg right now fearing the worst. Dried blood is caked on my forehead. I traced a long gash with my fingertips. I guess I could have suffered a concussion. I've pissed and shit my pants at some point. It stinks. I wonder what that nice flight attendant is thinking now. Florence was her name.

She was a looker. I can't believe she folded up my note without even looking at it. Bet she wished she had never read it. I bet those FBI agents are chomping at the bits to find me. I can't say that is such a bad idea right now. I could really use their help. Damn my leg hurts like hell. Head is getting light again. I've got to rest.

That must have been awful to be lying there in such pain and unable to do for himself, thought Mattie. What a shame to have had all that money and it didn't do him any good. You break the law. You pay the price. She walked back over to his skeletal remains.

"Well Dan Cooper, I don't guess you'll miss a few more shreds of that coat will you. I need to replenish my torch. Now we rest for a while."

"Mule is loaded," called out Nash. "And everyone has two additional backpacks to carry, except the big feller. I have him four stuffed and ready."

"Do we have all of it?"

"We have all that was ready to harvest. Do you want me to torch the rest?"

"Nah, that would be like sending up smoke signals in case we have more agents out there roaming the woods. I have a better idea. I'll booby trap the greenhouse with the dynamite. If we have company after we leave, that will hold them at bay for a while. I'll do the same with our little log home."

"Thought you might want to know," Nash said, taking a deep breath. "They dug up Cecelia's body last night. Grave is empty."

"What the hell is this, the damn *Invasion of the damn hairy Body Snatchers?*"

"I wouldn't do any booby trapping if I were you. Instead why don't we put some distance between us and this camp."

"Get the others. This won't take long."

"Bad idea. Just warning you."

Within thirty minutes they were on their way. Nash led the way, followed by Max towing the mule. Bam-Bam carried his four bundles of reefer effortlessly. Speedy brought up the rear, rubber necking all the way, certain they were being watched and probably stalked.

An eight-foot male Sasquatch roamed through the camp in broad daylight, confident the occupants had departed. Very agile at over four hundred pounds, it scavenged the premises. The once bountiful supply cabinet was empty from last night's raid. Curious, it pushed on the greenhouse doors attracted by the strange aroma from inside. It didn't smell food, but the odor enticed him like catnip. Almost a mile away, the explosion caused the pot smugglers to flinch and duck for cover. Smiling, Speedy glanced back in the direction of the camp.

"Bingo," he said. "Some nosey sonofabitch just got busted."

"Fireworks," smiled Bam-Bam.

"Do you think more FBI agents have arrived," asked Max.

"That or our hairy friends," answered Speedy.

"I hope it was FBI," muttered Nash.

The smaller female stood over the dismembered male, still deafened by the explosion. She let out a blood curdling scream, and then slammed her huge fists over and over on the ground.

"You hear that," laughed Speedy. "We got one."

"Shouldn't we go back and check," asked Max. "Like I said, name your price for even a carcass. "

"Mad Max, old buddy," said Speedy, as he placed his hand on Max's shoulder. "Be patient."

"I like Old Bertha," spoke up Bam-Bam. "Can we keep her, Max?"

"You better watch that trail closely now," warned Nash. "You just had to piss them off, didn't you? They'll be coming after us. Mark my word."

"Do you think that mule can carry a Bigfoot?"

Nash rolled his eyes at Speedy. "Let's get moving."

"Is that all the fireworks, Max?"

"I hope so, kiddo. Let's get moving like he said."

"Here, take this," said Nash, handing Max a pistol.

"What the hell are you doing," demanded Speedy.

"Evening things," answered Nash. "Max does the big guy know how to fire a weapon?"

"No, but he doesn't need one. He can handle himself just fine if he has to."

"Why can't I have a gun, Max? I've never had a real one before. I had that toy one from the fair I won picking up those little floating ducks."

"You've got to take care of Old Bertha." Max told Bam-Bam. "That's your job."

"Okeydokey. I like Old Bertha."

"We're going to need a hell of lot of good luck to get out of this one," whispered Nash.

Others from the foot clan gathered and expressed their outrage for their fallen member. The leader, the huge graying alpha male gathered up the smaller male's torso. Others collected the fragmented parts. Once they finished there would be no sign that the male had ever existed. Such was their way and their assurance for implying legend. Without hard evidence they did not exist. Tracks, sightings and even fuzzy photos could not prove they were real. The mystery would continue at least one more day.

Wednesday May 14th

Mattie had succumbed to the fatigue. Overwhelmed by the discovery she had slept through the wee hours of the next morning. Damien Dark had done the same.

Rejuvenated once again, she surveyed the tunnels she had seen previously and ventured a short way down the first. It dead-ended after forty feet or so. She backtracked and entered a second. This one shrank to an extremely small crawl space. Mattie wasn't desperate enough to do the belly crawl yet. Exiting the second tunnel she noticed Damien Dark tossing more wood on the fire, his back to her. She could not fathom why he was so disinterested in escaping. He seemed to enjoy this way too much. She guessed he had no life in the real world.

The torch flickered then fluttered loudly when she entered the third tunnel, apparently influenced by the effects of a draft. She figured this one offered a route to the outside. Just as she entered it, she heard a commotion. Someone or something was heading her way. Mattie Reynolds backed out and stood to one side, her back against the cavern wall. She held the torch like a Louisville Slugger, ready to swing for the fence. The figure emerged, and she started her swing.

Sports commentators would say she had not gone around or broken her wrist; no strike would be called. The camouflaged figure flinched as the torch swatted ever so close. Mattie recognized a boyish face and not that of a hairy *S'cwene'y'ti*. She took a deep breath, glad that she had not whacked him with her torch.

"You almost hit me," he exclaimed and then smiled. "But I sure am glad to see you."

"Sorry, I didn't know who or what you might be."

"My name is Bob. Bob Thomson. My stepdad is Bert Thomson. I don't know where he is now."

"You're the missing Thomson kid?"

"I reckon I am. Who are you?"

"You can call me Mattie," she said, rubbing her fingers through his thick blonde hair.

"What's down that tunnel?"

"Another big room like this one. The fire was getting low back there. I thought I heard somebody talking in here. I felt my way along the wall."

"You're a mighty brave lad."

"Thank you, but it's been really scary in here. Those others are gone right now, but I expect they will be back. They always come back sooner or later."

"Others. Haveyou've seen them too."

"Yeah, you know, the big hairy giants, they live in here."

"Have they harmed you in any way?"

He shrugged, "Not really I reckon. The big one made me take off my overalls and he ..."

"Yeah, they did the same thing to Damien."

"Who's Damien?"

She pointed toward the fire pit in the center of the cavern. "You haven't met Damien Dark."

"This is the first time I've been in here. I stayed put in that other one until I heard real people talking."

"Is anyone else in there?"

"Nope, just a bunch of bones I found in the pile and this," he said, handing her the metallic objects.

She examined them and remarked, "This one holds the scarf on a Cub Scout uniform and the other is the uniform's belt buckle. She sighed, "Tommy McAllister."

"Who is Tommy McAllister?"

"He was a young scout, a few years younger than you when he disappeared two years ago," she told him handing him the items. "I don't guess you saw him anywhere?"

"No. I just found these in the pile of bones. There was a lot of neat stuff back there."

"You'll have to take me there in a little while," she said, as she again rubbed her hand through his hair. "Did you see a way out in your cavern?"

"I did, but the big hairy giants always roll a big old rock in front of it. I tried to move it, but it was too heavy. Look, he's waving. Is that the Damien guy?"

She turned to see Damien waving frantically, motioning them to come to the fire pit. When they arrived, Damien had a long wooden limb prodding the coals of the fire.

"Who's the kid," inquired Damien.

"Bob Thomson meet fellow abductee, Damien Dark, famed UFO chaser."

"You're a famous UFO hunter?"

"Not yet," he boasted. "I've temporarily turned my attention to proving the existence of the Sasquatch."

"You've come to the right place to do that."

"Kicking and screaming most likely," chuckled Mattie.

"You may not think it is so funny if you plant your eyes on what I found in the fire pit," said a very serious toned Damien Dark pointing with the stick of wood he held firmly in his right hand.

Mattie followed the end of the wooden shaft to the glowing embers. Charred but still visible were fragments of bones and four skulls, five very human skulls. These were the remains of Booger Rhodes, Velvet Tucker, Cecelia Velazquez, Elijah Payne and Anson Parker. The fire pit had new meaning. She squatted on her haunches, unknown to her that one of these belonged to Anson. A cold chill ran down her spine. More human remains were burned in the pit and young Bob said another pile of bones were in the other chamber. She shivered, playing the possible scenario out in her very confused brain. What were these alleged creatures and just what were they capable of doing?

Matt McGregor had mentioned piles of human bones in that valley. He had never mentioned that they were capable of building fire or that possibly they were cannibalistic. Maybe both had been a product of evolution. What had she gotten herself into? The search for knowledge and closure might have dire consequences given the unnerving possibilities of this discovery,

----

"Did you hear that?"

"I heard it," answered Nash. "They've been flanking us on both sides for the better part of an hour."

"Asshole," barked Speedy. "Why haven't you said something?"

"I didn't want you to go crazy with that Uzi of yours and start shooting at shadows."

"What if I practice on you, Nash?"

"So far they have kept their distance," Nash said, trying to instill some common sense into Speedy. "If we don't provoke them, maybe they'll leave us be."

"Provoke them. Hell they are stalking us according to you. How many do you figure are out there?"

"Three or four at least," guessed Nash, "Maybe more."

"And you are worried about me harming them," exclaimed Speedy.

Bam-Bam laughed, "I saw Magilla Gorilla again, Max."

Using the 'N' word again, Speedy asked Max what was Bam-Bam babbling about now.

"I advised you not to call him that, didn't I? He doesn't like that name, nor do I, Mister Moore. Where did you see him this time, Bam-Bam?"

Bam-Bam pointed to a thicket no more than 15 yards away. He smiled, "Still naked though and he wasn't wearing his funny hat."

Nash chimed in, "When did you see this Magilla?"

"Just now," grinned Bam-Bam. "He poked his head out and looked at us."

"How big was Magilla? Was he as big as me?"

"Bigger than you, Mister Nash."

Nash didn't like that answer and asked, "As big as you then, Bam-Bam?"

"Bigger," said Bam-Bam, stretching his hand above his head to indicate just how tall.

"Hell no, that's impossible," barked Speedy. "That would make it at least nine or ten feet tall."

"He had funny gray fur on his face," added Bam-Bam. "The other Magilla didn't have gray hair and wasn't as big as this one."

"Other one," said Speedy. "What the hell is he talking about?"

"A couple of days before we stumbled into your camp, he told me he had seen Magilla Gorilla along the trail, but I didn't pay him any attention. He sometimes has a vivid imagination," explained Max.

"These woods must be very well populated," added Nash. "We're definitely trespassing on their turf and I don't think they're very happy about it. They've been trying to scare us off, but we didn't heed their warning. I say let's keep moving."

Speedy didn't like the developing situation. "Is there a shorter way out of here, Nash?"

"There is. It would be tougher terrain, but it could shave a couple of a days, maybe more, if we circled east of Mount Saint Helen and picked up an old logging road. Our regular way out might expose us to ambushes. The other route would eventually take us down by Harry Truman's place."

Speedy was losing his patience if he ever had any. "Who the hell is Harry Truman? I thought he was one of our dead presidents?"

Nash rolled his eyes. "He's an octogenarian that has lived up here forever. I've met him a couple of times. He's a tough old bird."

"An ocot-to-what-aian," asked Speedy.

"Old fart in his eighties," replied Nash. "He's a throwback and stubborn old cuss."

"Forget I asked. What's your gut tell you about that route? You're the mountain man with all the experience. I'm just a city boy with a trigger-happy finger. I don't trust these damn animals."

"I'd say it's worth a shot, but she's been rumbling pretty steady lately. You've felt the tremors. I heard on the radio that the experts keep saying she's going to blow real soon. I don't personally expect anything spectacular if she does. Mountain's been dormant forever. I like our chances better just the same. And for the record, the Sasquatch are not animals by a long shot."

A rock whizzed by Speedy's head. A second one grazed his shoulder. A third hit Nash on the left forearm. Speedy reached down and retrieved the rock, and then chunked it wildly back in the bushes. Hooting irrupted front and back and on both sides.

"That sounded like more than three or four to me," yelled Speedy, as he cut loose with the Uzi, shredding every bush and small tree for two thirds of the perimeter, almost taking out Old Bertha.

Bam-Bam grabbed the end of the barrel and forced the muzzle toward the ground. "You almost shot my mule."

Speedy attempted to shake the massive hand free, but it held firm like a vice. The once childish face displayed pure fury. Speedy stared into those burning dark brown eyes and decided not to push his luck. He eased his finger off the trigger and allowed the Uzi to go limp in his hands. Bam-Bam released the muzzle, but only after Max stepped over and placed his hand on the big guy's shoulder and whispered for him to release it.

Speed looked Bam-Bam dead in the eyes and then glanced over at Max, using the 'N' word and stating how Bam-Bam seemed to do whatever Max wanted him to do. "How convenient having muscle minus a brain at your beck and call.'

"Explicitly," replied Max. "And I've asked you not to call him that. Please, for your sake, just stop."

Speedy didn't take too kindly to someone like Max telling him what he should and shouldn't do. He would take great pleasure in wasting them once this was over. "That must come in very handy. How convenient, you have your own private muscle brigade with you, don't you?

"I don't like you very much," mumbled Bam-Bam, eyes blazing with hatred for Elwood Speed Moore. "You hurt things. You tried to shoot my mule and you call me that name."

"Yeah, we've been together for quite a while," added Max. "And I don't particularly appreciate your manners either. But we are partners in this, so I will honor our part of the bargain."

"You boys finished with your chatting," asked Nash. "We have more important things going on right now or have you forgotten about our pursuers?"

"Lead on mountain man. I think the ape men have gotten the damn message loud and clear. They are no match for my fire power."

Nash rolled his eyes thinking what a fool he had gotten hooked up with this time.

They continued the remainder of the day with no further incidents. Nash still wary that they were being trailed kept it to himself. He didn't want mister trigger happy to do anything stupid again. He sensed the Sasquatch had given them a little breathing room and was just following for now. Just maybe, he hoped, they were almost out of their territory. Little did he know that this was beyond territorial to the pursuers.

"It'll be dark in about an hour and a half," Nash told the trio. "Let's find a place that best offers us protection from any nighttime attacks."

"You still think they're following us, don't you?"

Nash admitted nothing. "Speedy, I just don't like to take chances."

The earth began to tremble, more violently than the trembles they had felt throughout the day. Bam-Bam looked wild eyed and rubbed Old Bertha on her neck. "It's the volcano," he whispered to the mule. "It's angry."

This tremor lasted almost a full minute. No one else said a thing until the earth stopped moving. Nash finally spoke up. "The old girl is rather pissed;" he said. "Maybe the experts are right about a pending eruption."

Speedy was getting more perturbed. "What the hell does that mean for us?"

"We should be able to make it to Truman's place in less than two days," Nash reassured the group. "We'll be safe enough down there."

"Volcanoes have lava," commented Bam-Bam. "It is very hot and kills dinosaurs and cavemen. Will the lava kill us?"

Speedy didn't listen and pushed it once again, referring to Bam-Bam with the one word he had been asked not to use, stating this time that Max's pal was such a wealth of damn information.

Bam-Bam hearing the "N" word again, clenched both fists and took one step toward him. Max seeing his anger, placed a hand on his arm and whispered, "Not yet. You'll have your chance with the bad man, I promise. For the last time, please don't call him that name. He doesn't take kindly to it and you're really riling him."

Speedy didn't acknowledge the request with a response. He did take note that he had rattled the big feller's cage again. He admitted to himself that he didn't really want to be on the receiving end of Bam-Bam's fury. The big guy could probably inflict some swift and serious damage if unleashed. Of course, this would give him the excuse to end this crap, but not before he got his precious reefer out of here.

Nash called out ahead. "I've found a place to camp. There's a huge rock formation ahead with a sheer drop off to one side and 20 yards of clear-cut covering two thirds of the perimeter. It would be tough for anyone or anything to sneak up on us without being seen."

"Perfect," replied Speedy. "Finally, you're earning your keep."

Nash barked "Max, you and Bam-Bam gather up as much wood as you can before dark. Have the big fellow drag that uprooted stump over here. It's perfectly seasoned lighter pine. It will burn like a flame thrower."

Bam-Bam liked the one called Nash. He never called him the bad word. He acted like Daniel Boone but didn't have a coon skinned hat. He still didn't understand why everyone was afraid of Magilla Gorilla or why he wasn't wearing his hat and suspendered pants.

"I'll be back in a minute," stated Speedy. "I've got to take a dump."

"Watch the type of leaf you pick for wiping," warned Nash. "There's plenty of poison oak and ivy out here."

"I have a handkerchief," he said, waving it at Nash as he walked toward the overgrowth.

Finding a small game trail, Speedy walked some 35 yards down it until he spotted a small fallen tree just perfect for parking his ass and letting it all hang out. Propping the Uzi at hands reach, he eased his pants and underwear down to his ankles.

Speedy removed a small case from his jacket. It contained five tightly rolled joints of reefer. He grabbed one and fired it up, toking on it while waiting for his bowels to kick in.
He hated crapping in the woods. His bowels typically froze tighter than a gnat's ass. The more he strained, the less likely he would receive results. He had the same problem pissing at public urinals. He didn't know why. He hoped the joint would relax him because his stomach cramped something fierce.

Halfway through the joint and still no luck, he heard something rustle the leaves directly in front of him. He already had one hand on the Uzi, scanning the bushes for movement. Suddenly the odor hit him like a runaway freight train. Obviously, the smell had not come from him because his bowels remained locked tight. The stench was worse than the morning after a night of drinking too much beer and eating beans and deviled eggs.

Straining to detect any sort of movement, Speedy was taken by surprise when the bushes meticulously parted, exposing a massive bodiless no necked hairy face over eight feet above the ground peering from the opening. His bowels immediately unleashed like a running faucet. He froze in terror as his hand still clutching the automatic weapon lost its grip and it plunked to the ground at his feet. The sound of the dropping Uzi and the fact it landed on both his feet shocked him back to life. He broke eye contact only long enough to reclaim his gun. Throwing the gun up and again looking toward the bushes, the face had disappeared. His finger frozen on the trigger. He could not will it to fire this time.

Forgoing the wiping process, he dropped his handkerchief, yanked up his pants with one hand, while still holding the Uzi with the other. He couldn't shake the image of the nightmare face he had just seen. Speedy decided at that instant, that capturing one of these things was no longer a good idea. Escape was the only valid option and the sooner, the better.

Mattie pondered the true meaning of the discovery in the fire pit and what Bob had described as the mountain of bones in the other chamber. She cringed at the possibilities. For now, Damien Dark had Bob's undivided attention with tales of UFO sightings, none by him of course. She took advantage of this diversion and pulled out Cooper's journal and picked up where she had left off. The next entry was two days later by the date at the top of the page.

I've slept more than I have been awake. I am concerned about my legs. The one is black and oozing fluid where the bone is jutted out. Someone keeps building up that fire while I'm asleep. I haven't seen them. More berries were left but I haven't been able to eat them. I'm running a fever and have been throwing up a lot. I'm unable to move from my current location. The chills prevented me from writing the last few days. I couldn't hold the pen steady. I don't know why that was so important for me to clarify. I've heard activity somewhere in the distance. I couldn't make out the language. It sounded more like grunts and growls, muffled. I'm probably just hallucinating. The chills are returning so I must stop.

I suppose I can be thankful I am not in Cooper's unfortunate shape, thought Mattie. Neither Bob nor Damien are injured either. We do need to find a way out though.

She read on. The next entry was dated as what he thought to be his fifth day in the cavern.

Remarkable. I had to wait until they left before I could report the extraordinary discovery. I'm being kept here by a horde of Bigfoots. Can you believe it? I have found the legendary Bigfoot, the missing link. They have not tried to harm me. A female much larger than me brought me some water in a folded leaf and more berries. I still can't eat. My leg smells bad. I've counted at least 11 different ones so far. Looks like 3 adult females, 6 adult males and 2 juveniles, one male and one female. There could be more. The leader is a monster standing over 9 feet tall. The other adults range between 5 and 8 feet. They have thick muscular bodies covered in hair except on their hands, feet and facial areas around the nose and eyes. They don't have much of a neck and have broad shoulders. Long powerful arms hang from their sides and they walk upright with ease. Their colors range from a dirty brown to reddish, except for the big male. He has some gray in the facial area and down his back like one of those silverback gorillas. I cannot guess their age. Something tells me they may have a longer life span than ours. What's more amazing is they keep a fire burning continuously in the center of the carven. I have not seen any of them make fire. They seemed to be determined to not let the one burn out in some sort of makeshift pit. One more remarkable observation, they seem to know sign language. I don't sign but I have been able to make out some of their hand motions and hopefully answered them correctly.

"Damn," Mattie spoke out loud, catching the attention of Damien and Bob.

She eased the journal down by her side and thought about Matt McGregor's writings of a mute mountain man who used sign language. She tried to recall the mute's name but couldn't. She did remember that he was a Frenchman. She also remembered how Matt had regretted leaving the mute behind when they escaped the hidden valley. She was now positive that the Frenchman had somehow survived and was the one responsible for teaching the S'cwene'y'ti sign language. These had to be their ancestors.

"I'm hungry," said Bob.

"Me too," added Damien. "I wonder when our host plan to feed us again. We're out of junk food."

Mattie didn't share the other two's concerns. "Why don't we concentrate on a way to get out of here?"

"Haven't you been listening to the kid? The Bigfoot keep the exit blocked with a huge boulder."

"Well just maybe if the three of us try we can move it." Mattie tired of Damien's pessimistic tone. "Look, I know you're just happy as a pig to be here and living out some great fantasy, but I'm not going to stay and end up like Cooper over there."

"Cooper," repeated Damien. "How do you know the skeleton's name?"

Oops she thought, such a damn foolish slip of the tongue. What was she thinking?

"Cooper as in D.B. Cooper," asked Damien.

There was no need to hide it now. "The very one," she replied.

"How do you know that?" asked Damien Dark.

"I found his wallet," she lied for now, not wanting to share the journal with the little publicity hungry flying saucer geek.

"Man, this just keeps getting better all the time," he giggled.

Bob wasn't following the conservation. "Who is D.B. Cooper?"

"Come with me little grasshopper while I enlighten you," motioned Damien, doing his best *David Carradine* portrayal of *Kwai Chang Caine* from the *Kung Fu* television series as the two returned to the fire side.

Mattie ceased the moment and huddled on the opposite side of the fire pit and continued her reading of Cooper's journal.

These creatures are far more intelligent than anyone could have ever imagined. They possess a structured culture and remind me of a primitive Indian tribe with their antics. They appear very social. The one female seems very interested in taking care of me. It's creeping me out a little because she almost seems to be sexually attracted to me. She has touched my privates a couple of times. Even in my sickened state I must admit she did arouse a stir. I must really be suffering disillusion. I've lost count of how many times I've soiled my clothing but my leg smells so awful it masks my own excrement. I am fearful that gangrene may have set in. The other leg hurts but doesn't appear infected. They've shown no signs of knowing how to medically treat the wounds with herbs. I don't expect to receive any remedies that may help me. The big female is heading this way with more water. I'll stop right now. My get rich scheme wasn't supposed to have such fatal ramifications. I survived the jump for Christ's sake. I didn't expect anything like this.

Cooper's scribbling jumped off the pages and affected Mattie just as Matt McGregor's had touched her. The writings of both men captivated her imagination. They had the uncanny ability to allow her to see the world through their eyes. She lived the adventure alongside them and realized Dan Cooper's situation had been terminal from the start. His gangrene leg had apparently caused his death. Her crash back to earth happened so suddenly it took her breath. Overcome by visions of Shawn, the tears flowed freely down both cheeks. If she couldn't find a way out, she would never see him again. She thought, he or others might eventually locate Anson Parker's stone grave but would never find her. She had no idea that Anson Parker's body had found a new resting place and had been cremated. All hope rested on her resourcefulness, but she just didn't know it.

A shaken and ashen faced Elwood Speed Moore made a hasty retreat, glancing over his shoulder the entire short distance he had to travel to rendezvous with the others. He spoke nothing of what he had just witnessed, terrified by what he had seen. He didn't care to share his shameful behavior with the others, even though the stickiness inside his pants reminded him all too well. Now terror stricken, he just wanted out of this wilderness hell. Even the pot didn't seem to be as important as it once had been, but still he wasn't ready to relinquish his claim on it just quite yet.

He planted himself with his back to the giant bolder overhang, Uzi in his lap. He said very little while the others built the fire and Nash prepared a pot of dried pinto beans for their meal. Nash noticed, however, but didn't say anything. He just went about business securing the campsite. Max and Bam-Bam had gathered more than enough dried wood to keep a fire burning all night. Bam-Bam now stood by Old Bertha, rubbing her and chatting endlessly to the old mule.

Nash marveled how childlike he acted, a kid trapped inside a monstrous human body, not a care in the world. Right now, he envied him, but still wondered when the Sasquatch would strike next. He figured it would come sometime after nightfall, when they least expected it. He wasn't convinced the four of them were any match for the wrath these creatures could unleash. He still opposed harming them. He would only act in self defense, but Speedy and

Max concerned him. Speedy was a loose cannon and Max wanted one of them to cash in on his gold mine.

The first couple of hours of nightfall proved to be uneventful. Speedy had eaten very little, said less, very uncharacteristic. The Uzi remained glued to his hands. Obvious to Nash, something had shaken up their fearless leader while taking his dump in the woods. He figured the time might be right to do a little prodding.

"Speedy, why not try to catch a little shut eye. I'll keep watch."

"Not sleepy," he barked. "You go ahead."

"Just what happened to you out there?"

"Nothing happened. What makes you think something happened?"

Nash chuckled, "Man, you're a bundle of nerves. Your face is still white as a sheet. You saw one, didn't you if I had to take a guess?"

"Shut the hell up. You don't know what you're talking about. I've got a damn automatic weapon here. Why would I be scared?"

"I didn't say you were scared. Those are your words. Yep, you saw one or maybe several," grinned Nash, now going in for the kill. "You still want to capture one and make your fortune under the big top? Ringling Brothers and Moore Circus doesn't quite have the same ring to it, does it?"

"I'm not going to tell you again, Nash. Shut the hell up!"

"In the center ring, the eighth wonder of the world," Nash, now mimicked a circus ringmaster, "Bigger and better than Kong, discovered in the northwestern woods of Washington by famed pot entrepreneur, Elwood Speed Moore."

Bam-Bam with a sparkle in his eye said, "I like the circus. I especially like the clowns. How do so many ride in that little biddy car? They have cotton candy at the circus. Max doesn't like me to have it because he says it is too sticky and messy. They have elephants too. Can me and Old Bertha be in your circus? I'll teach her to do tricks."

"For Christ's sake, please shut up that big ass nig..." catching himself, he finished, "nick-cum-poop before I do something I'll regret."

"Go check on Bertha," Max told him.

Nash laughed, "Nick-cum-poop. I have never heard you utter that before. That was hilarious coming from you. An edited version of your normal foul mouth. You continue to amaze me."

"Bite me," snapped Speedy, giving Nash the finger, while he still clutched the Uzi with his other hand.

The drumming started. The banging on a tree was soon followed by a second, a third, then a fourth. Although Nash was concerned as were the rest, he drew pleasure from the fear displayed on Speedy's face. It was simply priceless. Bam-Bam picked up a sick and began drumming on a tree in response. The hooting irrupted next. Bam-Bam imitated the hoots and answered. He laughed, continued to drum, and hooted some more.

Speedy relinquished his death grip on the Uzi and covered both ears. Closing his eyes tightly, he grimaced as if in pain. Nash's pleasure now extinguished; he witnessed a man being pushed over the edge. This spelled bad news. He might be capable of anything now. The thundering drumming suddenly stopped as quickly as it had started. The nightly sounds of the forest returned.

The remainder of the night went undisturbed. Everyone caught a little shut eye, except for the ringmaster, Elwood Speed Moore. He had developed a severe case of insomnia and watched the ever-changing shadows of night. His bowels were locked tight again.

Thursday May 15th

Shawn Reynolds, concerned about the reports of volcanic activity from Mount Saint Helens, had adjusted his office schedule to allow him time to go check on Mattie. She had been gone now for almost a week and a half, counting her seminar. She had supposedly hooked up with Anson Parker Sunday. She had called him before they departed Monday. He had not heard from her since and it concerned him. Hindsight, he should have gone with her. Shawn knew the importance for her finding proof of Bigfoot but had selfishly allowed his practice to sway his decision.

Mattie was much the hard head. Once she made up her mind to do something, hell or high water, she would do it. Confirming the existence of these creatures from McGregor's journal had possessed her with vengeance. He couldn't really blame her though. He would have probably felt the same way had it been from one of his ancestors. Shawn wasn't sure he believed in the legend or myth, but obviously McGregor had believed what he had documented. Maybe back in the 1800's some missing link had possibly existed and thrived in those vastly unexplored forest, but how could they stay concealed today?

Sure, there were sightings all the time in almost every state and numerous countries, but no civilization of giant ape like creatures could pull this off. Someone would have found a body or bones or something. A hunter would have killed one by now purposely or by accident. He would not solve the riddle sitting here on his ass. Shawn had a few loose ends to tidy up before leaving in the morning. What if she and Anson had not returned by the time he arrived? How could he possibly locate them on his own?

As a contingency, he decided he would call the local authorities and explain his dilemma. If they were unable to help in the search, he would ask if they could point him to a reputable guide. He would find his wife one way or another, if indeed she was really missing. Taking a deep breath, he ascertained how foolish to be acting like this. No, he wasn't acting foolish, but if he found her safe and sound he would never hear the end of it from Mattie. Shawn could live with that better than staying here and doing nothing.

Sitting in his office he watched television coverage of the awakening volcano. Authorities were asking for volunteer evacuation of the area. They interviewed a local, Harry Truman. The old codger told the reporter he had lived there for over fifty years and refused to leave his home. The camera cut to a panoramic view of the mountain. It didn't look so scary or ominous. The reporter mentioned that many campers and loggers remained in the area. Forestry officials were seeking them out and requesting that they pack it in and leave. The reporter mentioned a volcano expert vigilantly monitoring the activity near Coldwater Ridge.

Shawn surmised this was big news because volcanoes just didn't erupt in the lower forty-eight. He doubted this one would either, but still, it remained on the radar screen for the media. Mattie should be safe where she and Anson had planned to follow-up on the alleged Sasquatch sighting. Shawn shook his head, speaking out loud, "This is so ridiculous. I'm sitting here thinking volcanoes and Bigfoot, how screwed up is that? Doctor Demento, why not throw in little green men and flying saucers, ghosts and goblins for good measure. This is so not right."

Wednesday May 16th

Mattie was now consumed by Dan Cooper's journal just as she had been by Matt McGregor's. She had temporarily abandoned her search for an escape tunnel. She no longer attempted to conceal it from Damien Dark or little Bobby, often reading the entries out loud. Mattie had not had the pleasure of meeting a *S'cwene'y'ti* yet.

She would have already dismissed Cooper's scribbling as the rants from one badly disillusioned individual with mortal injuries, if not for the eyewitness accounts from Bob Thomson and Damien Dark. Where were they and why had she not seen one?

"Validation, I need validation," she mumbled.

Her belly growled loudly. They had not received any more food in the past day and half. Luckily the underground spring supplied water for them. She wondered if these creatures had abandoned them. Had something more urgent preoccupied them, or had they divvied out a death sentence to their prisoners?

Bob continued to be mesmerized by his new mentor, the self-proclaimed UFO hunter. Damien relished his new role and spewed countless stories of documented sightings and encounters of aliens. She left well enough alone, figuring it wasn't necessarily a bad thing to occupy the young boy's time, and divert him away from their unfortunate circumstances.
She certainly had not contemplated being kidnapped and imprisoned. But why not, after all, Matt had spelled it out precisely in his journal countless times. These creatures were notorious for abducting humans. Seeing is believing she supposed. Had she now become a believer? A close encounter would seal the deal for her, but did she really want this encounter?

"Please read us some more about the man and the parachute," begged Bob.

"Yeah," added Damien. "What else did he experience before he died?"

"Well one thing for sure, with gangrene setting in on that badly mangled leg, his time here was short lived. It certainly appears he probably died where they placed him here."

The calendar is of very little importance now. I fear my life could be measured in hours. Certainly, no more than a couple of days if I am lucky. My broken leg will be my death sentence here in this cavern. The female hardly ever leaves my side. She continues to bring me water and berries and just this morning offered me trout. They don't use the fire for cooking. They are vigilante and will not allow it to go out though. The female sniffs my rotting flesh and almost looks saddened knowing my eventual fate. The other members of the group pay me no attention. They come and go routinely. The dominant male appeared to be very disturbed earlier and has since disappeared accompanied by three other males.

Reading ahead, Mattie paused reading out loud and advised that her audience should attend to the dwindling fire. The creatures had left a good supply of wood for burning. She continued silently once the two males had taken to their task.

The female periodically fondles me trying to arouse me sexually. She seems obsessed with the task. Her massive hands caress my flaccid penis. I must say she's quite persistent. There's a strange urgency about it. Is she trying to grant a dying man one last wish? I managed to eat a little of the sushi without vomiting it back up. I placed the remainder of the raw fish on the worst of my oozing leg wounds. It seems I read somewhere about raw meat drawing out the poison. It is certainly worth a try. I fear it may be too far along to do any good. The female has stopped her massaging and just sits and stares at me. My eyes are growing tired. I must rest now. She is a good nurse. I just wish she had medical supplies.

My watch tells me I was out this time for over six hours. I feel slightly feverish. The female lies beside me asleep, one hand on my thigh. I wonder if they go into heat like animals. My bladder aches. I have an incredible piss hard right now. She might be impressed if awake. She must be telepathic. She is staring at me and signing. I must be stupid because I just can't make out her hand talk. She just placed her hand on my crotch. She's crouching over me. I must place my note pad down and see what happens.

"Okay," announced Bob "We're back."

"Read on Professor," added Damien.

Mattie skimmed through the pages until she found an appropriate passage for her young audience.

I hear noises from what sounds like another chamber or cave. I believe I hear a human's voice. The big leader just appeared carrying something. No, it is carrying someone. The other two have a second person. I cannot make out much in the shadows. That's better. They have released the two figures by the fire. By their dress, they look like they could be lumberjacks. A second female is very curious with one of them. She is groping the stranger like checking livestock. A smaller male has removed the cap from the second one. I can make out long flowing blonde hair. The second is a female. Yes, I can see her breasts now. The male is sniffing her like a dog does when it greets a new canine. The big male is now tugging at the man. I can't tell what's going on. The man is resisting. The other two males have ripped off the second's clothing. Definitely a female. They have positioned her naked body in front of the man. The giant leader is...

"That's enough reading for now," said Mattie, as she abruptly stopped, feeling very flushed.

"Got it," said Damien with a wink.

After the two grabbed a torch and ventured toward the far end of the cavern, she picked the journal back up to read on.

Unbelievable, they're using her nude body to arouse her male counterpart. The leader is masturbating the man. It's over. The big male is smelling and tasting his semen. It's rolling its lips and snorting in disgust. It didn't like what it sampled. With one flick of its massive hand it just snapped the poor fool's neck and tossed him into the fire. They don't seem very interested in the naked female and have just walked away. She just fell to her knees. I can hear her crying. I'll yell and see if I can get her attention.

"I don't get it," whispered Mattie out loud. "They are interested in the men but not the women. Then just like that they perform primitive masturbation, and then kill him. Slam, bam, burn you man."

The young blonde is in shock and asleep now. Her name is Mandy McDonald. The man was her husband Joe. She confirmed my suspicions. Joe had a vasectomy three years ago. He did not qualify as potential breeder stock if that is truly their intention as I do believe it is. I think I must still be in the ballgame or I too would be dead by their hands. I do not know why the male Bigfoots are sterile if that is the reason for this sexual interest and how it is possible for us to crossbreed with them. I have now mated twice with the female taking care of me. She is relentless with her advances. I am apparently lucky that I have good sperm count. It has bought me some precious time. The blonde told me that she and her husband were scouting the timber for a logging company when they were overpowered and kidnapped. Their field radio was unfortunately left behind. No one expected them back for a week. Mandy has been asleep for several hours. She wears what is left of her torn and tattered clothing which is not much. Mandy is alert but still in shock. The female has brought me water and food but has offered none to Mandy. I feel sorry for Mandy but can do little for her in my broken state.

Damn all mighty, the female just murdered Mandy. She slammed her body to the ground and crushed her skull with her enormous foot. The big female apparently didn't like how Mandy had curled up next to me and viewed her as a rival. I could do nothing to stop it. She now rests in the fire pit with her husband. The female constantly signs to me in what appears to be textbook sign language. I wish I could sign or fully understand what she tells me. I have not been able to achieve an erection in her past four attempts. My physical condition is worsening. She grows impatient with me but has not tried to harm me. I can hardly stand the stench that comes from my leg now. Pain is searing to my mid section. The chills and fever ravish me constantly. I am hardly able to keep my eyes open and fear my time is short.

My breathing is so labored. The pen is so heavy. I can hardly focus. If I am ever found and if these creatures survive, I hope mankind is as compassionate with them as they have been with me. These creatures are not animals. They are as human as we are, just more primitive. I do regret what I have done and hope the authorities find the money if it survived the jump I took. I was a desperate man taking desperate measures. I have paid for my sins. I am also blessed. I still marvel at these unique beings and the one I now call Angel. Please do not harm or cage them. They are God's children too. Man too often destroys what he does not understand. These creatures deserve to live. I wish I could too. I would carry their torch. God forgive me for what I have done.

There were no more entries. The man known as D.B. Cooper had obviously died not knowing how famous he had become in his botched attempt. He would have been even more famous with this discovery, if he had survived and chosen to publicize it. From his writing, she guessed he would have kept the *S'cwene'y'ti* secret for them and not because of him. In her eyes, he had died an honorable man. She questioned her own scruples and those of Matt McGregor. She had waited her career for such a defining moment. This had to be the find of a lifetime, discovering the existence of a new species and solving the mystery behind the greatest crime ever. The only obstacle standing in her way was finding an escape route.

Speedy had burned another joint, but only well after daylight had made its presence known. They proceeded on the route chosen by Nash. So far they had no new encounters with the Sasquatch.

"You think they are still following us."

"I can't be sure," Nash answered. "I haven't heard them or seen any signs. Cross your fingers."

"Why do you really think they've been messing with us?"

"Your guess is as good as mine, Speedy. I still think they are territorial, and they don't want us here."

"I thought we were going to capture one," interrupted Max. "I've got a couple of ideas how we might be able to pull it off, if you men are so inclined."

"Well, plans change," barked Speedy. "We're getting this dope out of here first."

"And our worthless hides," added Nash.

"But I thought..." Max attempted to say before Speedy cut him off.

"You don't have a say in this. You don't get paid to think. You just carry your load and shut the hell up."

"I didn't know we were getting paid at all," Max lashed back. "I thought the cash cow was going to be our big footed friends."

"Forget about the ape men. You'll get a cut of this once we get out of here," Speedy lied to Mad Max. *Yep, you'll get a cut all right he thought, right across that scrawny throat of yours and that big black sidekick gets it too.*

"I still say the big money is on us capturing one of these things, not your drugs."

"Cut the crap, Max. Just what the hell were you and your band of misfits really doing out here?"

"I guess it doesn't matter now if I tell you. We were here to locate D. B. Cooper's money."

"You've got to yanking my chain. What in the hell makes you think it was way up here?"

"We had our leads. Some of the money has been found out here."

"You're crazy. Cooper is somewhere in the Caribbean enjoying that money and the good life."

"Underhill didn't think so. He funded our expedition out of pocket."

"Whoa, hold on a damn minute. You're telling me that the narc was not here to sniff us out."

"We unfortunately stumbled into your little entrepreneurship by mere accident. What gave you the idea that we were trying to apprehend you?"

"That bastard Underhill," snarled Speedy. "I'll hand it to the asshole. He didn't break even when being tortured. They train their agents well."

"007, James Bond, Your Majesties Secret Service, shaken, not stirred," quoted Bam-Bam in his best British accent, "License to kill."

Speedy rolled his eyes. "What do you do, chain that boy in front of the TV?"

"We'll try again next week," spouted Bam-Bam.

"What the hell is he babbling about now?"

"That's Magilla Gorilla's catch phrase," explained Max. "He says it at the end of every show. Bam-Bam loves that cartoon."

"I don't give a damn if he loves Bugs Bunny or Daffy Duck, he's just plain loony tunes if you ask me."

"What's up Doc? You're despicable. That's just too funny," laughed Bam-Bam.

"That's frigging all folks. Now shut the hell up and you can quote me on that one."

"Enough boys," interrupted Nash. "Are you finished with your cartoon caravan? If so, it's time for us to get our asses moving."

The stench hit them like the mother of all farts. It almost burned their eyes and certainly instilled a gag reflex.

"The bastards are back," cursed Speedy. "I've smelled that stench before. It's worse than any damn skunk."

"Peppy Le Pew," shouted Bam-Bam, holding his nose, and then repeating, "Le Pew."

No breeze stirring made it impossible for Nash to pinpoint the location of the suffocating stench. This had to be their signature calling card to warn them they were still around. It worked. Nash braced for another onslaught of chunked rocks, but no incoming projectiles were detected. The creatures remained silent, no hoots or drumming this time. Nash would have rather had the latter because the silence was deafening and scarier than before.

"Someone cut the cheese," remarked Bam-Bam. "Blame it on the dog."

Speedy, finger on the Uzi trigger, had been tempted to spray the perimeter, but fought the urge this time. Remembering the peeping Tom from his crap break, he thought better of it. Wounding one of these things would possibly be the last thing he would want to do. Nash had probably been right on that assumption. Yeah, Nash may be right, he thought, and almost spoke it out aloud. Shooting one may just piss them off he kept telling himself. He then thought about the explosion back at their camp, the booby traps. Had he done just that? Had one been wounded or killed by that explosion? Is that why they wouldn't leave them alone? They were out for revenge. This was right out of a damn horror movie thought the distraught leader.

"Let's get the hell out of here, Nash. Now!"

"I think I've been saying that, haven't I?"

"Happy trails to you," sang Bam-Bam, "until we meet again..."

"We have our very own Son of the Pioneers," laughed Nash.

"He's going to be one very dead sonofabitch if he doesn't shut the hell up," said a very pissed off and frustrated Speedy.

Secluded in the thick brush the ten-foot-tall alpha male watched and listened to the antics of his smaller and more fragile cousins.

His graying face did not tell the whole story, an ancient by man's standards.

The *S'cwene'y'ti*

The huge male had no recollection of his birth parents or the beginning of his rein. He had always been the leader, never challenged by his peers. Of course, his peers had always been smaller. There had never been another ten-footer, at least not in the almost two hundred years of his existence. The great northern woods had always been his territory. He and his had dominated it. Other invading families had been driven out as quickly as they appeared. Families existed in almost every state and in most countries where great forest or mountain ranges were located.

His family's numbers had dwindled in the past decade due to the smaller cousins invading the forest and wreaking havoc on their habitat. While the smaller cousins played a vital role in the family's survival, sharing a world with them had proven to be impossible. The alpha male had found it more difficult in the past decade to acquire prime breeders. Too often, deformed or diseased young resulted. These were cullied from the family and the cousins responsible were killed.

The males of his species continued to be incapable of producing offspring, but they remained sexually active. Often the males acted on these desires with captured female cousins. They were incapable of impregnating the female cousins but quenched their sexual needs just the same. Sexual intercourse with the much smaller females frequently ended in their death or led to their insanity. Either way, they never survived the experience.

Family females not carrying young were targets of their sexual urges when no cousins were at their disposal. This practice was not encouraged by the elder but was tolerated to stabilize the family core. Concealing the abductions of the breeders had become more challenging. In the earlier days the cousins feared them. Now, the cousins were more curious and tended to seek them out. It had become more vital than ever that the family destroy all evidence of their existence. The cousins had never found a dead family member or captured a live one.

The leaving of strategically placed footprints or allowing glimpses of themselves to their cousins symbolized a family member's maturity and rite of passage. Failure to succeed was not an option. This became the family's ultimate game, one that they always won.

Only once could the alpha male recall a family member allowing themselves too much exposure. In that incident, the three cousins were quickly captured and disposed of and the offender had been dealt a death sentence as well.

The big male missed the earlier time shared with the red skinned cousins. These cousins had respected them and never hunted them. They could have probably coexisted with them if not for the arrival of the more dominant white cousins. The family's blood line had been at its purest with that of the red skinned breeders. The leader experienced sudden sadness when he reminisced about the one eyed, tongue-less one who had taught the family to talk with their hands. The alpha male had made an exception of him when he had been identified as a non-breeder. He had found something fascinating about that one and his hand language.

They had learned much of their cousin's ways from him. The eternal glowing pit had been of his making. While most family members disliked the taste of food from it, they cherished the warmth and light. They rarely allowed it to die, maintaining an ample supply of wood. If they by chance allowed the fire to go out, the tongue-less one had taught them how to make more. Sadly, he had not the life span as them.

He remembered the arrival of the tongue-less one. Three others had been captured along with him. A red skinned one soon had to be killed. He had resisted the great canyon spirits and refused to breed. A second white cousin rebelled and tried to harm family members during the great escape. He had been taken quickly. His young offspring had escaped. The third, a large one like the tongue-less had served to be a loyal cousin after the canyon spirits. A perfect breeder, he had produced three strong cubs before taking ill and dying of an odd white cousin disease.

The tongue-less one lived a long life by the cousin's life span. He had grown old, gray and frail before sleeping and never awakening. He never attempted to escape and eventually accompanied the raiding parties. He lured other cousins for the taking. The tongue-less one had not been allowed to couple with family females. He had been allowed to possess cousin females when he so desired. Destroying them afterwards was part of the family's ritual.

The alpha male remembered the arrival of the cousin from the sky. No other had ever come to them from above. While this one did not live with them long, the family worshipped him like their God. He produced one offspring, a strong and powerful young female, still too young to breed yet. He died of sickness soon after his arrival. His leg smelled of death just days after they brought him to the cave. This one did not fully understand the hand talk even though he made attempts to communicate using his hands. To commemorate his greatness, the family had allowed his body to remain where he had drawn his last breath.

Another special one had been the tiny cousin of not long ago. This one wore the bright colors with animal faces and shiny things. He had the flaming hair and speckled face. While small, he never feared the family. This one would have made excellent breeding stock once he reached maturity. A short time after being accepted into the family, the red haired one became sick and he too died quickly. Sickness always ran its course among the tiny white family. They had no means to stop it. Sometimes the elders of the family were taken before they became too feeble. Outliving their usefulness, they became a liability.

The young one that had been recently taken demonstrated some of the same strengths and qualities of the smaller red headed version. He would be groomed for breeding. The other older male had passed the test of the breeder. His seed had been pure, but he seemed a bit too scrawny. The family could not endure more disappointing births, so he wasn't sure of this one's final fate yet.

The female cousin had been taken for his own personal indulgence. He had not partaken of a female, family or cousin, for too long. He now felt the stir in his loins to relieve his male cravings. He sensed her prime cousin stock and just recanting her smell aroused him. He deferred his thoughts back to the ones he now watched and extinguished his burning desire. He would couple with her soon enough.

The alpha male was intrigued by the large dark cousin in the herd they now pursued. He had not seen a cousin this large since the days of the tongue-less one. He and the dark one had made eye contact several times. He sensed compassion in those eyes. He hoped the dark one had good seed. If so, he would be spared.

The others may not be as fortunate, especially the one that smelled of the strange leaf and fired the thunder splitter. He had smelled this one's scent on the carnage left at the cousin's layer, the place where the family member had fallen lifeless to the loud thunder. Protecting the family, this cousin would be held accountable. The older alpha cousin interested him as well. He sensed this one could be a breeder. The remaining cousin appeared protective of the large darker cousin. That cousin smelled of deceit and worthy of watching. Instinct would ultimately cull the cousins.

Three additional males accompanied the huge alpha male. The largest was eight and half feet tall and weighing over four hundred pounds. The other two were seven footers but formable just the same. The remainder of the family presently occupied a chamber beyond the two caverns holding the captured cousins. Cautiously the four measured their smaller cousins for potential weakness. The thunder splitter had prevented them from swooping in and taking them by surprise. Be assured, they would be taken eventually. These cousins would not be allowed to leave the northern woods.

Mattie unable to sleep, just remembered she had not read the pages she had skipped. Excited, she retrieved the journal and thumbed back through the pages until she located her stopping point. The young males slept noisily on the other side of the fire pit. She still had not seen one of the creatures yet and wondered why.

Mattie desperately needed to see one. Evidence, she must have evidence for her own validation. Matt and Cooper had seen them and had lived among them. She had their journals to support it. The two boys snoring loudly had both said they had seen them. Why not her yet?

She thought, was this my death wish? What makes me think there are as interested in me as I may be in them? I should be plotting my escape she thought, and then she gazed back at the pages of the open journal. It tugged on her like a magnet. Taking a deep breath she began to read.

I cannot believe what just happened. I'm torn between shameful thoughts and those of shear astonishment. I've just been screwed by a female Bigfoot. She did all the work. She ripped open my trousers then straddled me. Those catcher's mitt sized hands are magical. I feel like she has granted a dying man his final wish. Slam, bam, thank you ma'am and she just strolled off afterwards. She made me forget about the searing pain in my leg and hip at least for a while. It is back with vengeance now. The gosh-awful smelly ooze is flowing freely from the open sores. I am surprised they haven't tossed me in the fire pit with the others. I guess I'm special. I can't image why. Time is a blur and I fear running short for me. I still can't believe my luck.I hear noises from what sounds like another chamber or cave. I believe I hear a human's voice. The big leader just appeared carrying something. No, it is carrying someone.

"Incredible," she whispered.

She walked back to D.B. Cooper's remains. Standing over them she tried to visualize what she had just read. This man had basically been raped by a female *S'cwene'y'ti,* more than once. She now understood what had happened to Matt and the other men. Shamed by the experience, her ancestor had apparently been unable to pen it. She placed the journal where she had found it, wrapped inside the parachute, still indecisive if she would reclaim it once she found a way out of the caverns. She placed her hand on her growling stomach and wondered where her captors were hiding.

Mattie prepared three new torches from Cooper's black suit jacket and decided to explore the adjoining cavern to see firsthand the bone pile Bob had described, and to search for a way out. Supposedly a large boulder blocked the exit way or so had described little Bob.

She found the second room much smaller than the one she had just exited. Her torch offered the only light but exposed enough for her to assess the outer reaches. Moving along the closest wall Mattie searched for any exit tunnels.

Detecting movement ahead, just around a jutting corner, she paused to listen. She heard the scrapping again, followed by a guttural moan. Had she finally located one of the creatures? How will it react to her being here? How would she react to seeing one? She cocked her head and listened. The moan erupted again, but this time had more of a human quality. That made sense, didn't it? They were humanlike creatures in some ways. Inches from the corner now, her heart raced, her breathing almost stopped. She was about to encounter the *S'cwene'y'ti.*

Holding the torch out in front she peeked around the corner. Lying on the ground she spotted the source of all the commotion. Somewhere between disappointment and jubilation she mustered up an, "Are you all right?"

The figure lying on its side quickly turned on its back to eyeball the source of the sound. Blinded by the torch he could not see its owner. His hand clutched a fist sized rock. More were piled to his left.

"Are you, all right?" repeated Mattie, holding the torch up high so he could see her.

"You're a woman," spoke a raspy voice. "I thought you were them."

"If you're disappointed, I'll leave," replied Mattie.

"Who are you?" asked the stranger, now sitting up gingerly.

"I'm Mattie Reynolds and you?"

"Underhill, Spencer Underhill."

Nash had picked up the pace. He no longer smelled the stench that had almost sickened him earlier. Everyone was on pins and needles, glancing over their shoulders, jumping at every twig snap, seeing shadows, and imagining bush movement. Nash's own confidence shaken he was no longer sure they would survive the ordeal.

Speedy held the roach in his fingertips, sucking in the homegrown weed, dulling his senses, and snuffing out his fears. "Come on guys," he babbled, eyes almost closed from the effects of the reefer. "We have automatic weapons. Those bastards out there have sticks and stones. They're no frigging match for us."

Tell that to Booger Rhodes thought Nash. These things are not a pack of wolves. They think. They plan. They react to the situation. They calculate their next move. They don't intend for us to escape. He didn't waste his breath sharing it with Speedy. He was too high and delusional to comprehend.

"We have about two hours of daylight remaining," spoke up Nash. "We best locate a strategic place to make camp. These creatures tend to perform better in the dark."

"How much further to reach that damn logging road?"

"Terrain was a little tougher than I expected, so I apologize for it taking longer this way. We should be there by Saturday morning if our friends don't slow our progress. From there, we could make it to Truman's place by nightfall. Then it's a matter of arranging some transportation."

Max explained their situation to Bam-Bam. "Okay, look, your job is to keep Old Bertha moving so we can be home by the weekend. Just three more days. And you tell me if you see any Magilla Gorillas, okay?"

"I can watch TV when we get home," smiled Bam-Bam. "Magilla Gorilla was just over there," pointed the big man. "He didn't have the gray face like the other one did. I didn't like his face. He looked mean."

Max strained his eyes but saw nothing. He checked the cartridges in his pistol. "You tell me next time when you see one."

"Okay Max. I'm hungry. When do we eat?"

Over the next hour Nash scanned the forest for a good camp sight, but the denseness of the woods offered little hope. Few breaks were found/ He feared if they had to camp with the forest so close to them, they'd never ward off an ambush. Finally, they came to a small brook. Visibility in any direction was less than ten yards, but it would have to do. He had seen nothing better. One problem, the babbling brook offered just enough noise to potentially mask an attack.

Nash didn't like their odds. He ordered Max and Bam-Bam to clear any small saplings or underbrush around the perimeter. Bam-Bam, using the machete he gave him, bush hogged the area much better than he would have expected. Nash gathered wood for a fire. Speedy sat on a log, fired up another joint, removed his shoes, and began soaking his feet in the brook. His finger remained diligently on the Uzi's trigger. He had transformed into a paranoid basket case.

Darkness fell abruptly. The overcast sky offered no relief, masking the almost full moon. Frogs serenaded them, making it impossible to detect any movement in their forest surroundings A hooting owl raised the hair on the back of Speedy's neck. He tightened his grip on the Uzi and toked on another joint, stoned out of his mind. Max, exhausted and not accustomed to this rigorous hiking routine, snored comfortably on the ground close to the blazing fire. Bam-Bam, wide awake, sat by the fire listening to it crackle and watched the glowing embers. He smiled as he watched the shadows move without sound.

Nash observed Speedy and his concerns grew. His present pot consumption reduced their profit margins. He had become a chain toker. Nash never used the stuff himself, but if he had, this would probably have been a good time to do so. He opted for staying sharp. He decided he could easily sacrifice the others to save his own sorry hide, if it came to that.

Old Bertha reacted to movement in the darkness nearby. Her ears flicked, attempting to home in on the sound's source. She stomped her left front hoof to display her discontent with what lurked nearby.

Nash watched Bam-Bam ease from the fire and walk over to where the mule was tethered. Talking to the mule, he began stroking her neck and rubbing her long snout. The gentle giant soon calmed Old Bertha. He smiled and whispered something in her ear. Nash turned his attention to Speedy when he heard splashing water. Speedy wavered as he stood there pissing in the little stream. He staggered twice, almost falling backwards, cursing when he pissed on his shoes.

Nash contemplated rushing Speedy. He could probably catch him off guard and overpower him. Then he thought, was he a worse liability in this state or would having to tend to him as a prisoner be more troublesome. He opted for leaving well enough alone for now. Extra fire power couldn't hurt if worst came to worst. He glanced back to Bam-Bam and the mule. Bam-Bam was gone. He scanned the campsite but didn't see the big guy anywhere. Walking over, he found the mule still securely tied but no Bam-Bam.

Speedy zipped up, turned and spotted Nash by the mule. "What the hell's going on over there?"

"Bam-Bam is missing. He was just here a couple of minutes ago petting the mule."

"That dumb ass retard probably just wandered off," said a still unsteady Speedy. "Good riddance is all I can say. I hated that sonofabitch."

Bam-Bam had followed the ten-foot, gray faced Magilla Gorilla with no reservation. He had hand signaled him from the bushes to come and he had done just that. They were now 100 yards from camp and Bam-Bam found it difficult to make his way in the darkness. Ahead, Magilla paced him by only a couple of strides.

"Where are we going?"

Magilla paused, and then hand signaled him to come with him. He understood the motion and continued to follow. Two smaller Magillas trailed quietly behind him.

Nash nudged the still snoring Max with his boot. Max sprung up as if he had received some sort of electrical shock. "What?" he murmured. "Are we under attack?"

"Guess what Mad Max, your bodyguard is gone," smiled Speedy.

Max sprung to his feet, whipping around, searching the campsite for Bam-Bam. "What did you do to him you bastard?" screamed Max, with his finger in Speedy's face.

"Unless you want that finger of yours snapped off and shoved up your ass, I would suggest you remove it from my face."

Max more intimidated than brave, dropped his hand by his side. "Where is he?"

"We don't know," answered Nash. "One minute he was standing there petting the mule, the next he was gone. I never heard a sound."

"We've got to go look for him," begged Max. "He's afraid of the dark. What if they've gotten him?"

"Hold on dipshit," warned Speedy. "We're not stumbling around out there in this pitch black looking for that damn brainless wonder of yours."

"He's right, Max" added Nash. "It would be suicide. Come daybreak we'll search for him."

"Like hell we will," barked Speedy. "If he doesn't show back up on his own, we leave without him."

Nash shrugged. "Well I guess that's that."

"But..." Max attempted to say.

"But, damn nothing," Speedy warned with his finger now pressed against Max's chest.

"You're either in this with us or you're on your own. Choose wisely, Mad Max."

"I'm looking for him at first light," challenged Max. "You can leave without me. I owe him that much." I should have let him snap your worthless neck, thought Max.

"Suit yourself," answered Speedy. "Be warned. We'll not waste a second looking for either one of you. And you forfeit your cut." This would work just fine thought Speedy. The Sasquatch would do his work for him.

"Well tell me Spencer Underhill," remarked Mattie. "How did you get here?"

Underhill pondered if he should tell this stranger the truth or embellish the version. A no-brainer, he opted for embellishment, but first he wanted to hear her story.

"You first," he replied, getting to his feet quite gingerly.

Mattie was not sure how honest she should be with this man. He seemed out of place. She too opted to modify her version temporarily until she knew more about him.

"An associate and I were hiking and unfortunately he lost his footing and fell into a ravine, was killed on impact. I buried him, covered his body with rocks to deter any scavenging animals. I was overcome by exhaustion and possibly shock. When I awoke, I was in an adjoining cavern with two other strangers, a young boy and another young man. I have no recollection of how I got here."

"Where are the other two?"

"Asleep in another part of the cavern," she said, pointing in the direction of the others.

"What about you and where's your ear?"

He felt where his ear had been. "I was hiking with some friends too. I got separated from the others and took a fall myself. Lost my ear and got pretty battered up, and then I found this cave for shelter."

"Then you know the way out."

"Not exactly," he scrambled for a reply. "I suppose I was traumatized too and wondered around in the darkness, disoriented. I have no clue where the entrance is."

Suspicious now, she commented, "You were lying in front of it," she motioned with a nod. "Behind you, that boulder blocks the entrance."

"Was there a cave in," he asked, still trying to play the dumb game.

She sensed he was not telling all he knew and wondered if he sensed the same thing.

"Might have been, we've had some quakes."

"Right, that volcano has been acting up," he chimed in, trying to change the subject. "So, how do we get out of here?"

"We'll have to work on that little problem I suppose. Are you hungry?"

"No, not really," Underhill replied.

"Good, we don't have any food," she smiled. "But we do have water. There's a little underground spring in the other cavern, and we have a fire."

"Very resourceful. Shall we go join the others?"

Reluctantly she answered, "Yeah, I guess we should. Maybe we can put our heads together and come up with a plan."

"Don't either one of the others know a way out?"

"I'm afraid not," she replied, knowing this was about to become a very sticky situation with all the lies being thrown about.

Mattie fired up a second torch just before her first one flickered out. She led the way back to the cavern. The pit fire had dwindled somewhat. She could tell the others must still be asleep. Upon arriving, she tossed some more wood on the fire illuminating the enormousness of the cavern.

Damien Dark stirred, sat up and yawned. Rubbing his eyes, he caught sight of the stranger standing by the professor woman. He stood and brushed himself off.

"Who is he?"

"Spencer Underhill meet Damien Dark and that's young Bob Thomson sawing logs over there."

"Where'd he come from? Did they bring him here too?"

Oops, thought Mattie. The cat was out of the bag right out of the chute. She turned and made eye contact with Spencer Underhill. He didn't look happy.

"They?"

"The Bigfoots," answered Damien, not believing the stranger did not know about them.

"This must be a joke."

"Man, they really messed you up, didn't they? What happened to your ear? You must have put up quite a fight."

Mattie eyed old one ear for his next response. She hoped he confessed and stopped his lying.

"Like I told the young lady, I injured myself in a fall and found this cave for shelter."

Damien smiled. "Then you know the way out?"

"Sorry, I don't."

"Mister Underhill says he became disoriented in the dark and can't remember where the exit is. Isn't that right Mister Underhill?"

"Precisely. I lost my way."

Damien shook his head. "You're telling me you don't know anything about the Bigfoots?"

"Only what I've read in the tabloids," he now replied. "I thought the going thing was to be abducted by little green men."

"Now you're talking my field of expertise," boasted Damien. "I'm a UFO investigator."

"Let me get this straight. You were searching for flying saucers and you're now telling me you got kidnapped by Bigfoot. This is simply priceless, something out of the National Inquirer."

Damien, becoming pissed off by the stranger's skepticism added, "And you haven't even heard the best part yet."

Mattie rolled her eyes, knowing what was coming next. The jig was about to be up, and all the cards would have to be placed on the table.

"We've solved another one of the great mysteries," Damien grinned from ear to ear.

"Don't tell me the Loch Ness Monster is in here too," smarted Underhill.

"Better," boasted Damien. "We found D.B. Cooper's remains. The Bigfoots brought him here too."

Mattie watched as the color drained from Spencer Underhill's face. His expression transformed from mocking to suddenly interested in what Damien said.

"Repeat that again young man."

"Don't tell me you've never heard of D.B. Cooper, the most famous hijacker ever?"

"You've seen his body?"

Damien smiled, "Actually the professor made the discovery."

"Professor?"

"Professor Reynolds, the woman who found you," said Damien, shaking his head in disbelief. "Are you suffering from amnesia too?"

"Where did you find the body?"

"You can forget it," explained Damien. "We didn't find the money."

Mattie giving the hand signal for a timeout said, "Hold on guys. The man is dead, okay. Damien is right. We didn't find any money. Can we forget about him right now? We need to focus on the task at hand, and that's how we get out of here."

In a very assertive tone, Underhill asked, "Where's the body?"

Damien pointed. "I don't get it. You're not impressed that we discovered Bigfoot, but you're creaming in your pants over us finding D.B. Cooper. You're really screwed up, man."

Underhill said nothing. He grabbed Mattie's torch and walked to where the UFO kid had pointed. Sure enough, there lay the remains of someone. He knelt to examine the skeleton remains. He fumbled in what was left of his clothing, searching inside the cadaver's ragged pockets. Frustrated that he found no identification, he yelled back to the others, "How do you know this is him?"

Mattie didn't want to share the journal with the stranger, but she couldn't stop Damien from blurting it out. "The professor found his diary."

Underhill stood abruptly, placing one hand on his hip, "Where is it?"

Mattie now took the lead. "First of all, you tell me who you are and how you really got here. And don't give me that pathetic hiking with friends, falling off the cliff lame excuse for a story."

She had struck a nerve. His face ablaze with fury made the torch seem dimly lit. This man was hiding something for sure.

"The diary. Now!" Underhill held out his open hand.

Bob was wide awake and watching the antics of the three adults. "Why is everyone yelling? And who's the man with only one ear?"

Friday morning had arrived.

Nash had managed a little shut eye and now stretched as he poked at the fire and added some more dry lighter pine kindling. Speedy was standing near Old Bertha, smoking a joint and fondling the Uzi.

"Where's Max?"

Nodding toward the dense forest Speedy said, "Gone to look for that damn black ass retard, just like he said he would do."

"Do you have to keep calling him names? And why didn't you try to stop him?"

Speedy shrugged, "He's a big boy. He can make his own decisions; damn fool idea he had going out there, though."

"That crap has fried what few brain cells you have left. You know as well as I do that the Sasquatch probably already got their hands on him."

"And that's a damn shame;" pointed out Speedy, "Those two came in real handy helping us carry our dope."

"You're a piece of work, you know it, Speedy?"

"I'll add their share to the mule and we better limit ourselves to one satchel a piece. Put the rest on the nag. We need to keep our trigger fingers free."

"That's quite a load for Old Bertha, you do realize that?"

"Hey man, why do you think they call them pack mules," grinned Speedy, inhaling the last of the roach he held between his fingers.

Their conversation was interrupted by the sound of gun fire, one shot followed by three more. Speedy cocked his head listening for more, but the forest went quiet again.

"Mad Max, meet Sasquatch," snickered Speedy. "Let's get the hell out of here while they're occupied with our wayward friend. I wonder if they'll cash in on a gold mine, having old Max on display."

Trapped in the caverns day verses night had no meaning. The fact that Friday morning had arrived made little impact on the two strangers confronting one another.

"You're really trying my patience. You really don't want to do that I assure you."

"I guess losing that ear has impaired your hearing," said Mattie. "You were brought here just like the rest of us, weren't you? And you've seen them, haven't you?"

Underhill now fuming, trying to compose himself, responded, "Fine. I admit it. I didn't just wonder in here on my own. Are you happy?"

"And," she prompted him.

"Look. It doesn't matter how I got here and what happened before I got here," he said, elevating his voice again. "I'm retired FBI. This case is especially important to me. I was there when Cooper hijacked that plane."

"Cool," commented Damien.

"You're a real FBI agent," said Bob.

"Retired," said Underhill, taking a deep breath. "I've spent the last ten years trying to locate Cooper and break this case. That's why I'm here. I was following a lead."

"If you're FBI, then you should have some credentials to support your story."

"I lost my identification."

"You're telling me the *S'cwene'y'ti* picked your pockets when they abducted you. Get real, agent Underhill."

"The what?"

"Another name for Bigfoot," clarified Damien Dark.

Underhill was getting nowhere beating around the bush. What did it matter if he told them the whole story? This thing was so beyond bizarre now anyway.

"Here's the deal. Like I said, my purpose for being here was finding evidence of Cooper, the money, a parachute, his body, something. Three other men accompanied me. We unfortunately stumbled upon some real bad asses growing marijuana out there. One of my party members was shot and killed. The other two were taken hostage and are probably dead too."

Mattie stood there with her arms crossed. "How did you escape, Agent Underhill?"

"The pot growers discovered I was an agent, my wallet mystery solved. That didn't set so well with their leader."

"They sliced off your ear, didn't they," asked Bob.

Underhill rubbed the side of his head and nodded. "They took my revolver, my ID, and yes, my ear."

"So how did you get away," asked an excited Bob

"I didn't," he paused. "You were right. They brought me here. The others left me tied up like a neat little gift package. These things took the bait, me."

"So, you have seen them?"

"Yeah, I've seen them all right. One tossed me over its shoulder like I was nothing. Three moved that boulder and dumped me inside, and then rolled it back in place. It would take half a dozen grown men to budge it. Their leader, a gray faced one, must be ten or eleven feet tall."

Mattie finally satisfied said, "The journal is wrapped in that parachute behind you. Dan Cooper or whoever he was, documented his last days in here. He eventually died from injuries he received from his landing. Gangrene most likely got him. And I told you the truth, I don't remember being brought here. I have not seen them yet. The man who accompanied me did fall to his death in a ravine. I'm just not sure how accidental it may have been given what I have learned since being here."

"They got me near Mount Saint Helens," added Damien. "I was following leads about some UFO sightings. I have seen them too. They're awesome. I think they have something in common with the UFO sightings. It's not unusual, you know. There have been reports of them seen coming out of a space craft."

"My stepdad and me were cutting wood when they stole me," said Bob. "He didn't even try to stop them. He just ran the other way. I'm glad I'm here and not with him."

Damien saw the puzzled look on Mattie's face. "Why don't we give Agent Underhill time to read that journal? Bobby, how about watching the fire while the professor and I have a little chat?"

"Okay, Damien, what's up," she asked, after they put some distance between them and Bob.

"The kid confided in me, Professor. It seems his mom died a couple of years ago. He was left with his stepfather to raise him. The bastard has been sexually molesting him."

"Poor lad," she remarked.

"It didn't just start after the mom died. It was going on for several years before she got sick. Typical scenario, she was in denial and covered it up. She allowed the sicko to get away with it, with her own son. He doesn't want to go back because he's afraid of ending back up with that worthless piece of elephant dung."

187

"What now? How can we protect him?"

"I'll take him in," said Damien. "He's really into UFOs and investigating the unknown, just like me. I have always wanted a kid brother. When he gets older, I will make him a full-fledged partner. We'll solve the mysteries of the universe."

"That is very noble of you, Damien, but how do you expect to keep him hidden when we return? The stepfather is still the legal guardian."

"You mean if we get out of here. Besides, me and the kid are staying here to study them. This is the chance of a lifetime."

"Absolutely not. That's just plain stupid."

"Look, I'm not an abused child or anything like that, but I don't really have anything waiting for me out there. This is my life. Please don't deny me. If we do get out, we'll just lay low for awhile until we can blend back into society. Trust me. It's easy. I've been there."

"What about Bob, Damien? You can't make that decision for him."

"Why, because I'm not a relative. All he's got is that perverted stepdad. What kind of future is that? This is the only way to protect the kid."

"I can't deal with this right now," she said, throwing up her hands. "We'll discuss it later."

"Our minds are made up. You've got to do what's best for you, Professor. I hope it doesn't include telling the world about this place."

"This place, I don't even know where this place is," said Mattie, walking away without acknowledging his last request.

Bob stood diligently over the fire. She patted him on the head and took a deep breath. This certainly had not gone as expected. Agent Underhill sat on the other side of the fire enthralled with the journal. She had been there already. Rubbing her eyes with her fingers she sighed, "What a bunch of misfits we are. I've got to find a way out of here before they return." She thought, funny, I don't seem so eager to meet them now that I know they're real.

Gray Face watched the two remaining cousins tug the four legged one along loaded with the strange smelling leaf. Only two males remained by his side. The third male had been directed to return to the lair with the dead cousin and the large dark cousin. The small cousin had tried to harm them with the thunder stick. Gray Face fingered the open wound in his right shoulder, smelled, and then tasted his own blood. The bullet had lodged in the fleshy portion of his shoulder and remained there. It had not struck any vital organs or bone. It would heal in time, once the bleeding stopped.

He inhaled. He could smell fear from the one that smelled of the leaf. The older gray haired one smelled only of body stench. He might be too old to serve as a breeder. The other had bad blood and would not be considered for breeding. Gray Face let out a blood curdling roar to intimidate the cousins. It worked. They picked up their pace and would be more careless now. The other two stood by his side, awaiting instructions from the alpha male.

"It sounded pretty damn pissed," said Speedy, looking behind frantically.

"Like I've been saying all along," Nash reminded his worthless leader, "You don't want to cross them."

"What do you think they're going to do," asked a very panicky and paranoid Speedy, firing up another joint.

"You really need to lay off that stuff. It dulls your senses and makes you as jumpy as a kangaroo."

"They're not going to let us get out of here, are they, Nash?"

"Would you?"

"We've got to kill them, kill all of them."

"Look around you boss man. And then there were two. I think they control the show, not us. They're picking us off or have you not noticed?"

"I still have some explosives," he smiled. "If we can even up things, just maybe they'll think twice about screwing with us."

"How are you going to blow up a ghost? I'm one hell of an outdoorsman and a damn good tracker, but they've beat me on every move. Let's face it. This is their world, their rules, their endgame."

"You're just throwing in the damn towel, just like that."

"No. I still think we can reason with them if it's not already too late."

"Let me get this straight, you really think you can talk to these giant monkeys. You're the one that needs to smoke some dope to clear your head of that crazy notion."

"We could lay down our weapons and show them we mean them no harm. Maybe it's not too late."

"Suicidal," scoffed Speedy, picking up his pace another notch. "You're getting me out of here first, and then if you want to come back here and talk to the animals, fund your own little expedition, Doctor Doolittle. You're on my damn clock right now."

"So, you keep telling me," acknowledged Nash, tugging on an overloaded Old Bertha. "I say we forget about this reefer. It's just slowing us down."

"Just keep moving," warned Speedy, fingering the trigger on the Uzi. "And keep thinking about your cut."

"Not much use is it to a dead man," Nash grinned, making eye contact with the pathetic basket case walking behind him.

Saturday Morning May 17th

Mattie had given into the fatigue and exhaustion again. The lack of food contributed to her deteriorating physical and mental condition. She questioned why none of the creatures had returned. Could this be how they treated their captives, leaving them to starve, and then tossing them in the fire pit?

"Are you awake," said a voice, shocking her from her dream state.

Mattie sat up and rubbed her eyes. She really felt like crap. She turned to see the FBI agent standing over her.

"Some account," he remarked, waving the journal.

"Yeah," she responded in a much weaker and raspier voice.

"Now I know what happened to Cooper or whoever he really was, but I still don't know what happened to the money. You didn't see anything else besides the chute?"

"That's all I've seen, but I didn't really look for the money," Mattie answered, rubbing her stiff neck. "The creatures could have burned it for all I know. I'm sure they've been on no shopping spree."

"I really thought he may have pulled this thing off. There's a part of me that wished he had."

"You wanted him to get away with it?"

"No, that's not it at all," explained Underhill. "I wanted to be the one that captured him. He owed me that. He stole that from me, just like he had the money."

"So, the bad man hurt your feelings and tarnished your reputation," she taunted him.

"Something like that," he admitted. "I was there when he pulled this off, and yes, it has been a thorn in my side, my career and I suppose my ego."

"Get over it," she told him, her voice breaking up and becoming hoarser, "You now know how it ended. Can't you just be happy with that?"

"I might, if I had also recovered the money."

"Who knows," she threw up her hands. "This is a big place. I am sure they're other caverns and tunnels. Knock yourself out super sleuth. Me, I'm going to find a way out."

"And if you don't?"

"Then I guess I should think about completing my own chronicle, my last rites and so forth," she said, mustering up a mocking smile.

"Hey guys," interrupted Damien. "We may have a little problem."

"And that would be what," asked Underhill.

"We're running out of fuel for our fire. I'm not sure we have more that three or four hours left at the rate we're going through it. Unless the Bigfoots return with more, it's going to get mighty dark and cold in here."

"Maybe that's their plan," remarked Underhill.

Mattie had a minor panic attack. Only three torches remained. She had stripped Cooper's bones clean of all clothing. She had no more material to burn unless she started removing her own. Time had become more urgent.

Underhill scooped up one of the torches. "I'm searching for the money."

Mattie tried to reclaim her torch, but he held it out of her reach, restraining her with his free hand. In her weakened condition, she posed no threat to the agent with one wounded hand and the missing ear. Damien started to protest, but one look from Underhill signaled he better stay out of it.

"Boys," she said to Damien and Bob, "You've got to come with me."

"I'm staying," replied Damien. "They'll be back. They won't let the fire go out."

"Me too," echoed young Bob.

"Suit yourselves," she said, not having the strength to argue. "I'll send help once I get out." Her voice was fading fast.

"Please don't. Just forget about this place, okay."

"I won't promise that," she said, her voice now fading to a mere whisper. "I can't."

She fired up one of the two remaining torches and returned to the small tunnels she had discovered earlier. She followed the first until it funneled to no more than three feet high and abruptly ended. Backtracking, she entered the second of the four she had discovered. It held promise until hair pinning, and it too ended in a stone wall. Her first torch flickered as she entered a third tunnel. This tunnel continued much further than the first two. She was weak, almost too weak, but she pushed onward.

Mattie fired up her last torch with the dwindling first one. She continued her trek, deeper into the tunnel. The sides had narrowed to not much wider than her shoulders. The tunnel's height gradually slopped. She grouched to keep from bumping her head. The torch's flame showed no indication of a draft from the dark cavity. She had come too far now to turn back. Darkness would surely engulf her, whether she continued or back tracked. Desperately she pushed on, do or die.

She could no longer stand and now inched along on all fours, her shoulders and hips scrapping against the stone and jagged sides. One forearm now bled. She had snagged her shirt ripping a gap from shoulder to elbow. The contour remained level. She crept deeper. Another 30 feet and she crawled on her belly like a serpent. She could barely hold the torch in front of her. It didn't matter because it too began to flicker. She thought, if this became her tomb, no one would ever find her. Poor Shawn would never know what happened to his wife.

Now turning on her side, she inched along pushing the torch ahead. Smoldering, it almost took her breath. She coughed, lowering her head, trying to suck in smokeless air from behind. It really didn't matter. The torch extinguished like flipping off a light switch. There was only blackness. Coming to a dead stop, she lost all hope and began to whimper, but could muster up no tears. Whispering, she said, "Shawn, I love you."

Nether Nash or Speedy slept. The Sasquatch had not slept either. Hooting, growling and grunting filled the night from every possible direction. Rocks periodically pelted the encampment. The tree thumping erupted numerous times, but they did not launch a direct attack. That puzzled Nash. This reminded him of tactics often used during war times. The surrounding enemy would institute sleep deprivation to push soldiers over the edge. Nash tried to focus on the positive. They should make the logging road by late morning. Then it should be smooth sailing to Truman's place.

Nash regretted now that he hadn't chosen the other route. It would have been easier going than this way, but as he had told Speedy, it would have offered too many ideal opportunities for ambushes with all the overhangs and narrow passages. The Vegas odds sucked no matter which route they had decided to take. Ole wasted and trigger happy posed even worse consequences. It had been tough enough to rationalize with a clear headed Speedy, but now he could forget it. Pot head refused to listen to reason. Nash now thought it may be time to cut his loses and leave the wild man to fend for himself.

"Get the mule ready and let's get the hell out of here," commanded Speedy.

"Don't you think you should eat something first?"

"I'll eat when we're at President Truman's place," sputtered Speedy. "How much damn further do we have to go?"

"We should reach the logging road in three or four hours, tops. It's winding and all down hill the rest of the way then We should be in clear cut terrain then, and able to detect the creatures if they try anything."

Nash suspected they would be attacked before they reached the logging road. That's what he would do if he was them. He decided he would part company with Speedy before that happened. He just hoped he could pull his escape plan off discretely and undetected by his traveling companion and the Sasquatch. He had little faith in any of his options but liked distancing himself from the trigger-happy wild man smoking the joints. On his own seemed the lesser of the two evils. Either way, luck was not on his side.

The stress and strain had taken its toll on his aging body. Mentally he wasn't at his best right now either. Still sharp for a man his age, better than most, he had the will to survive. Unlike the non-stop second-hand reefer smoker, his head was clear. He was convinced his traveling pal suspected nothing. He also knew he would have only one shot at pulling it off. Failure would mean a certain death from the whizzing barrel of that Uzi. Nash maintained a steady pace, but the old mule dragged on him like a boat anchor. The weight of the marijuana satchels bore down on her fragile state. Her previous master had probably not treated her as recklessly as her present custodians.

Nash jumped and twirled, pistol in hand, when he heard a loud rustling noise from behind. Speedy tried to right himself after stumbling and crashing to the ground. His legs were even more rubbery than the mules. Squinted and blood shocked eyes stared back at him. His left palm bled from attempting to break his fall. The knee was ripped out of one pant's leg.

"I'm fine," he waved to Nash. "Keep moving."

I am far from fine, thought Nash, thankful that his trigger finger did not cut both him and Old Bertha to shreds. Nash eyed the trail ahead for any opportune venues for escape but spotted none. He would have to exercise patience, but he had to do it before they reached the logging trail. A large rock caught Nash square on the right temple. He fell to the ground in front of the trailing mule. Speedy sprayed the Uzi in the direction of the tossed rock, emptying the cartridge and quickly replacing it, almost mechanically.

He nudged Nash with a boot, and then leaned down. Speedy saw the blood trickling from his ear and his nose, a large reddening knot forming on the side of his head. Nash was out cold if not dead figured Speedy. He frantically twirled around. His finger was on the trigger. He was expecting an attack, but all remained silent. Too quiet for his taste. Feeling he could do nothing for the Nash, he retrieved his revolver, grabbed the mule's reins, and hoped he was headed in the right direction.

Speedy glanced one last time back at Nash's lifeless body, and then sprayed the trail ahead with bullets as a precaution. He pulled a joint from his pocket, fingered it for a second, and then tossed it to the ground. He trekked onward pausing every so often to spray the perimeter with bullets. Old Bertha now became his personal boat anchor and a liability.

Underhill searched every possible alcove for any signs of the stolen loot but had so far found nothing. His torch flickered. He finally had to call off the search while he could still find his way back to the fire pit. He had Cooper's diary, so why worry about the money, he kept trying to convince himself.

Damien Dark and Bob Thomson tossed the last four chunks of wood into the pit and the glowing embers ignited immediately. Shadows danced on the cavern walls, resembling ghostly figures. In less than an hour the cavern would most surely go dark.

Underhill walked over and tossed his spent torch into the flames. "So, this is it."

Damien nodded. He didn't really care for the agent. Spencer Underhill cramped his style. He feared the agent would disrupt his research. He had Bob to mentor now and didn't need interference from the FBI. Movement caught their attention from the direction of the adjoining cavern. Underhill turned expecting to see the professor. Instead, a behemoth figure approached with something or someone tossed over its shoulder.

Unarmed, all any of them could do was watch the creature from the outer reaches of the firelight. Bob huddled behind Damien. Damien tried to muster up a defiant pose and crossed his arms, but his legs felt like Jell-O. Underhill dreaded the potential encounter. He knew they were no match for these creatures. He felt so naked without his service revolver. His new mission would be to capture that pot head leader once he got out of this mess.

The giant stepped from the shadows. "FBI man, where's your ear?"

"Is he some sort of Bigfoot hybrid," asked Damien.

"I'm not a high-bread but I do have big feet. I'm Bam-Bam. This here is my friend Max. He's dead," he said, easing Max Paxton's lifeless body to the cavern floor.

"Where are the others, the two men and woman?"

"Me and Max buried the crazy lady. The bad man called Speedy shot her all too pieces with a Tommy-gun. I don't like him. He called me bad names. Max told me I should break his neck. I should have."

Underhill asked, "So where is he now, if you didn't break his neck?"

"He and the Davey Crocket man have got my mule. The big old gray face Magilla Gorilla is following them. I don't think he likes him either. I miss Old Bertha. She was a good mule. I never had a mule before. Max was going to let me keep her, but Max is dead. He shot the gray face Magilla and made him mad. He hurt Max really bad and made him dead."

Underhill had a fleeting memory of Elijah Franklin Payne, the rugged mountain man, Old Bertha's former owner. He had taken a liking to that frontiersman throw back. He recalled his last candid conversation with Payne. What a waste of life?

"So, you know this man," Damien Dark asked the FBI Agent.

"My name is Bam-Bam Benson," he said offering a handshake. "Like Ray Benson, Asleep at the Wheel. He's tall like me and sings cowboy swing songs. Pleased to meet you."

"Damien Dark, like wise, and this is Bobby Thomson."

"Just Bob," corrected the younger, dropping his stepfather's last name.

"Pleased to meet you Just Bob," said Bam-Bam, shaking both their hands vigorously.

"He was part of my group," acknowledged Underhill. "So was Max Paxton. The third was our guide, Payne. He was murdered by the pot heads, So was his dog. The mule belonged to him originally What do the Bigfoots run here, a catch and release program,"

"Unfortunately, all catch and no release so far," clarified Damien. "By the way, that hole where your ear used to be looks badly infected."

Underhill rubbed his hand across it and felt the festering ooze, and immediately thought about Cooper's leg. He was in bad need of antibiotics or at least an antibacterial cream. He had neither. Underhill checked the gun shot wound in his arm. It appeared to be fairing better.

"Tell me, Bam-Bam," asked Underhill, "Did the creatures bring you here too?"

He nodded. "They can talk with their hands like my deaf and dumb friend Larry Price."

"They can. Do you understand sign language?"

Bam-Bam nodded to confirm. "My friend Larry Price taught me. They are not as good as Larry though."

More figures emerged from the darkness, a large male and what appeared to be a least five adult females. Some were carrying an assortment of wood and limbs for the fire. Others carried berries and raw fish.

"Magilla Gorillas," smiled Bam-Bam, pointing to the entourage. "The big gray face is not with them. He's bigger than me and Ray Benson. He can't sing like Ray Benson though. I don't know if he can sing at all." Bam-Bam stretched his hand up to show the others how much bigger.

The size and mere girth of these wondrous creatures captivated the onlookers. The females had huge gravity challenged breasts, hairless around their large darkened nipples and areola. The smallest female stood nearly seven feet tall. Three were obviously with child by the looks of their swollen bellies.

"See," pointed out Damien. "They are not the monsters portrayed in movies and our culture. They are socially structured creatures with more human behavioral habits than apes. You can see the human intelligence in those dark brown eyes."

"You should," spoke up Underhill. "We apparently father their children. The males of their species must be sterile. We're mere breeder stock to them. Man is responsible for their continued existence. At least that's what Cooper believed."

"We were wrong with the missing link theory," added Damien. "We are them. They are us. Together we created the link and we continue to do so."

"Should we break into a chorus of *We are the World*," smarted off Underhill.

Bob swallowed deeply. "You mean we have to screw them."

"I think you're a little too young for that right now," hedged Damien.

"But I'll soon be thirteen," said a still disbelieving Bob.

"Puberty," chuckled Underhill. "It all begins very soon. To be young and promiscuous again, now that's a thought."

"This isn't funny," whined Bob, experiencing flashbacks of his stepfather, Bert Thomson.

Damien picked up on the kid's fears from the distraught look on his face. The whole sexual thing scared the crap out of Bob, and it should, considering what he had gone through with his perverted stepfather.

"Don't worry kid," consoled Damien, placing his hand on Bob's shoulder. "I won't let anything like that happen to you." He had just lied to the kid. How could he stop it if the creatures chose that path? He would cross that bridge in due time.

Once the fire had been replenished, the male Sasquatch retrieved Max Paxton's body from Bam-Bam and tossed it into the pit. Shocked by the ritual, no one uttered a word, except Bam-Bam.

"That's how they bury people and other Magilla Gorillas."

Underhill asked, "What gave you that idea?"

"They told me with their hand talk," he responded, trying to replicate the hand signs for the agent.

"Amazing," remarked Bob. "You can talk to them. Can you teach me?"

Bam-Bam nodded and signed something back at Bob.

In another section of cavern hell laid Professor Mattie Reynolds, frozen by the suffocating pitch blackness and confinement of her tunnel grave. She would have been in a fetal position if the space had allowed. Cold, hungry and just plain paralyzed, she remained positioned on her side, still clutching the fireless torch. She could neither make herself inch forward or backward. Time in her world had come to a standstill.

Mattie Reynolds had briefly felt warmth from releasing her bloated bladder, but now the dampness between her legs made her shiver even more. It was not her character to give up and lose all hope, but these were indeed unusual circumstances. She thought about the woman mentioned by Dan Cooper in his journal. The female S'cwene'y'ti had so nonchalantly taken her life. Human females served no real purpose in their society. If she would have stayed with the others, she most likely would have been eventually killed.

These thoughts jolted her. She had done the right thing looking for a way out. Escape was her only option. Retreating would serve no purpose. Wiggling, she tried to restore circulation to her tingling limbs. Using the torch as a blind man uses a cane, she began to inch her way forward. Her arms stretched ahead. She could not withdraw either of them. Still on her side, progress was slow and extremely difficult. The tunnel only got smaller.

Her shoulders scraped against the tunnel's ceiling and floor. She pressed her back against the wall and her breast frequently undulated against the contour of the opposite wall. Her shirt and pants snagged constantly on the jagged surfaces. Fresh scratches opened and spilled droplets of her precious blood. If the tunnel closed by another couple of inches in any direction, her progress would certainly be halted. Worst fear, what if she crawled into a bottomless crevice? The good news, no S'cwene'y'ti could possibly follow her in here. She thought, thank God, I'm not claustrophobic.

The height of the tunnel had begun to gradually increase. Her right shoulder no longer touched the ceiling. It remained narrow. Mattie breathed heavily from the strain of her worm like maneuvering. Suddenly, she thought she heard a noise and held her breath to listen. Very faint, but it sounded like running water. She prayed no sudden rush of water now funneled in her direction. Drowning in this tunnel struck terror in her mind. She picked up her pace just in case. The tunnel without warning widened. She could now rotate to her belly and brace herself under her elbows. It felt wonderful. Pausing, she took a well-deserved deep breath and sucked in cold moist air. Flowers had never smelled better than what filled her nostrils and lungs.

Yes, it was water. She could hear it loudly rushing and splattering on rocks somewhere ahead. Mattie could see no daylight. She laughed, realizing she had her eyes closed tightly. Opening them, she could just make out a faint light source spilling into her private little worm hole.

Smiling, she muttered out loud, "Thank you Lord."

Several minutes passed. All was quiet. Nash opened the eye not pressed closely to the ground. He could see very little due to the high grass where his body had landed. Raising and up righting his head at a snail's pace, he could detect no movement directly ahead.

Playing possum had apparently fooled Speedy, but had it buffaloed the Sasquatch party? He continued to hear bursts of Uzi fire in the distance. The creatures could be distracted. He certainly hoped Speedy kept them preoccupied.

His head ached something fierce. Nash hoped he had not sustained a concussion from the blow. At least he had escaped from the company of his cohort in crime. He could not have planned this incident any better. After a couple of more minutes he decided to chance it and stand. During his first attempt, he settled noisily back on his butt when his rubbery legs would not support him. He glanced around quickly for the creatures, fearing they had heard his crash. So far, so good, he hadn't seen them. He hoped he never did.

Kneeling on one knee, balancing with his hand, clutching a small sapling, he scanned the surrounding woods. No creatures burst onto the scene. He breathed deeply and then successfully up righted himself. Weaponless, he contemplated his options. None were very promising. Obviously, he couldn't continue the present course, not with the Sasquatch potentially dogging Speedy. Returning to base camp seemed stupid. It could be swarming with more Sasquatch. Trying to pick up the original escape route from here would be challenging due to the terrain, no food, water or a weapon.

Heading West away from the rumbling volcano seemed to be his best option. Even he now admitted an eruption might be imminent. He thought he should put some distance between him and the mountain. Without a map, he just wasn't sure where westward would take him. This was not Alaska. His head and face still hurt, but he sucked it up and made hast. He figured sooner or later the Sasquatch would take note that he was missing. Confident in their intelligence and demonstrated persistence, he suspected that they would back track and pick up his trail.

Muffled somewhere behind him he barely detected another series of Uzi rounds being fired. Speedy was still alive and apparently keeping them at bay. He would quickly run out of ammunition if he maintained the frequent barrage. Speedy's safety didn't really concern him though. He had to concentrate on his own survival.

Shawn Reynolds had arrived at the sheriff's office and explained the urgency in locating Mattie and Anson Parker. The sheriff concurred and assigned a deputy. He then recruited a couple of local game management officials to accompany him to the area they were supposed to be scouting. Shawn did not divulge Mattie's true intent, searching for Bigfoot. He lied and said he had suddenly lost radio contact with the twosome after a distress call.

That little white lie prompted immediate action by the authorities, especially after he painted her up to be a celebrity, insinuating she was a famous professor and speaker. What he didn't know, Mattie was far from her original destination, and Anson Parker was no longer among the living. His make belief distress call was closer to truth than fiction.

Underhill sat, eating the trout sushi provided by their host. He could have cooked it over the fire, but eating wasn't his top priority. Escape was. He had D.B. Cooper's journal tucked into the back of his trousers' waste band. Eyeing the antics of the humanoid apes, he perceived less contempt in their demeanor than he had experienced in his previous ordeal. He owed payback to that bastard who had severed his ear. That would certainly be on his priority list once he escaped, but not before taking credit for Cooper's discovery.

Underhill pondered the fate of the professor. She had not returned since trekking off to locate an escape route. He didn't know whether that equated to her being successful or encountering some unfortunate accident. Hindsight, he should have gone with her. Attempting to do so now in the presence of these numerous creatures could be problematic. Searching for the money had prevented him from completely thinking rationally. While here, he may as well make the most of it.

Glancing over at the boy, he noticed he ate only the berries and avoided the raw fish. Fire, cook, get it, he almost had said. The geek sampled both as did Bam-Bam. He watched diligently while Bam-Bam carried on a hand sign discussion with one of the pregnant females. The apes seemed to favor the big guy. He could possibly parley this to his advantage. He wondered if these creatures had always used sign or had been taught.

Underhill could have never guessed that a mute French mountain man by the name of Bénard Chouteau had taught them sign language some 130 years ago. Of course, grunts, snorts and high-pitched whistles seemed to be part of their language too. Either way, Underhill understood very little of their communications.

Tilting his head to one side, he felt more of that nasty fluid running down his neck from the hole where his ear used to be. Infection was winning the battle. He also felt a little feverish. He rubbed the wound. Smelling the fresh goop on his fingertips he again thought about what had happened to Cooper.

Underhill noticed one of the females eyeing him. Standing what he calculated at just shy of seven feet, she probably easily topped the scales at nearly 400 pounds. She periodically sniffed the air, and then emitted a short series of grunts, reminding him of the apes on National Geographic.

Damien Dark plopped down beside the agent and nudged him in the side with his elbow. "I think she likes you," he smiled.

"What the hell is that supposed to mean?"

"Love is in the air. I do believe she might be in heat and in need of a mate."

"You can't be serious? Get away from me with your foolish talk."

"Take a look around. All but those two over there appear to be heavy with child. Remember what Cooper said. They abduct mature human males as breeders. Guess what agent, you fit the build. It's not so funny now since you're on the menu, is it?"

"Looks to me that they have their mind set on Bam-Bam," said Underhill, attempting to shift the conversation "Maybe size does matter."

"Possible Down syndrome, or haven't you noticed," said Damien. "I don't think he can contribute to their gene pool."

"Well just maybe they don't know that," snapped Underhill.

"They have ways of finding out, trust me," grinned Damien, simulating jerking himself off. "I've been tested. I've apparently passed their inspection. You're next."

"I'm not going to discuss this with you, boy."

"Like I said, it isn't quite so funny now, is it? You didn't think that way earlier when you were giving Bob crap about reaching puberty."

"Just get the hell away from me," demanded Underhill. "I've got to think."

Damien nudged the agent one last time. "You better be thinking how many ways do I love thee."

The female now standing, had her sights set on Agent Spencer Underhill.

He wasn't ready to go x-rated with a sub species in front of a viewing audience. He needed a diversion and he needed one now.

Inching her way out of the worm hole, Professor Mattie Reynolds emerged into a larger cave. Still lying on her stomach, she tried to adjust her eyes to the dimly filtered light. Sounds of the running water filled her ears, as did the dampness in the air and on her face.

Suffering severe leg cramps, Mattie attempted to sit up. Her clothes were ripped and torn from the agonizing crawl. For each rip she had a cut or scrape to match. Thankfully, she was not a free bleeder. Most had already clotted.

Massaging her legs, she suddenly realized she had lost her left shoe. In her panicked condition she had not remembered doing so. She looked back into the mouth of the narrow tunnel and quickly decided she would not be re-entering and conducting a search. The cramps had almost subsided. With abundant headroom she attempted to stand. One last cramp nailed her in her left leg. She hopped around on her right leg, while holding her left. She resembled a young girl playing hopscotch.

Mattie grabbed hold of a section of rock jutting from the cave wall to balance. Gradually the knot in the back of her leg relaxed. She eased her shoeless left foot to the smooth rock floor. Her eyes had become adjusted to her surroundings. She estimated her new cave as being approximately twelve to fifteen feet wide and varying up to ten feet high. Where she stood must be just over seven feet because she stood comfortably and hadn't bumped her head during her kangaroo jumping ordeal.

She could not yet see the end of the cave because it took a slight right-hand bend, but light filtered from just beyond that corner. The source of the water was hidden by that turn also. She moved cautiously because she couldn't be sure if her exit exposed her to the *S'cwene'y'ti*.

Surveying her new surroundings, Mattie surmised that water had carved the tunnel, the surface being too smooth, with almost a polished appearance. Moving toward the nearest wall, she could make out what appeared to be cave drawings. She first thought it could be graffiti, until she got a little closer.

"Amazing," she spoke. Her voice sounded like that of a smoker, deep, gruff, hoarse, and almost gone.

Walking along the wall and running her fingers over the drawings, the illustrations depicted pulled her into the story lines. The figures were of ancient men or Indians interacting with what appeared to be the *S'cwene'y'ti*. Scenes of human sacrifices and abductions were obvious. Most of the human counterparts shown were males. In a few, females were among those kidnapped, but that was more the exception than the rule. She figured the drawings must be very old because none showed fire. Animals such deer and bear were prevalent. Scenes with Wooly Mammoth and several other creatures she could not identify gave credence to just how old they must be. A smoking and erupting volcano appeared in others. The clincher, in every scene, the painters had portrayed a specific *S'cwene'y'ti,* one that always stood head and shoulder taller than the other similar creatures. The alpha male apparently attracted a lot of attention and commanded respect from those who had drawn the paintings. Another repeating theme had caught her eye. At first Mattie thought it represented the sun or maybe the moon. Upon closer examination she discovered it represented neither.

"Oh my God," she gasped, realizing the object was a flying craft. "Damien Dark would crap a brick if he saw this."

Old Bertha had dropped anchor. No amount of tugging her reins or switching the old mule on her rump influenced her decision to stop here and hold her ground. She had had enough.

"You damn sorry piece of dog food. Just what the hell is your damn problem?"

Old Bertha flicked her ears as if offended by the obscene cursing, but her legs held their position, unmovable. Speedy swatted her several more times with a limb from a hardwood sapling. She twitched with each blow but refused to move. Frustrated, Speedy howled at the top of his lungs. A chorus of Sasquatch answered with mimicking howls of their own. Speedy could tell they were close, but out of gunshot range. They still had him surrounded.

"You damn jackass, do you hear that? That's the dinner bell ringing and we're the main course. Do you really want to be ripped to pieces by a horde of Bigfoots?"

Old Bertha held firm.

Speedy began unloading several satchels of his crop, deciding to carry what he could and shoot the mule for being such a disloyal pain in his ass. He had just removed the third satchel when it began raining rocks; very big rocks. Covering his head with a satchel, he tried to avoid the onslaught. Rocks caught him solidly in his left hip and right foot. Another nailed him dead center of his lower back. He fired a quick burst, but the rocks continued to pound him.

After maybe a half a minute, it stopped. He eased the bundle off his head and took a deep breath. Battered and bruised, he turned to the mule, but the mule wasn't there. Old Bertha had taken flight while he had been distracted with the attack. Speedy stood there looking at the three satchels. This was almost not worth carrying. Not only that, he had been robbed of the satisfaction of killing the mule. Hooting mocked his situation. He fired again yelling, "You bastards!" The Uzi clicked empty.

He reached in his pocket and pulled out a clip. Staring at it, he became terror stricken. This was his last Uzi clip. The others were on the mule. He checked, confirming he had two remaining clips for his pistol and possessed a hunting knife. He had never felt so naked and helpless. Nash had warned to leave them alone. Maybe the old coot had been right after all. He was not a quitter. He was far from being licked yet.

He scooped up the satchels and tossed them over one shoulder. He held the Uzi out front and tried to get his bearings. Speedy picked a direction and hoped it was the correct one. There were no clearly marked trails and he was not an outdoorsman. At best his pick was a dice roll. He was headed downhill. He desperately hoped he would see the logging road soon.

Speedy smelled them. They had emitted that stifling odor again. It engulfed him like an invisible fog. He would need more than just luck to escape their clutches. He wasn't sure just how much luck he had left. Still he was a man and they weren't. Monkeys had their limitations regardless to how smart Nash thought they were.

After traveling only 30 minutes he discarded one of the three satchels. Shouldering the Uzi, he leaned over, clutching both knees, trying to catch his breath. Every bone and muscle ached. He licked his lips. He was thirsty. The water and food were with that damn mule. It was time to suck it up and do what he had to do to get out of here. He had faced worst challenges or maybe he hadn't come to think of it.

He did have a flask of bourbon in his coat pocket but hesitated when his hand touched it. He should stay sober. He laughed out loud, thinking about how many joints he had already burned. With that, he unscrewed the cap and took a long swig. It burned his parched throat and only worsened his thirst. It did serve to embolden him though.

One more swig and the flask had been emptied. He threw it into the bushes, mocking retaliation for the rock throwing. He grabbed up the satchel he had discarded and rotated it like a windmill, and then tossed it as far as he could, like performing in the shot-put competition.

Speedy recalled he had a nephew who had participated last year in the Special Olympics and had won four gold medallions. His two tosses would not have gotten him through the first round. His nephew could certainly run circles around him right now. He then thought about the halfwit, but somehow what he had felt about Bam-Bam didn't seem so important now.

Taking a deep breath, he thought about Ceil and how he missed her laughter and constant nagging. He had practically raised her and had saved her from the tough street life. He remembered how her body laid lifeless, shot to pieces from his fit of anger. Speedy quickly justified his actions. He had saved her from this hell, so it must have been the right thing to do.

He had no remorse about killing that other bitch, Velvet. She and Booger were in cahoots and were going to claim the fruit of his labor. Looking at the two remaining satchels, he said, "So what, just one damn cluster, and the sooner I'm out of here, the better."

If he got off this mountain just what would he do then? Ceil was gone. Nash was gone. His crop was gone. That stupid ass mule was gone. What if more FBI agents were waiting for him to return to his apartment? What if they were trailing him right now? Maybe the big hairy monkeys and the agents would mount a standoff. Max had said no other agents were involved. It was probably some sort of damn trick. D.B Cooper was just a made-up cover.

"Oh, enough of this damn pity party crap," he spoke loudly. "Hey, you hairy, hooting rock throwing bastards, if you want a piece of Elwood Speed Moore's ass, you're going to have to step up your game. You hear me out there you Big footed, big ass, son of a bitches. Bring it on."

Continuing down the sloped wooded grade, he blocked out his pain, kept his finger on the Uzi trigger and unleashed a relentless tirade of Sasquatch cursing. He tittered on a tightrope, insane or not, without a safety net to catch his fall. This was far from over and he always came out on top. This would end the same way. He hadn't come this far in life to be beaten by something that wasn't even supposed to be real. He yelled a challenge one more time just because he could and to make his point.

Waving his arms, Underhill motioned for Bam-Bam. He signed one last series of hand signals, and then ambled over to where Underhill impatiently waited.

"Do you really understand what they're saying?"

Bam-Bam frowned, not sure about the agent's question. "They can't talk."

Underhill rolled his eyes. "The sign language," he mimicked with his hands. "Do you understand what they are telling you with all those hand motions?"

"Some of it. They do it too fast."

Underhill rubbed his chin, pondering his next move. The female still watched him. "Can you ask them if they found any money?"

"Silly question," replied a grinning Bam-Bam. "I don't think they use money up here. They don't have any stores."

Underhill, realizing it was probably a stupid request said, "All right then, can they show us a way out of here?"

"I know the way out. It's behind the big rock. They moved it when they brought me in here, and then rolled it back. They sure do use real heavy doors."

"What do they intend to do with us?"

Bam-Bam shrugged. He didn't know or didn't understand the question. "Does that hole where your ear used to be hurt? It looks like it would hurt to me," he said, holding his own ear. "Max always said God gave you two ears and only one mouth because you were supposed to listen twice as much as you talked. I reckon you talk and listen the same way now. I sure do miss Max and my mule, Old Bertha."

This was getting him nowhere fast thought Underhill. He would probably have better luck talking to a Bigfoot than trying to communicate with this big lug.

"I think the woman Magilla likes you Mister Secret Agent Man," commented Bam-Bam.

"Tell her I'm spoken for. Offer her the geek over there," he said, pointing at Damien Dark.

Bam-Bam had the deer in the headlights look. He did not comprehend Underhill's concern or understand the agent's dialogue. Underhill was wasting his breath.

"Forget it," remarked Underhill. "I think erectile dysfunction will take care of this situation. I would require a bag over her head and another over mine to muster up one for the cause. Sick them on Dark."

"You are a funny man, Mister Secret Agent Man, talking about bags over your heads," laughed Bam-Bam. "You say stuff like Max used to say. I like you. Will you be my new friend like Max?"

Damian overheard his name being mentioned and walked over. "What did you say about me, Mister Underhill?"

"I was just telling Bam-Bam that you hunted UFO's, and you were probably up for almost anything. He's been communicating with them with that sign language. Accompany him over there. He's going to try to teach you how to communicate with them."

"Fantastic. This is better that I could ever have hoped. My fantasies are coming true."

More than you could ever imagine, thought Underhill. I hope you enjoy your discovery. Underhill preoccupied, never saw the male Sasquatch approaching from the opposite direction.

Mattie now viewed the drawings on the opposite cave wall. These captivated her more than the first ones. "Oh my gosh," she gasped, seeing details of the flying objects, beaming lights toward humanoids, surrounded by an assortment of *S'cwene'y'ti*. Woozy, she had to take a seat on an outcropped ledge.

"Damian was on to something. The UFO sightings he was investigating are related to the creatures and their legends. Could the *S'cwene'y'ti* really be aliens?"

She discounted this theory quickly. Creatures capable of building space craft would not live so primitively in caves and the wilderness. "But there must be a connection. It's right there in those drawings."

Mattie had temporarily forgotten her hunger, thirst and fatigue. This discovery had overwhelmed her senses. She tried to remind herself that these were just cave drawings, and that she had no concrete evidence that they were anything more than Indian folklore, worshipping mythical creatures. She only had secondhand accounts. Matt's journal, as well as Cooper's, and the testimony of eyewitnesses didn't produce a live *S'cwene'y'ti* or any physical evidence that UFOs were real. She didn't even have Cooper's journal. Agent Spencer Underhill did.

She wondered how the world would accept the existence of these legendary creatures and UFO's, and their possible connection. She could think of no good outcome from a discovery such as this. It would bring her fame and fortune, but did she really want that, when it would most certainly put these creature's lives in jeopardy, creatures she had yet to see. Thinking soon exhausted her.

She leaned her head back against the cool cave wall, closed her eyes for another power nap, but instead gave in to deep slumber. The afternoon light began to fade, and the cave darkened. Eyes closed she never saw the darkness approaching. If she had, she would have surely made a hasty exit.

Nash Hudson made his way through the narrowing and winding canyon, following the stream flowing in his direction. He at least had an abundance of water to drink. He had seen a few frogs and crayfish, but his hunger didn't command eating raw critters just yet. A fleeting thought told him he might regret this decision.

Darkness approached. He now searched for shelter. Luckily, so far, he had not sensed being followed. Nash had traveled in the stream when possible to mask his tracks. His head still ached periodically from the stone that had struck him, but he had managed to maintain a steady pace.

He could no longer see Mount Saint Helens. Nash wondered if the experts were right about an imminent eruption. If they were, would he be out of harms way? Surely it would be nothing very impressive. Volcano eruptions weren't common here, were they? Nash figured it would make for a mention on the local television stations, and then some child murderer or small no name country threatening war would captivate the viewing audience. People enjoyed bad news more, not nature stories.

Glancing at his watch, it wasn't quite as late as it seemed. The canyon blotted out the setting sun and the shadows darkened his little world. It didn't dispel his urgency to find shelter. He knelt and cupped some water in his hands, drank, and then splashed some on face. An impressive bullfrog sat motionless a mere foot away. He wasn't hungry right now, but would be later, so he snatched it up and stuffed it in a pocket and zipped it up. It moved frantically trying to escape.

He ignored its spastic behavior, seeing a second one. He quickly captured it and slipped it into to the same pocket. The zipper strained as he tried to seal them safely inside. He saw a third one, but it must have caught onto his little plan. It quickly leapt and disappeared into a small pool.

Nash picked up his pace and followed the contour and flow of the stream. Rounding a turn his hope turned to despair. He was in a box canyon. A towering three-story waterfall fed the stream, water plummeting into a quarter acre pool. It was too late in the day for him to retrace his steps.

Nash must hunker down here, risk climbing out or wait until daybreak, and then back track. He hated all three options. Clutching his pocket and the annoying frantic frogs, he sat down to ponder his dilemma for a few precious minutes.

Speedy suddenly emerged through heavy brush into an open clear cut. The entire mountainside and valley had been scavenged by loggers. He had arrived at his destination. The thought of civilization nearby suddenly sent tingles through his bones. Even if he couldn't find a logging road, all he had to do was follow the clear cut down the mountain. He moved quickly to distance himself from the denseness of the forest. Nightfall would come crashing down in less than an hour, so he would need to prepare a camp and a last stand.

With firewood a plenty, compliments of the loggers, he could build a massive fire to light the surroundings and ward off the intruders. He picked a spot on a slight rise, posing a lookout in any direction. Speedy strategically placed three perimeter fires and had them crackling and blazing by dusk. With plenty of dried wood at hands reach, he could fuel them easily throughout the night. Sitting on a log, Uzi clutched to his bosom, thirst overtook him without warning. He had forgotten he had had nothing to drink or eat lately. Speedy would find no water here and he dared to venture into the woods to search for a stream.

He saw on a movie once, this guy stranded in the desert, placed a smooth stone in his mouth and sucked on it for moisture. He searched the immediate terrain but found no smooth stones. He found a couple of jagged rocks but thought better about putting one of them in his mouth. Speedy sat with his back to the largest fire, the other two roaring and spaced 20 feet in front of him. He waited for the hooting, rock throwing and an ambush. Other than the usual sounds of the night, all remained silent. Speedy hoped that the fires and open land would keep the ape men at bay. So far, his plan was working.

He had one remaining sheet of rolling paper. Speedy opened one of the satchels and removed enough leaf to roll one last joint. He had nothing else to do, so why not. He only had to fear the munchies brought on by smoking the weed. Hours passed and Speedy had heard not a peep from them. Had they given up or were they watching and waiting for him to drop his guard. Pulling a couple of twenties from his wallet he improvised and rolled two more joints. "Money to burn," he remarked. "Life of the not so rich and famous."

Firing up his twenty-dollar bill joint and taking a pull, he then replenished the fires. He fired a quick burst from his Uzi and yelled, "What are you waiting for? I'm here. Bring it on and let's settle this thing, Fur Face."

He watched and listened for a reaction to his challenge, but the night remained deathly silent. He twirled, completing a 360, but detected no movement. What were they waiting for? Mocking a series of hoots, he taunted them. He even chunked several rocks into the pitch-black surroundings, but they did not counter. He shouted, "Is this some sort of new strategy, or are you hairy bastards giving up?"

He hooted again, and then banged the butt of his Uzi on a log, attempting to imitate their tree thumping. The Uzi's clip popped out, falling behind the log. Panic stricken, he scrambled to retrieve it, convinced they would rush him now. He could not immediately locate the clip, trying to eye the darkness for an onslaught.

Finally, his fingers found what they were feeling for, and he snapped the clip back in place. The night had not exploded into a frenzy of attackers. He stood alone in the clear cut. Collapsing on the log, he fired up his second twenty dollar joint and wiped the sweat from his brow. He mumbled, "You stinking bastards, do you know who you're messing with?"

Agent Spencer Underhill, humiliated, recovered his tidy whitey boxers and pants from around his ankles. Embarrassed, he couldn't fathom how effortlessly the male Sasquatch had aroused him and then completed the unthinkable. The male still stood there, staring him down. Underhill slipped D. B. Cooper's journal back into his waistband. His treasure would solve part of the mystery once he made it public. Still, the missing puzzle, the money, what had happened to the stolen money? Underhill glanced over at Damien Dark, Bam-Bam and the kid. They had witnessed the degrading incident. He absolutely could not allow them to ever share this story with the outside or he would be ruined. It would certainly blemish his discovery and tarnish his image. He would convince Dark to lay claim to the Sasquatch discovery, in exchange to exclude this episode, while Dark did the same with the hijacker. Deals would be struck.

How disgusting he thought, witnessing the male smelling and tasting his semen. Its nose crinkled, and lips rolled in a most unpleasant manner. Underhill thought, I would probably have that same reaction, big fellow. He even smiled, just glad the ordeal was over, and he could now focus on an escape plan. The male extended his huge hairy hand and clutched Underhill by the scruff of his neck. Underhill in turn slipped his left hand to clutch the journal behind his back. What now he wondered.

Agent Spencer Underhill stared into the cold dark brown eyes, trying to read its thoughts. He started to flag down Bam-Bam, figuring he could interpret. The thick lips parted exposing a full mouth of discolored teeth. Its breath could surely use a dose of mouth wash.

"What do you want big fellow? Are we about to become friends, maybe?"

 I'm for it if it gets me out of here, thought the agent. The creature's massive thumb rested on the side of Underhill's neck. Underhill could feel his own pulse throbbing under the applied pressure. The gigantic humanlike hand easily forced his head to one side, and then back, while scrutinizing its subject.

Underhill impressed by the power in that hand, never broke eye contact, caught in a stare down, just like kids do when trying to see who will laugh first. This didn't seem like a laughing matter though. He started to place his hand on the creature's powerful arm but decided it may not be the best of ideas. He didn't need to rile it while they seemed to be making a little progress.

Suddenly it clicked with Spencer Underhill. He recalled the incident in the journal and Cooper's description of the man killed in his presence. Taking a deep breath, he remembered why. He thought of his own vasectomy and tried to free himself from the male's death grip, but his hopes quickly faded.

"Please don't do this," he whispered. "The truth belongs to me. It is my destiny. I earned it. We can work this out. I know we can."

Still locked in the creature's stare, in one quick flick of its wrist, Underhill's neck snapped, and then he hung limply in the clutches of the Sasquatch. The alpha male discarded the agent like yesterday's trash and tossed his lifeless body into the awaiting fire. With him, D.B. Cooper's journal perished in the blazing fire.

Mattie opened her eyes, but all remained dark. She shivered. The night's temperature penetrated her weary bones. She could hear, but no longer see the cascading waterfall, the caves entry way. She did detect movement and felt a presence. Shrinking against the cave wall, she tried to blend into the smooth stone background.

She frantically strained her eyes, attempting to draw on any sliver of light, but she could muster up no visions of what shared her lair. Trembling, Mattie began to grind her teeth to prevent them from chattering noisily. Aware now that her bladder ached for relief her panicky state teetered. She was now on the brink of screaming out loud.

She heard it again. It was movement and very close by the sounds of it. Mattie visualized the entity shifting its weight, feet grinding against the cave's floor. Unnerved she curled up the toes of her shoeless foot and the toe's joint cracked inside its sock. It sounded like Shawn cracking his knuckles, a habit of his that drove her up the walls. The air changed. The entity had heard her toes snap, crackle, and pop too.

She blindly touched the floor's surface within arm's reach, searching for anything she could use as a weapon, but found nothing. She considered removing her only shoe to ward off the intruder but thought better of it. It would only be affective against an invading insect or small rodent. She hoped for either.

Her swollen bladder made it difficult to think rationally. A tear rolled down her cheek. She fought sniffling. Anxiety taking its toll, Mattie needed a paper bag to control her breathing, on the verge of hyperventilating. The silence was broken by a command so close she could feel the turbulence from the expelled words. "Get out of here, whatever you are," screamed what sounded like a man's voice.

Mattie countered the unexpected warning yell with the warm flow of pee, drawing comfort from its release and the fact that the intruder sounded human. "Who are you," she managed with her weak raspy voice.

"Are you alone," asked the shadow monster.

"I am. Are you?"

"Yeah. Name's Nash. Who are you?"

"Mattie. Where did you come from?"

"I was about to ask you the same thing. I found the entrance to the cave when I was climbing out of the box canyon. It was already too dark for me to see inside, but I just took a chance, figuring nothing would be alive on the other side of the waterfall."

"Thank goodness you were wrong."

"What's your story?"

"You wouldn't believe me even if my voice would hold out long enough for me to tell you. Short version, a friend and I were hiking, and he took a fall, was killed. I became lost and trapped in a cavern that adjoins this cave. I made it this far before dark. What about you?"

"Similar story," he recounted. "My group fell on some ill misfortunes. I became separated from them. Do you have any food?"

"We have a waterfall, I suppose, but no, I have no food. What about you?"

"How do you feel about eating frog legs or any other parts of the frog as for as that goes?"

"Sounds wonderful," she licked and smacked her lips in the darkness.

"I don't have matches for fire."

"Doesn't matter," she answered. "I don't have any wood."

"Sounds like frog then," he laughed.

"Sushi in the dark with a stranger," Mattie replied. "It'll probably taste just like chicken."

"I bet it will. You wouldn't happen to have a knife or something sharp, would you?"

"Afraid not. Guess we're taking roughing it to a new level."

"You got that right. Our supper is still alive and kicking and inside my pocket."

"Spare me the visual effects please," said Mattie, now picturing the slimy, squirming critters.

Nash slid in the direction of her voice and reached out to locate her position. "Sorry," he apologized, realizing he had copped a feel of one of her breasts.

"Are you sure you can't see what you're doing?"

"Well, the blind routine usually works on dumb blondes. Guess you must not be one. By the way, I usually grab both."

"Brunette, married and you better count your fingers."

"This is certainly an interesting predicament we have here. Pitch dark, no matches, no weapons, a couple of frogs and a brunette by my side."

"A married brunette," she reminded Nash, her voice almost fading out.

"Do you always sound like that, or do you smoke three packs a day?"

"You're referring to my sexy raspy voice. Fatigue and exhaustion have taken its toll I'm afraid. I've never smoked. You certainly do have your way with the woman, don't you?"

"Guess I'm not accustomed to the married kind in my neck of the woods."

"And where would that neck be?"

"Spent much of my life in the Alaskan wilderness, so I suppose I'm a hermit of sorts. I've lost touch with how to treat a lady."

"So blind man, you have elevated me from potential dumb blonde status to a lady. My we have come a long way in a very short time."

"What you say we have a little frog?"

"I really do hope it taste like chicken."

Rubbing his beard, Nash, regretted that neither his hazel nor brown eye could see the face behind this alluring gravelly voice. He dispelled his evil thoughts and retrieved the first frog, and then took out his frustrations by whacking it against the stone wall.

"Dinner is served," he told his female companion, the lady of darkness.

The smell of Underhill's burning flesh still lingered. Damien Dark, torn between the horror of the murderous slaying and the sweet aroma of cooked meat, tried to comfort a shaken Bob. Bam-Bam had resumed his hand talking with one of the pregnant females.

Damien assessed their situation, trying not to be influenced by what he had just witnessed. The scientific value of this discovery outweighed the death of the agent and solving the D.B. Cooper mystery. Convinced this had to be the chance of a lifetime, he felt compelled to comply with the creatures' culture. This hedged their chances for survival. He decided he would put up no resistance nor would he try to escape.

Secondly, he wanted to protect young Bob. The kid should be in no immediate threat to the females' sexual interest, but on the other hand, would eventually be a focal point. He doubted that the slow-witted Negro would be deemed breeder material, but he could not discount it. He still was not sure how the Sasquatch males were able to grade sperm quality, if that's what they were doing.

Damien began playing out the scenario in his head. First things first. Would the creatures allow them to live, and if so, for how long? Would they ever see the light of day again? Food, they were dependent on the Sasquatch for this. How long could they really survive on berries and raw fish before their systems began to break down? Raw fish he chuckled. We have fire.

So far, the creatures had not tried to restrict their movement or actions. Why should they? They were trapped, or were they? The professor had never returned. Had she found a way out, or had she died trying? Too many questions and very few answers.

Bob finally broke the silence. "Are they going to kill us too?"

"If they had that in mind for us I think we would already be dead," he attempted to assure young Bob and himself.

"Why did they kill the FBI agent?"

Being candid, Damien tried to offer an explanation. "I believe, for whatever reason, Agent Underhill failed their inspection and no longer served a purpose in their higher achy."

"Huh," Bob reacted.

Trying again, Damian said, "They have their needs and rules that they follow, and apparently Underhill just didn't fit any of them, so they got rid of him."

"Do we fit?"

"For now," he said, thinking that was the wrong answer. He tried to back peddle. "I don't believe we are in any danger, if we do what they want us to do. We have Bam-Bam on our side. They really seem to be warming up to the big fellow."

"Maybe Bam-Bam will teach us sign language, so we can talk to them too."

Damien nodded, "Maybe he will."

On cue, Bam-Bam approached them. "They are really scared."

"Of what?" asked Damien. "What could possibly scare them?"

I don't know," answered Bam-Bam, throwing his hands in the air. "I don't know what they are telling me, but it must really, really be bad. I'm scared too."

The three turned hearing an echoing sound approaching from the other cavern. It sounded like someone wearing tap dancing shoes. Damien saw the confused look on the faces of the Sasquatch. They did not recognize the sound either. This could not be good.

Speedy Moore woke to the sunlight in his eyes. He could not believe he had fallen asleep. More startling, he could not believe he was still alive. Relieved that no big gray face stood over him, he sprung to his feet, Mister Commando ready for action. The fires smoldered. The flames had long been gone. Scanning the countryside, he saw no signs of any of the hairy ape men. Running his tongue over his teeth, and then his lips, it tasted like a heard of elephants had crapped in his mouth.

Rubbing the crust from his eyes, Speedy stretched to the sound of cracking bones. Taking a quick piss, one hand still on the Uzi, he desperately needed something to drink to quench his parched throat. He tossed the satchels of reefer over his shoulder and headed down the clear cut in search of a water source.

After walking for about a while he noticed he had not seen any wildlife, nor had he even heard any chirping birds. That seemed too weird. He stopped and perused the landscape, getting his bearings by zeroing in on the ominous mountain dominating the horizon.

He glanced at his watch. It was 8:31 AM and still there were no signs of his pursuers. Waving a middle finger salute, Speedy smiled. He was satisfied that he had escaped the wrath of the stinking ape men. He spoke out loud, "You're no match for the Mighty Speed Moore. I belong to the superior race. You're just a step above a slug underneath my shoe."

In response, Mount Saint Helens, one minute later, exploded, a catastrophic eruption, shaking the ground with an earthquake measuring 5.1 on the Richter scale.

"Oh crap," exclaimed Elwood Speed Moore, hopelessly clutching his stash of reefer. "I have absolutely no frigging luck." He regretted he had burned his last joint. He saw it coming but could do absolutely nothing. Within minutes the hot ash cloud struck his position, the shear force flattening the surrounding forest and burying the landscape beneath its volcanic fury. Not a living thing escaped its destructive power, not even the Mighty Speedy Moore.

Mattie awoke with the aftertaste of frog disrupting her taste buds. Unfortunately, it had not tasted at all like chicken. Light filtered through the cascading waterfall. Sitting up, she caught the first actual glance of the man she had shared dinner and a cave, standing on the opposite side of their refuge. Nash was running his fingers along the cave paintings. He apparently had heard her movement and turned to face her.

He was not at all what she had envisioned. His dress did fit the picture of a mountain man, but his physical characteristics were quite the opposite of the voice. His multi-colored eyes held her attention. He was much older than she had expected, but he looked to be in great physical shape, considering their ordeal.

"Not what you expected my dear," he asked, seeing the telltale astonishment in her facial expressions. "I look a lot better in the pitch of dark."

"I bet you wish I were that dumb blonde, don't you?"

"It sounds like your voice is coming back."

"Frog juice works wonders I suppose. I see you're inspecting our décor."

"Pretty amazing. How old do you think they are?"

"Much older than you or I. These weren't all done at one time or by the same people or tribe. They were painted over many generations, almost like updating the history books."

"Do you think they're real?"

"The paintings?"

"No, what's in the paintings? Do you believe the stories that they tell?"

"Native American history is filled with legend and folklore. They believed in what they painted, just as we believe in our God and the countless stories in our own biblical history. Some of those are pretty amazing if you think about it."

"Have you ever seen one?"

"Seen one what," she countered, unwilling to so quickly admit what she believed.

"An unidentified flying object or a Sasquatch. Have you ever had one of those encounters with either one?"

"No, I can honestly say I have never seen either. Have you?"

"Nope, me either," he answered truthfully, because he had never seen the creatures that had attacked and followed them. "Do you believe they exist?"

This was where the conversation got a little tricky. She chose her words carefully. "There are plenty of unexplained things out there I suppose. Without concrete evidence of their existence, who can say what is real and what isn't."

Nash sensed she was hiding something. She tip-toed around the subject as deliberately as he. He could see it in her eyes and her body language. Sitting there in the daylight she wasn't what he had visualized in the pitch black either.

"What about you? Do you believe that there is a possibility that a family of Sasquatch could go undetected in this wilderness?"

"Interesting that you would imply a family and confine their existence to just here. Are you keeping something from me, cave buddy?"

Before she could answer, the earth trembled, and a thunderous roar tipped them off that all was not well. Mattie scrambled to her feet, wide eyed, and trembling. Nash too felt the end of the world approaching.

"The volcano. I'll be damned. It has really blown its top."

He took a couple of steps in the direction of the cave entrance concealed by the waterfall, but the rushing water transformed into a cloud of steam, the hot ash storm vaporizing the flowing stream from above the cliffs and plummeting them into darkness once again. Mattie screamed, but Nash never heard her panic-stricken voice, too mesmerized by the unfolding scene, and their uncertain fate.

Damien Dark held his breath, listening to the click clacking of the approaching unknown. He glanced at the boy and saw the terror on his face. Turning his attention to Bam-Bam, the big galoot grinned from ear to ear, teeth gleaming as if posing for a tooth paste commercial.

"Old Bertha," he laughed out loud.

"What's an Old Bertha?"

"My mule, Mr. Dark" he answered, clapping his hands. "But Blue Boy is dead."

"What's a Blue Boy?"

From the shadows emerged two more male Sasquatch, one tugged on the reins of a mule, loaded down with what appeared to be supplies.

"Old Bertha," said Damian.

"Old Bertha," repeated Bam-Bam, now walking toward the two males.

"No," warned Damien.

Bam-Bam turned and smiled, and then said something to the males in hand language. The one holding the reins dropped them and walked pass Bam-Bam, signing something back in response. Bam-Bam hugged the old mule and began stroking it behind its ears and down its neck. The mule snorted and shook its head in recognition. The males walked over and stood toe to toe with Damien and a terrified young Bob. Locked in eye contact, they sniffed them like dogs do when they greet one another then they made a series of whistles and grunts before walking away.

The females greeted them with incoherent grunts and groans. The earth began to shake, and thunderous echoes rang in their ears. Damien pushed Bob to the ground and lay on top of him, protecting him from any falling debris. No debris fell. The rumble seemed endless, but apparently, they were in no danger deep inside the cavern. Finally, Damien shifted his weight and rolled off the top of Bob. Bob covered his ears but said nothing.

Damien pulled his hands down and said, "Earthquake. I think it's over."

He walked over to Bam-Bam, but he paid him no attention, staring into the darkness. "What now? What do you see?"

Smiling again, Bam-Bam said, "The gray faced Magilla Gorilla is here."

The gargantuan gray faced alpha lumbered into view. Standing in the glow of the fire, Damien saw its blood-stained shoulder. He was awestruck by the creature's size. It was gigantic.

Shawn Reynolds, miles away and safely watching the volcano spewing continuously on the television screen, thought this wasn't good. This wasn't good at all for his Mattie. May the 18, 1980, Mount Saint Helens made its mark as the deadliest and most economically destructive volcanic event in the history of the United States. When it was over, fifty-seven people had been killed or never found.

The death totals would exclude the marijuana growers, the D.B. Cooper expedition, Damien Dark, young Bob Thompson, and the

Anson Parker party. All toll, 250 homes, 47 bridges, 15 miles of railways, and 185 miles of highway had been destroyed as result of the eruption. The stubborn 83-year-old octogenarian, Harry R. Truman would never be found, nor would the volcanologist David A. Johnston. His last uttered words would be infamous, "Vancouver! Vancouver! This is it!"

A volcano eruption overshadowed far more important events, the discovery of Sasquatch and the fate of D.B. Cooper. Shawn Reynolds watching from the comfort of his motel room knew the reality of neither. He sat on the edge of his bed, troubled by the whereabouts of his wife and Anson Parker. Mount Saint Helens would erupt for nine hours changing the landscape forever. It would be etched in the memory of America like no other known natural catastrophe to date. None of this historical mumbo jumbo mattered to Shawn. He just needed to find Mattie.

The cave remained dark. The volcano's continuous eruption turned day into night as the ash fell nonstop.

"Are you okay?"

"I'm alive, if that's what you're asking," responded Mattie.

"I never really expected the old girl to show her ass. We are damn lucky to be where we are, or we would have been deader than hell, probably vaporized or snuffed out by the ash."

"Deader than hell not being good, I'm glad luck played in our favor."

"I'd say we're not going any where, any time soon. Is there another way out?"

Mattie hesitated. She had no desire in crawling blindly through that worm hole and into the world of the *S'cwene'y'ti*. Why not, she had not seen one of these wondrous creatures yet. She had only read what Cooper had written and heard Damien Dark's tails. She had no physical evidence that they existed. Wasn't that why she had ventured here? Struggling with her conviction to find the truth and her immediate urge to be in Shawn's arms, she answered Nash.

"Our best bet is to wait out this eruption, and then try to exit the canyon through the falls. We have no light, so stumbling and bumbling our way though this cave and those caverns would be insane."

"We have no idea how the old girl has transformed the landscape out there and how long we'll experience more eruptions and quakes, and you with the one shoe."

"Don't worry about me. When it comes time to get out, I will be ready. Just call me shoeless Joe Reynolds."

"Hold onto that humor. It just might come in handy."

"What do you really think our chances are of getting out of here?"

"Well, I'm somewhat of a survivalist. I know my way around the wilderness, but..."

"But?"

"I've never tangled with an erupting volcano before or its aftermath. I'm on virgin ground with this little predicament we have gotten ourselves into. What about your husband?"

"What?"

"Won't he be looking for you or are you two separated? I see you still wear a wedding band, so I suspect you're still an item."

"Oh, you mean Shawn. He knows I'm here somewhere, but I might just win this little round of hide and go seek."

"Even if he knew, I'm not sure your hubby could get here with the ongoing fireworks show."

The mountain thundered and shook just to make a point. The waterfall remained dry, either blocked upstream or indeed vaporized too. If blocked upstream, a pending breach and flood could await them. They had no way of knowing. Venturing outside for now most likely spelled a death sentence.

Damien Dark watched as the big gray face surveyed the surroundings. It rubbed its chin, appearing somewhat puzzled. Damien finally figured out it must be missing the professor and the FBI agent. The agent was mere ashes now and he didn't know what had become of the professor.

Bam-Bam stroked Old Bertha behind her ears and smiled, not a care in the world. He liked the Magilla Gorillas. He could talk to them with his hands and they talked back, making him feel important. He had never had a mule for a pet before and liked Old Bertha.

Bob stood, his face buried in Damien's shoulder, peeping at the King Kong sized Bigfoot. His fear of the Bigfoot dwarfed in comparison to the terror he endured from his abusive elder. Damien Dark had promised to protect him. Bobe believed the UFO hunter spoke the truth.

Gray Face rubbed his wounded shoulder, and then smelled the dried metallic blood odor. In time it would heal. A hardy species, they rarely succumbed to any type of infection. If they did, the sky people had healing powers. The others of the tribal clan tossed fresh wood on the fire and ambled around doing nothing else of any significance. Damien watched them intensely, noting they reminded him of a family of caged gorillas he had viewed at the San Diego Zoo. The giant leader acted much like the dominant silver back.

Damien tittered between despair and astonishment. His gut told him that he and young Bob and the slow-witted Negro should plot an escape, but his scientific ego screamed opportunity of a lifetime. His ego won out. He would be here for the long haul or until he felt threatened. Damien took a final census and counted only nine of these unique creatures. He wondered if others existed or were, they the last of their kind and on the brink of extinction. He vowed he would protect them, just as he had promised young Bob.

Gray Face, the alpha male approached him. He felt so tiny and insignificant in its presence. A gigantic hand cupped his chin and tilted his head to the left, and then to the right. Damien replayed the Underhill scene in his mind. It eyed Bob, trembling behind him. Bam-Bam walked over and placed his hand on Big Gray's arm and shook his head to indicate his disapproval of Gray Face's actions. Gray Face snarled and clutched Bam-Bam's hand, removing it from his arm. Bam-Bam signed something and Gray Face responded with a sign of his own, nodded, and then lumbered away toward the other males.

Damien gulped then asked, "What did you tell him?"

"Friend," smiled Bam-Bam. "I told him you and the boy were my friends."

"He was okay with that?"

"Yep. Now I'm hungry."

"Me too," whispered Bob, stepping from behind Damien.

"That makes three of us," nodded Damien Dark, as he patted young Bob affectionately on the head. "We're going to be just fine. We are with friends."

Bob frowned, "Guess that means I've got to learn to like raw fish."

"Heck no," grinned Damien. "We have fire remember and I cook a mean trout."

"Are trout really mean," asked Bam-Bam.

Young Bob and the UFO hunter burst into contagious laughter. The hand talker would have joined in but wasn't sure what was so funny. Sniffing the air, old Gray Face searched for the female he had brought to the cavern but could not detect her scent. This prompted an angry snarl. The females cowered, one signing they had not harmed her. Another sighed she was unaware of what had happened to his prize. A third female backed up to him offering herself to him. Big Gray ignored her and brushed her aside and sought solitude instead.

"It's getting lighter outside," commented Nash. "I think she may be quieting down."

"About time. This has been going on for over eight hours and my frog has been long gone. My tummy is rumbling as loudly as that volcano."

"Well, I wouldn't get your hopes up. I'm not sure what we might find out there."

"I suppose we should take a peek don't you think?"

"Guess we might as well. Sould be pretty damn interesting."

Easing over to the still waterless entrance, Nash poked his head outside first. The ravine below had been buried in several inches of ash, but otherwise looked about the same. The sky was dark with some ash still falling like dirty snowflakes.

"What do you see?"

"Trouble for us I'm afraid."

The cave dwellers emerged, resembling hibernating bears. Nash led the way and they cautiously completed the short climb to the top of the now defunct waterfall. Standing at the top of the canyon, the silence overwhelmed their ears. Surveying the horizon, the visual impact brought tears to Mattie's eyes.

She spoke first. "It looks like we've been marooned on some Godforsaken uninhabitable planet."

"Worse, this is good old planet earth and we're a long way from civilization. We won't find any frogs or drinkable water any time soon."

"Such power, it wiped out everything."

"I've never seen anything like this before either. I wonder how many causalities she has claimed."

"This is catastrophic, isn't it?"

"Would be my guess, and it's taken a deadly toll on the wildlife for sure."

"Where do we go now?"

"Even for an old mountain man like me it's going to be tough to get my bearings," he said, as he rubbed both hands through his hair. "Landscape all looks the same and the sun is blotted out by the ash cloud."

"We're screwed, aren't we?"

"Pretty much and I'm not the pessimistic type. I'm not a quitter but I must admit I'm feeling my age right now, older than dirt and about as worthless."

"Matt McGregor would have gotten out of this mess and we will too."

"Who the hell is this McGregor fellow?"

"He was my ancestor and had been captured by...never mind," she paused in mid sentence.

"Indians?"

"Yeah. Indians and he was a seasoned trapper, a mountain man like you. He would not let something like this lick him and we won't either."

"Well you must have his spunk, good genes it appears."

She gazed back toward the cave. She was fretting the fate of those she had deserted. Mattie regretted she had not seen one of the creatures that she had so urgently hoped to find, but she had no doubt they existed.

"What have you left back there," asked Nash, noticing her concern.

"Thinking about Anson Parker's body, probably lost forever."

"Yeah, I fear those in my party may not have survived, if they didn't get clear of the mountain. I don't see how anything could have survived this."

"We're lucky we were in that cave."

"Speaking of, what do you really think about those drawings? I mean, do you believe the artist really saw those things, UFOs and what looked like a Sasquatch?"

"To be honest, my ancestors believed, but like I said, I never experienced what he said he saw. I came here to find out for myself."

"And did you find what you were looking for?"

"Sometimes legends and folklore are best left alone."

Raising an eyebrow, Nash asked, "So are you saying you saw something?"

"I'm saying I won't be coming back to the great northern woods. Let's just leave it at that."

"Same here," he winked. "If we're going to walk out of here, we've got to fix that shoeless foot of yours."

Ripping a sleeve out of his shirt he began wrapping it around her foot and then he tore several strips and laced the extra padding, securing it. "It wouldn't make a fashion statement but should work. As John Wayne would say, daylight is burning."

"You lead, and I'll follow, Pilgrim," she responded, glancing one more time over her shoulder.

Nash mockingly tipped an imaginary hat, thinking retirement back in Alaska didn't sound half bad. Deep down, he hoped the legend had survived. A thunderous roar confirmed his wishes. Mattie Reynolds and Nash Hudson made eye contact, but neither said a word.

Nash then Mattie began waving frantically at the copter. It veered in their direction. Shawn waved back, overcome by tears, realizing that the stranger standing beside her was not Anson Parker. Right now, that didn't matter. He screamed, "Mattie." She recognized him hunkered in the copter's open door. This nightmare was over...or was it?

Gray Face had stepped from the shadows of the concealed entrance. He too no longer recognized the terrain. Intelligent enough to know this spelled trouble for his kind. He let out an impressive roar. It reverberated over the vast moonscape. The ancient ten-footer sensed food would be scarce. Starvation could be inevitable. His kind faced their toughest challenge. Extinction loomed. He grunted, rubbed his wounded shoulder, before disappearing back inside the cave into obscurity, a living legend.

Stay east of the big water. Do not travel into the mountains of the north woods for the S'cwene'y'ti lives there. The sacred ones welcome no intruder to their land. Anger them and they take your spirit. You disappear as does the melting snow.

July 12, 2016

SEATTLE – The FBI says it's no longer actively investigating the unsolved mystery of 1970s plane hijacker D.B. Cooper.

The bureau announced Tuesday that it's "exhaustively reviewed all credible leads" during its 45-year investigation and has redirected those resources to other priorities.

The FBI has investigated since a man calling himself Dan Cooper hijacked a Boeing 727 over the Northwest on Nov. 24, 1971. He later jumped out the back of the plane wearing a business suit and a parachute after receiving $200,000 in ransom money.

No sign of Cooper has emerged, though bundles of his cash, matched by serial numbers, were found in 1980.

The FBI says it has conducted searches, collected all available evidence,nd interviewed all identified witnesses. It says the agency chased an immense number of tips, but none have resulted in identifying the hijacker.

About T. Allen Winn T. Allen

Winn began writing in 2003 while being cooped up in hotels during business travel. His first book 'Road Rage' was published in 2011. His first seven books were published by Prose Press. In 2016 T. Allen Winn established Buttermilk Books, his publishing company and to date has published 23 books with short stories published in three other books. He does not write under any specific genre. He writes what strikes his fancy. If you do not see something that fits your reading wheelhouse, just tell him what you like, and he might just write it for you. He and his wife reside in Myrtle Beach, South Carolina.

His books are available on Amazon or online where books are sold. Select books are available at Southern Succotash on Washington Street in Abbeville, S.C. and in Tabor City, N.C. at Grapefull Sisters Vineyard. Or *Message* T. Allen Winn on Facebook to arrange delivery of signed copies.

Fiction from T. Allen Winn

The Detective Trudy Wagner series

Road Rage
North of the Border
Tithes and Offerings

Foot Series

Foot, Tree Knockers and Rock Throwers
Another Foot, What Really Happened to D. B. Copper?

More Fiction from T. Allen Winn

The Perfect Spook House
Dark Thirty
Lou Who
Raw Ride, a Wild West Zombie Apocalyptic Shoot'um Up
The Man Who Met the Mouse
Mister Twix Mystery, a Cat Scene Investigation
The Tenth Elemental
The Lord's Last Acres

Non-Fiction from T. Allen Winn

Being Bentley, A Dog Like No Other
It's All About the 'A', Faith, Family, Football and Forever to Thee
with coauthor, Benji Greeson
It's All About the Angels in the Backfield, Dawn of a Dynasty
with coauthor, Benji Greeson
December's Darkest Day, While I Breathe, I Hope
The Hardwood Walker of Port Harrelson Road (based on true
events in Bucksport, S.C.)
Cuz, My Brother, Life is Good, God is Good

Memoirs

The Caregiver's Son, Outside the Window Looking In
Cornbread and Buttermilk, Good Ole Fashion Home Cooked
Nostalgic Nonsense
The Endless Mulligan, Short Shots from the Golf Whomper
Don't Sit Naked in a Grits Tree, More Nostalgic Nonsense Vol 2

Short Stories

For Your Amusement featured in Beach Author Network's book titled 'Shorts'

Ciled Me a Bar featured in friend and author, Danny Kuhn's Headline Book's *Mountain Mysts*, Honorable Mention in Fiction at the 2015 London Book Festival and the book is endorsed by *Joyce Dewitt* of the sitcom *Three's Company*

Short story about Granny Bowie in friend and author Robert Sharpe's book, *The Heart and Soul of Caring*, about caregivers and their challenges